Outside Man

Outside Man

Marc Heberden

Camerado Press

Marc Christine

And before :

Mary & Arthur Schultz

Maguy & Jacques de Villemandy

&

George Whitman

Preface to the 40th Anniversary Edition

On a sunny December morning forty years ago, in a house overlooking the Mediterranean in the southern French town of Nice, a young man opened wide the glass-paneled doors of his room facing out onto a veranda, letting the cool air in, and sat down to a small table. There, with barely a pause, he began to write about another young man, who was driving a car down from the Rocky Mountains of northern Idaho into the Palouse country of eastern Washington. The young writer knew that faraway country well. The other knew it not at all. And if the two young men had anything in common it was that they were both roaming into new and unfamiliar countries.

The young writer was me. Roughly two months before, with the plan of seeing the world, I had left behind a job working as a newspaper editor and reporter in a mountain town east of Everett, Washington. In this case, seeing the world only consisted of an invitation to visit a family in France, but that was already more of the world than I had ever known. I hadn't the slightest premonition at that time of how events, one after another, would result in France becoming my home. But on that morning, taking up a pen—not really knowing what sort of story would flow from that effort—it was simply with a feeling of freedom... to not be writing something tied to the pressing concerns of deadlines or the formulaic process of news reporting.

As for the young man in the book, named Sam Lawrence right from the start, while he was not me in any specific way, I knew he would be experiencing things I was familiar with in the Palouse, and in ways that could only happen in that time and in that place depicted. The town he came into I named, also from the start, Gainesville, modeling it roughly on several small towns I knew in the wheatfield and scabland country west of Spokane.

Regardless of how little information a writer provides about a character, they know everything there is to know about that person. I did not choose to write much about Sam at first. I also did not know what might happen. But I did know that Sam's only hope for making the best of that new country was to accept how things were and be open to it all. It was not lost on me at the time, and was never forgotten, that the way I went about writing about Sam was in many ways similar to what I was experiencing there in those days in France... meeting new people and learning new ways of looking at the world.

I would finish writing the book, called by then Outside Man, by mid-July of 1984. As things were, despite encouragement from people like the writer William Wharton, the book was not brought out by a well-known publisher and appeared in a highly abridged form with only a limited distribution. However, through new means, the book is now making its way into the hands of a more significant readership. For that reason alone it seemed only right, if not deserving, that on its 40th anniversary it be brought out in a restored edition hewing much more closely to the initial vision of that young writer and returning the book to its original intent. Considering all the things I could thank that young man, my younger self, for—especially for all the other doors he opened for me—I can't think of a better way than this.

Marc Heberden
Boullay-lès-Troux, France
December 2023

OUTSIDE MAN

Deepest thanks to Snowy White for his permission to use his song lyrics.

Bird of Paradise

Saw you flying by
Flash of turquoise blue
I just had to try
To keep your life in view
My bird of paradise
Sweet bird of paradise

Wish that I could fly
I'd be beside you now
But I can only sigh
And watch you circle 'round
My bird of paradise
Sweet bird of paradise

So you fly away
When will you come again
So I can watch you play
In the pouring rain
My bird of paradise
Sweet bird of paradise
My bird of paradise

Chapter 1

FARMERS do not believe in luck. They do believe in fate, mostly as a function of the weather. But when it comes to their own fortunes, because of their immediate involvement with the land, they see their efforts as the thing most responsible for personal success or failure. It is a hardy, productive point of view, both self-reliant and efficient, but at the same time deeply causal and in the end uninspired. Myths and superstitions, goddesses of fertility worship, the colorings of the human imagination for thousands of years, died with the weather report and the McCormack Reaper. Luckily, here and there, a few men and women survive of that ancient race for whom accidents still might mean something, and portents might exist.

Across the endless hills of the Palouse country of Washington, low, slow-moving clouds were wetting the cool ground. On the dark flanks of the hills the first green shadings of sprouting winter wheat were beginning to show; and in the deep, unfarmed valleys white blossoming trees with yellow and white carpets of wildflowers at their feet braced beneath the occasional, soft coming and going of the showers.

In that early spring, out from beyond Bozeman with four hundred dollars, a couple of fishing poles, and a suitcase stuffed with year-old work clothes, he drove his dusty, maroon-colored car along the straight, flat highway stretching west from Spokane. He had driven all night, coming over the Rockies in a pelting downpour, the storm having blown out just before dawn. With the morning half gone, the sun breaking strongly through the swiftly scattering overcast, the tires of his car whined through the intermittent wet stretches remaining on the road.

It was about noon when he first saw the town, a few miles distant, as the highway went over yet another of the tirelessly rolling hills. From that distance, other than the towering grain elevators, nothing else could be seen of it except a massing of heavy trees. He had felt hungry for hours and took the off-ramp for the town when it came along.

His car sat in the dusty parking lot alongside an old diner on the outskirts of the town. In the front seat, unshaven and a bit disheveled, he slumped behind the wheel, fast asleep. The day was hot and his windows were down. He breathed with slight groans of exhaustion while a fly buzzed against the windshield.

Across the lot, the door of the diner opened and a pudgy cook stepped out onto the porch, wiping his hands with a rag. He took a long look at the car, sighed, flung the rag over his shoulder, and stepped off the porch to walk over towards the car, his shoes shuffling the gravel.

He looked inside and rapped his knuckles on the roof of the car. The man inside opened his eyes and squinted.

The cook's mouth pulled to one side. "You planning to eat something?"

"Sorry?"

"Because if you're going to sleep, there's a hotel in town."

The man blinked and looked at his wristwatch.

"Oh..."

"Yeah, oh. You've been here for an hour."

The cook walked away. The man pushed his door open and got out. He stretched, arching a stiff back, and then headed towards the diner. A while later he walked out of the place with a burger in one hand and a drink in the other. He set the drink down on his car hood, unwrapped and took a bite out of the burger, and looked around. Next to the access road back to the highway were signs, one saying Spokane East and the other Seattle West. The sign for Spokane said 45 miles. He turned to look into the town.

From where he stood he could see all the way down the main street, four or five blocks of old storefronted buildings. On either side of Main he could see some of the rest of the town, houses with big trees lining the streets and at the far end a white, windowed spire rose over the main door of a red brick church. He took another bite and looked away towards the countryside. He could see several miles across large, unfarmed flats to the beginnings of distant wheat hills. He looked back at the town. A weather-beaten sign put up long ago by the local Kiwanis Club identified it as Gainesville, 1883, population 546.

He ate the rest of his lunch there in the hot sun, chewing slowly and looking around. When he finished he took his faded old green bandana out of his pocket and poured the ice from the cup into it, folded it, and ran it across his face and neck. Cooled, he wrung out the bandana and got back in the car, spreading the bandana on the dash to dry. It was an old bandana but he took care of it, unable anymore to remember a time he did not have it with him, and just looking at it reminded him of every place he had been and, in a way, seemed the connection he had to those places, even to his unchanging way of life.

He turned the key in the ignition and watched the needle on the gas gauge move up to just under half a tank. He scrunched over, pulled out his wallet from his back pocket and looked inside.

"Shit."

He threw the wallet onto the passenger side, stared at the highway sign, and then started the car and steered it out onto the street going into town. He cruised slowly between the brick commercial buildings and then went off on a side street, parking in back of the drugstore. He grabbed his wallet and got out, leaving the windows all down, and walked back to Main.

There, he looked up and down the street. A block down from him, on the other side, was a faded red and yellow sign for a restaurant called The Hearth with a cocktail lounge called the Flame Room. He crossed the street and went down to it.

Chapter 2

NOBODY was in the small restaurant area and he walked past the tables and chairs towards the cocktail lounge. Next to its doorway was a bulletin board and he paused to read the ads and notices pinned to it.

"Chevy 1-ton flatbed for sale. 300,000 miles."

"Part-time help needed, with a strong back. OK Tires."

"Divorce sale: kids bedroom furniture."

"Rich farmer looking for wife."

He grunted a laugh.

"Reliable stockman needed."

He unpinned the last one and a woman's voice suddenly came from inside the lounge.

"That's only if you really like cows."

The woman was behind the bar. He looked at the notice again.

"Says stockman."

"It's a dairy."

He inhaled through his teeth, stuck it back, and walked into the dim, reddish glow of the lounge. Compared to the restaurant area the lounge was a large room full of tables with red vinyl chairs and red vinyl booths along the walls, and at the far end was a dance floor in front of a small stage. Except for the barmaid the place was empty. The bar consisted of a black Formica counter with red vinyl bar stools. The barmaid sat at the far end of the bar watching television. As he sat down she slid around the back of the bar. She was a cute thirty-ish curly-blond. She gave him a professional smile.

"Not a dairyman, huh? Want something?"

4

"A draft, I guess."

The tap only foamed at first, forcing her to dump out the first few glasses. At last pulling a beer she felt was reasonable, she brought it over and set it on a coaster.

"Looking for work?"

"I just came into town." He took a sip of his beer.

She leaned against the bar, picking up a cigarette. "So what are you selling?"

"I don't sell anything."

She took a drag on her cigarette and smiled. "Good thing for you. Nobody here buys anything."

"I look like a salesman?"

"You look new."

"You know everybody in town?"

"It's hard not to," she laughed. "Even if you don't want to."

"I suppose so, when you're from a place this size."

"My turn. Do I look like I'm from a place like this?"

"I'd say so."

She shrugged. "Fair enough. It doesn't take long to seem like you're from here if you stay long enough. Hard to figure you'd be here, otherwise, I guess."

"How long have you been here?"

"Ten years." She stared at him as though he might say something, but saw he wasn't about to, and she shrugged. "Where're you from?"

"Here and there."

"But mostly there," she nodded. "I get it."

He thought she looked a little irritated. "No, it's not that. Just nowhere interesting. Was in Montana, last."

"And you've come here?"

"No. But sort of tapped out. So who knows."

"Tapped out ..." She smiled. "So who knows? What's your name?"

"Sam. Sam Lawrence."

She stuck her hand out. "Pleased to meet you, Sam Lawrence. I'm Lonni. For Lonni Scarlet-Mae Gonkle."

He stared at her.

She smiled. "I try to get it all out, right from the start."

"Well," he smiled. "Lonni's unusual."

She laughed. "Believe it or not, it's really Lorilei."

Sam let out a laugh of his own.

Lonni nodded. "I know, right?"

Sam looked around. "Not too busy."

"Here? Mid-day? Never. And if you're actually looking for work there's another restaurant down the street with a better bulletin board. Here, the drunks put up jokes."

"I was beginning to think that, but..."

"Hey ho," came a voice from the door.

Lonni looked over. "Hi, Hon. Starting early?"

Sam turned and saw two women. One was a dark, auburn-haired woman who looked like she could be in fashion magazines. Her friend was pretty with thick black hair cut to a page-boy style.

As the first woman passed, she gave him a quick look-over and a nod, friendly in an indifferent sort of way.

Sam looked back at the bar and suddenly up at the mirror, giving himself a sort of holy-smoke look. She wasn't the sort of woman you normally ran into in these sorts of town.

Unfortunately for him, she had also looked into the mirror and caught him at it. The woman said to Lonni: "No, just wandering around." And then turned to Sam. "As for you, mister big brown eyes...," she leaned in. "Thank you."

Sam felt himself cringe.

"Sam," Lonni said, "this is Marilyn. Marilyn, Sam." She nodded towards the other woman. "And this is Julie."

He nodded at everybody. "Hello."

"Sam's from here and there," Lonni went on, "and is not sure if he's coming or going. And that's all we know about him."

Marilyn laughed pleasantly. "That's OK. Sometimes the best thing to know about people is that we don't have to know about them."

Sam had absolutely nothing to say, but nobody seemed to care, and the two women both just smiled back at him, although Julie seemed to be giving him more of an examination. For half a second Sam wondered what she was seeing in him, and then in another found out.

"Not bad for a change," she said to Lonni. "You plan to snatch him up before anyone else gets a chance?" She gave Sam a smile. "She tends to do that. Has the advantage of location."

"I see," Sam said. He wished he had something else he could say other than that, but then found it was not necessary. Marilyn gave a nod to Lonni and all three of the women went down to the other end of the bar. Unfortunately, that was also the end where the television was, and Sam had nothing he could look at except his reflection from the mirror behind the bar.

Sam gave himself a grim smile. He felt as though he had just been run over by a hit-and-run. He glanced down the bar, saw he did not exist anymore, finished his beer and got up.

Outside on the sidewalk and back in the heat of the afternoon, he remembered what Lonni had said and walked farther down the street to find the other restaurant. Five minutes later, he came out looking at a piece of paper. He stuck it in his pocket, took a breath, and went for a walk.

He went along Main for a few blocks and then took a corner, walking into the side streets. There, old houses with close-trimmed lawns slept beneath large-limbed trees. A few streets back was the town park which was quiet and cool, the grass spreading beneath big maple and chestnut trees, their young leaves already filling out so early in the spring. Along one side of the park, a high-riding river flowed silently. He walked over to look at it, surprised at its size. Somewhere back in the hills, he thought, there were probably good trout pools. He left the park and, making his way back towards his car, he came across a blue and gray stucco building with large, weather-beaten wood balconies on all three stories. The St. Charles Hotel.

He stopped in front, looking it over, and then felt the fatigue hit him for real. He went up the steps and into the lobby. The deskman, bald and oily-looking, was reading a paper behind the counter and made no sign of movement until Sam had crossed the wide, red-carpeted lobby, scattered with tables and old reading chairs. Then the paper was slowly folded up.

"Any rooms?"

"You've got your choice. No difference in price."

"Yeah?"

"Yeah." The deskman looked at Sam a moment, taking in his workman's clothes. "I've got a corner room on the top floor, at the front, that has a fridge and hotplate. Fifteen for the night. But if you give me fifty I'll let you have it for a week."

Sam brought out his wallet and pulled out three bills. The deskman took the bills, pushed a ledger across for Sam to sign into and reached back for a room key. "Third floor to the right, all the way at the end."

It was a big, L-shaped room with a high ceiling. So big it could have been an apartment. A wide bed was placed halfway down the longest wall and there were a couple of old armchairs and a folding-top desk along the other. He opened doors and found the L-shape was caused by a bathroom and kitchen built into one corner of what had been an even larger room. The bathroom was small, tiled from floor to ceiling, and the kitchen was equipped. The room itself was well-lit, one big window facing the street, a smaller one above the bed, and there was a pair of French doors... small glass panes made private with white muslin door curtains... leading out onto the balcony. He threw the shades back, letting the sun come warmly into the room, but did not open the window or the doors, just going over to lie down on the bed. As he settled down, he suddenly remembered his car, but then yawned and rolled to the side, turning his back to the light coming in through the balcony doors.

Chapter 3

THE clicking and rattling across the roadbeds of a train passing through town woke him. The room was dark. Out through the main window, the eastern sky was a deep blue, rich with the coming evening, two stars showing themselves above the dark silhouettes of the trees across the street. He pulled himself upright and rubbed the rough stubble on his neck, then went and opened the French doors and stepped out onto the balcony.

With an overhanging roof, the balcony started at his door and disappeared around the far corner. Cane chairs and tables, shoved back against the side of the hotel, spread down the length of it. He could see into none of the other doors, all unoccupied, with heavy drapes pulled shut. He walked down the balcony, finding it went around the corner and along that side of the building, stopping at the back, where a lone door marked a room.

Back in front of his own room he leaned on the railing, looking out at the town. Streetlights, beginning to gather strength beneath darkening skies, showed in glimpses up through the trees. Brighter lights and the sound of traffic came from the downtown, half a block away. From a house across the street he could hear the banging of pans and cupboards as someone began to prepare dinner. He went back into the room, shutting the doors behind himself, and went down out of the hotel.

Cars parked on Main were mostly crowded around The Hearth, and he went down the street to the other place, called the Country Kitchen, which had a cocktail lounge called the Fireside Room. Unlike the place Lonni worked at, this place was mainly a restaurant,

9

warmly lit and decorated with old farm implements, with dozens of tables spread around and a full-length lunch counter running down one side of the room. He took a seat at the counter and picked up the menu. Along with everything else, breakfast plates were served all day and he ordered a Spanish omelet with hash browns. Afterwards, he walked down Main towards where he'd left his car.

By that time the sky had become black and clear and, even there on Main with the street lights, full of stars. He turned off Main to go behind the drugstore. Up and down the tree-lined backstreets, the houses glowed, some yellow, others the dim blue of televisions. He found his car and drove back to the hotel, parking in the lot behind the building. Pulling out his fishing poles and suitcase, he went up into the hotel. Inside his room, he set the suitcase in a corner and leaned the poles against it. He kicked off his shoes and opened the balcony doors, and then went and sat in one of the armchairs and looked out over the town. It was quiet out there and it was quiet in the hotel, and he rested his right foot up onto his left knee and took a deep breath.

Maybe he should have stopped in Spokane. Or just kept going and gone over the mountains to Seattle. But he had not thought of stopping when he was going through Spokane and now having paid for that room, he did not have enough to go anywhere, let alone Seattle, and be able to afford a room for any comfortable amount of time. And having come to realize that was all there was to it, he did not think much more and after a while nodded off and it wasn't until about three in the morning that he stumbled over to the bed.

Barely past dawn, he took a long shower, letting the hot water stream over his shoulders and back. Afterwards, looking in the mirror, he decided he could go a while longer without a haircut, just pushing his dark hair back, but he had to get some razors. Out in the room, he picked up his suitcase and opened it flat on the bed. His clothes were still in good shape and he put on a heavy shirt and a pair of jeans and, wiping off the dust, his walking boots. They were heavily creased but the leather was clean. He stuck his old bandana in his pocket and went down.

The morning sidewalks on Main were bathed in bright sunshine. So early, the stores were closed. He walked to the restaurant where some cars were already nosed up to the sidewalk. A dozen or so men sat around the tables and along the counter. Some were eating but most just drank coffee and smoked.

He sat at the counter and ordered toast and coffee. Half a newspaper lay on the counter next to him and he glanced at it, but there was nothing in it for him. As he ate his toast, letting the waitress refill his coffee cup, he listened to the conversation nearby. Mostly it was about farming and other farmers. He heard some talk about hunting and fishing, and sometimes they even talked about the economy, or politics, but those lasted about as long as it took to make a joke, and then it all went back to farming, and who was doing what, and where, and who had been able to start and who had not. The same sort of talk he had heard everywhere he had ever been. He did not start a conversation with anyone and, those men being polite, no one started one with him, a stranger. He finished his coffee and left.

The grocery was open by then, and he went in to get a razor. He also went to the cooler in back for some beer. Up front, the owner, an enormously fat man in a green apron, black glasses nearly falling off his nose, rang up his things.

"Beer and razors," the grocer said. "Man can go a long way on those."

"I've tried."

"And our mothers are so proud of us."

He pushed his money across the counter, noticing a display of fishing lures behind the grocer.

"Any lakes around here?"

"The rivers are better."

"All the way over here?"

The grocer shrugged. "Not many come to fish for the trout hereabouts. Most go over past Spokane. Above Coeur d'Alene."

"Do you fish?"

"Yep."

"Around here?"

The grocer bagged his purchases. "Oh, here and there. Depends, you know?"

He reached for his bag. "Yeah. Where's the gas station?"

"Out beyond the equipment dealer."

Sam went and gassed up, and then went back into town. The day before he had seen a bridge going across the river from the park with a road on the other side looking to go straight out into the countryside. Although he knew he should not be doing such things, his money now running so low, he went and found the bridge and crossed the river and drove out through the first fields there close to town.

For two or three miles out from Gainesville, the land was flat. More sprouting wheat showed there and the land was drier and he saw a distant tractor out cultivating. The farther he drove, the more the Palouse countryside began to rise and fold upon itself until, finally, the road was just worrying its way between the high, cultivated hillsides. The fields there were alive with short green wheat, their furrowed regularity combing the hills in big swipes. The unplanted fallow lands were green also, but there it was with the spottiness of wild grass, mustard, or even the occasional patch of sprouting Canadian thistle. If rain held the tractors off the hills, that ground would soon need weeding on top of the normal spring farming.

His old car was almost as high centered as a pickup and he rolled off the paved highway onto a dry looking dirt road and drove up through a deep, tree-lined gully, tall grass in the road brushing the underside of his car. Near the top, where the gully petered out, the road, now barely a dirt track, followed a fence line across the summit ridges of a long series of grass-covered hills that, he thought, could not be much different from what the first French trappers had seen coming into the country.

The Palouse. He couldn't remember exactly how he had picked it up but he knew that when the French trappers had first seen those grass covered hills they had called them that: the pelouse—the grass. And they named everything, from places—Loup loup, the Pend d'oreille and Coeur d'Alene, down to the Dalles and the Grande ronde—or features like the coulees, buttes, or cascades, and then even the locals, the bone-pierced-nose Nez Percé, with their horse: the cheval de la pelouse ... the appaloosa.

He had always wanted to see the Palouse and had never thought he actually would. But Montana had finally drawn him far enough north and westward that it was in fact easier to go west than trail southward again and he had not felt interested in going southwest again and certainly not southeast and he liked the idea of going somewhere that had nothing to do with anything. Maybe in fact, and finally, trying out an actual city. Seattle perhaps. Just drive out of it all and into something completely different.

He was far out in the hills by then and after a while the fence line he had been following quit itself in nothing but a last post and some tangled shreds of barbed wire, as if announcing that not even fences would keep him company out to where he was going. There, a ways across the top of that hill, was a rocky outcrop with a few scraggly ponderosa pines.

He turned off his motor and it ticked itself into the silence of what seemed the most forgotten place on earth. He took a beer and walked toward the outcrop, going then into some brush and thick grass, at one point flushing a big hen pheasant which took off with a blast of wings and a cackle.

From the outcrop, Sam looked out over the land. An ocean of green and light brown waves going out in an endless series of folds and winding valleys. Here and there in the far distant bottoms were groupings of trees around farmhouses, and then he noticed just a ways up the small valley below some trees unmistakably marking the spot where an old farm had once stood, only some ruined barns remaining. It had been a long, long time since he had seen anything like that.

Where he had come from, history had long since gotten plowed beneath ten-thousand-acre fields. Turning to walk back to the car, deliberately ignoring the pregnant coyote that had been watching him all that time from beneath a downed log, he looked down the plunging hill in the other direction and saw a half-mile thicket of bushes and weeds in the deep bottom where a small creek trickled through it all, and barely visible through the greening brush glimmered, with an almost turquoise sheen, what appeared to be a small, inviting pond.

Chapter 4

BACK in town, and even though he did not need to, he went to the gas station again and topped up. Regardless of whatever else happened, he could get to Seattle and he would have a week or so to look around. He'd never needed more than that. He went from the gas station over to the burger stop. Recognizing him from the day before, the cook nodded from behind the counter. "What'd you do? Get lost?"

"I stayed at the hotel."

"A population explosion."

He ordered and the cook slapped patties onto the grill.

"Where you from?" the cook yelled at him.

He shrugged.

"I mean last."

"Montana."

The cook nodded over the splattering burgers and yelled again. "I like it there, but I like it better in the San Luis Obispo area."

"Where?"

"San Luis Obispo."

"No, you like it better than where?"

"Monterey."

Sam nodded. "Me too."

He took the burgers back to the hotel and ate in the dark lobby. He was sitting there later in the shadows of that lobby, with the big doors open out onto the bright street, thinking about Seattle, when the desk clerk appeared behind the counter. He nodded at the clerk. "Afternoon."

"Yeah," the clerk answered. The clerk had a newspaper in his hand. He looked down at it for a moment, and then looked back at him. "Everything all right?"

"Just fine."

With a slow movement of his head, the clerk yawned. "Quiet around here, huh?" He was obviously not used to having someone sitting there in the lobby.

"It's nice."

The clerk leaned across the desk, looking out the door onto the street.

"If you need anything," he said after a moment, "just ring, you know." He continued to lean there, as though expecting something else to happen.

Sam stood up and went towards the stairs.

Up in his room, he opened the French doors and lay down on the bed.

He shut his eyes, listening to the sound of the breeze rustling the young leaves in the trees below his balcony, and fell asleep. When he woke, it was evening, and even though he had not done much of anything that day, he was hungry again and went down to the restaurant and got a bowl of beef stew. After dinner, with the sun throwing long shadows across the town, he went to the park and walked along the river.

The river was wide, the spring runoff high, but the channel he'd been so surprised by was deep, and the banks were very steep. He knew the river would maintain its size even after it began to go down. He stopped and put his hand in. Only up to his wrist, the water made his elbow joint tighten, sending a shiver along the back of his legs.

"Ooh, ma'am," he said softly, drawing his hand out, reddened from the icy contact. "You're still a cold bitch, aren't you?"

He dried his hand with his bandana and walked away along the bank. The trees around the river, with their young, small leaves, had a pleasant, dark effect on the water, and in that darkness he could see right through the glassy transparency of the surface to a clean, rocky bottom.

He walked all the way around the park, breathing in the evening air, and then walked back into town to the bar, where a small neon sign stuck out high above the door, saying the place was called Bob's. There, the wedged-open front doors let him inside, where lights over the pool tables and the bar cast smoky pools of luminescence below the dark ceiling beams.

The bar itself was old and heavy with a brass foot-rail bolted along the base. He went and sat on a barstool, ordering a beer from a tall, thin barman with black hair slicked back behind his ears. He wore a cowboy shirt buttoned tight at the wrists and throat.

Sam put some bills on the counter and waited, and the barman returned with a pint glass, foam-topped and beading quickly around the sides. Grabbing a bill, the barman picked a couple more from the register tray and slid them onto the bar beside his glass.

Sam eyed his change. "That's almost charity."

"We call it marketing."

A few men sat at the bar. They glanced at him and the closest nodded.

"Plenty here for so early in the evening," Sam said to him.

"Ground's still too wet," the man said, but then went back talking to the man beside him.

Over the man's shoulder, Sam saw an old man come in through the back door. His overalls were dry and dusty above the knees but dark brown below, almost wet at the bottom. Someone, at least, had been working.

"What have you been doing, Fred?" someone called out. "Playing in the mud?"

"Playing with himself," someone else said.

"Playing with your old lady." The old man stamped off his boots at the door.

One of the younger men poured out and gave a glass of beer to the old man and offered him a chair, but he just nodded, taking the beer and heading for the bar. He took the stool next to Sam.

He was heavy but not fat, his flushed cheeks showing a week's worth of white stubble. He rubbed his hand over his chin with thick, hard fingers and took a long drink. "That's better," he said, looking at Sam. His look showed no curiosity, but just a general sort of friendliness.

"Long day already?"

"Just the first ones. The ground's still wet underneath. You end up carrying a pound of mud on your feet."

"Are you farming?"

"Oh no. Not for another week, maybe. We've been making fences. We're going to put some cows on turnips."

"Turnips? I thought this was wheat country. How do you harvest turnips on these hillsides?"

"No, it's just for the cows. We seed the hills by airplane and the cows do the rest. Never heard of that? No? You should see the size of some of the turnips the cows dig up. And you should see the cows out there, rooting around in the dirt like a bunch of pigs."

"How much fence are you building?"

The old man thought for a moment. "About a mile."

"Not too bad."

"No. Got some rocks though."

"How're you getting the posts in?"

"I'm not. I have to build goddamn stone-anchored pen-posts right over the top of it. I only got a couple hundred yards today. And that was in the so-called dirt." He went back to his beer.

Someone put on an old Charlie Pride number and the old man listened, keeping some sort of time with his fingers. Sam finished his beer and tapped his empty glass on the bar. The barman broke off from a game of Horse, sweeping the dice off the bar.

"Want another?" Sam asked the old man.

"Sounds good."

"Make it two more," he said to the barman. The barman walked into a patch of light and Sam noticed for the first time that the barman had a dark swelling under one eye.

The barman went off and the old man glanced over. "Bob's not quite himself today."

"Looks like he walked into a door."

"Wrong door all right. And I can tell you her name."

The barman came back and the old man squinted.

The barman squinted back. "What's the matter, Fred? Got something wrong with your eye?" He looked at the old man for a moment and then went back down the bar.

"Whole damn family's like him," the old man said. "Not a lick of sense in any of them."

Sam took a drink of his beer. "I think you're the only person here who's worked today. You know of anyone hereabouts who could use some help?"

"I could, yes. Me."

"Yeah?"

"But I don't have anything to do with the hiring. Which won't happen until we start farming."

"But you can use some help."

"We can always use help. But right now our schedule says we aren't farming."

"But you can use some help."

The old man smiled. "Where you from?"

"Lately, east Montana."

"Barely farming back there. Just fields along the Yellowstone. Ain't much like here. This is the Palouse, and it's nothing but hills. Not the same thing at all."

Sam looked back placidly.

"All right. All right. Hold on." The old man swiveled around and headed back towards the toilets where a payphone hung in the corner. Sam watched him pull down the receiver, stick in a coin, and start dialing. Sam looked back at the bar until the man came back.

"What's your name?"

"Sam Lawrence."

"I'm Fred Rosenbauer. Where are you staying?"

"The St. Charles."

"Be in front of here at six and we'll see how it goes."

Someone back at the pool tables shouted Fred's name and he turned to look. He looked back at Sam and nodded and turned off his stool again. Sam could see, from them glancing over, that the other men down the bar were taking more notice of him now. Sam drank off his beer and left.

19

He stood for a while on his balcony looking out across the town. Streetlights clouded the night air, but he could see out to where, against the black darkness of the distant hills, a few farm lights burned dimly.

Closer, he could see the lighted highway exchange just east of town. There, and along a strip of highway, he could see the lights of cars making their way east in the direction of Spokane, or west towards Moses Lake, or even ... beyond ...

Maybe one of those cars, some Nitecapping voyager, was heading for the mountain passes far to the west, heading for Seattle. Although that was a long drive. Six hours? Normally, only truckers would be doing that. But someone leaving Gainesville right about then would be driving into Seattle early in the morning. Early, but never too early to get a motel room. Drive around and find one on one of the highways into the city. They must not be that hard to find, even within the city limits. Just have to keep an eye out for the state routes through town, get off the interstate. He stopped looking at the drivers out on I-90 and turned his eyes back towards the dim, distant farm lights out against the dark horizons of the countryside. Far off on some hill the lights of a car rounding a curve flashed briefly and then disappeared, swallowed up in the blackness. He wondered how far off in those hills he would be finding himself in the morning.

In the trees lining the street below him, a bird suddenly warbled an evening song, late and out of place. At the sound of the bird, he suddenly was thinking how, no matter what, he would not let it go like the last time, thinking that things would be different. He looked down at his car.

"Just a couple of weeks, old girl. I promise."

He would just have to remember it. No place was ever different. Things were never different. They were only either a little better or a little worse.

He went inside, shut off the lights, and lay down, and did his best for a few minutes to try to look at it like that. But finally it all fell apart, and he was thinking how he could have already been in Seattle if he had paid for one night instead of the whole week.

Accidentally here, indeed.

He thought about that but then did not want to think about it so he thought about other things and even then about the women at the bar the other day, but not too much. Then darkness closed over him.

Chapter 5

BEFORE dawn, he followed the tail-lights of Fred's pickup out to the Petersen farm.

Not far off the road, all the main buildings were down in a wide, rock-rimmed canyon. The cavernous opening of the high-peaked barn revealed the depletion of its winter supply of hay. The other buildings—shops, sheds, round-sided steel grain bins, the bunkhouse and a chicken coop—spread along each side of the canyon.

At the far end of the canyon, where it began opening towards an expanding series of dry pasture and rocky scabland, stood the farmhouse with its big, bay windows and deep front porch. A wide, lush lawn surrounded it, spreading out to where old, high-limbed and heavy black cottonwoods stood along the fence lines.

Fred and Sam walked across the dewy grass to the back porch of the house and picked up lunchboxes set out on the top step. They drove out to the fence line in Fred's truck and worked all day, pounding in steel poles or building wood pens and stringing barbed wire. That evening, they drove back to the farm. When they got out of the pickup Fred nodded at Sam.

"All right. See you in the morning right here."

Sam could see people inside the house and could hear crockery being set for dinner.

"All right. Same time, I guess."

"Yep." Fred turned and started walking towards the house. Sam watched him for a second, and then called out.

"I'm getting paid for this, right?"

Fred half turned. "Friday night work?"

"Sure."

Over the following week, Sam and Fred worked side by side on fence lines. Having finished the one they moved on to others, repairing, building or removing. As the days went by, with no more than a few passing clouds in the warming skies, the ground gradually dried out. No longer, when he pulled out an old fence pole, did he find wet, black dirt clinging at the bottom. It was still rich dirt, but lighter in color and dryer.

On Friday evening, Fred went into the farmhouse for a few minutes and came out and handed Sam a paycheck. And a week later, he did the same thing.

After two weeks, Sam still did not have any idea how long he would be working with Fred, but the pay was good and had more than made up for the hotel and food and gas, and in another week or so he would have enough to clear out of town and get over to Seattle, and have enough to get by with until he could find some real work and not just the first thing that came along. Maybe two more weeks, better three, he was thinking.

Then one morning, when Fred and Sam were loading wire bales into the back of Fred's pickup, a young man, tall and dark, came out of the farmhouse across the way. Getting closer, he gave them both a crooked grin that was more confident than friendly, with eyes roaming up and down Sam. He stuck out his hand.

"Sam, right? I'm Dan Petersen. You boys almost finished out there, I hear."

"Pretty much," Fred said.

Dan raised his eyebrows, looking at Sam. "Fred says you can drive tractor. Is that right?"

"I've done it."

"Follow me."

They walked towards a big, steel-clad shed. Inside sat a huge four-wheel drive hillside wheel-tractor, its doubled front and rear tires, eight in all, nearly six feet tall. Dan climbed up the ladder and opened the cabin door. He pointed at the various levers for raising or lowering implements and running the big diesel.

"You know this? It's articulated. You don't turn the wheels, the whole thing articulates in the middle."

"Nothing this big. And not up on hills like yours." Sam looked at the tractor. Its doubled wheels on the front and back spanned sixteen or seventeen feet across.

"That's why it's so big and all the wheels are doubled. But, it's the same thing. Just... see that button down there?"

On the floor was a wide, round pedal in the place where, in a car, would be the accelerator.

"When you get up higher," Dan said, "you stand on that to get all wheels driving. You'll be nearly standing instead of sitting."

Sam stared at the cab for a bit. Dan looked over at Fred and then back at Sam.

"So?"

Sam nodded.

"I can give it a shot if you want."

"It's not hard once you get going. You know how to farm a field, is the main thing."

Sam nodded.

Dan looked at Fred. "All right. If you're done with him, you need to get going yourself by the Miller's. I'm going to get him going over by the Larson's." Fred made a sound and Dan raised his eyebrows. "What?"

"Nothing. Just that the big flat over by Williams Lake is dry now and what hills there are don't have eyebrows."

Sam took his eyes off all the levers inside the cab and turned to them. "Eyebrows?"

Fred raised his hand, cupping it upside down. "Places high up where it gets so steep we don't plant. Way up. They look like eyebrows." He looked at Dan. "You want him starting there?"

"Over by Larson's isn't that bad and I want to get it out of the way. So, let's go. Follow me with your car."

Dan turned and walked off. Sam gave Fred a quick grin and followed. Dan got into a big, red, four-wheel drive pickup and drove off up the road before Sam had barely gotten to his car. He jumped in and sped off to catch up.

Fred watched them go, then turned and grabbed another bale of wire, mumbling, "not that bad, my ass."

Dan and Sam parked just inside a wide gap in a fence that opened onto several dozen acres of flatland, overloomed, just a ways off, by immense hills seeming to rise nearly vertical from them. They walked toward a big, articulated wheel-tractor with a cultivator implement attached. The cultivator tines were armed with curving spikes, glinting in the sunlight. Dan pointed at them.

"We weeded last year so we don't have to drag wide points. We just want to soften things up so we can get seeding."

Sam looked toward the tall and steep hillsides, furrowing and bending out of sight. Dan crouched down and with the palm of his hand smoothed a wide patch of dirt, drew a large, irregular octagon, and then drew a shape like a big, six-fingered hand inside it.

"This is the hill. None of it is cut off by fences so you can go all the way around. All you have to do is drive." He dragged his finger along a contour. "Start like this: go halfway up the hill, put the cultivator down and make your first mark all the way around at that level. Then just keep going around and spiral up from the mark. When that's done, do the same from the mark down. If you find yourself crossing the same ground, lift the cultivator so you don't powderize the dirt. Got it?"

"I think so."

"Well, even if you don't, you will soon enough. Do you have a lunch? Enough water?"

"I didn't really bring much. Fred would bring that."

Dan turned towards his pickup.

"Get the tractor warming."

Sam grabbed the handrail and climbed up into the cab. It was the biggest machine he'd ever been in, and seemed even bigger just sitting in it.

"Jesus."

He looked things over, making sure the drive was in neutral, and reached down and turned the key to the on position, set the throttle to low, pulled out the fuel control and pushed the start button. The big diesel coughed its way around a couple of times and

25

then roared to life. While the engine warmed, he adjusted his seat and looked back to see the implement reacting to the way he moved the hydraulic control, watching the wheels rise until the hundreds of tines held the implement off the ground, and then setting the wheels back down, lifting the tines clear.

Dan came back swinging a plastic gallon jug of water, and a lunchbox. He climbed up and set them inside, next to the hydraulic levers Sam was testing. He had to raise his voice to be heard.

"You're not going to be able to run much past six tonight. Just bring these back and leave them on the porch. Tomorrow morning, you'll find them waiting for you on the porch. And ..." he pointed at the all-wheel foot pedal on the floor, "don't forget." At Sam's nod, he jumped down and headed back to his pickup.

Sam pulled the door shut, and things became much quieter. After a few minutes, with the engine temperature needle in the running range, Sam pulled the throttle lever wide open, stepped on the clutch, set the speed level into low, and let out the clutch. With a slight jerk he started rolling.

He looked back at the cultivator, ninety feet wide, then forward at the looming hillside.

With the tines out of the ground, the tractor ran easily across the flatland, and Sam had it throttled three-quarters of the way up and in the next-to-high gear by the time he began climbing the hillside. He climbed smoothly, but he could feel the front set of wheels beginning to drift, and he stepped on that all-wheel button and felt how the tractor now firmly gripped the ground even there on that increasingly steep hillside.

When he reached halfway up, he turned the machine to run on a horizontal line around the hill and pushed forward the implement lever, lowering the cultivator tines into the dirt.

The tractor took on a deeper roar, only slowing a bit, and he was now farming there on the side of a Palouse hill, with the tractor angled over and him sitting half on the seat and half on the arm of the seat, his foot hard on that button. It was like steering a sailboat in a crosswind. He gave out a laugh.

"Holy smoke..."

He pushed the throttle all the way up and slapped the machine into full drive.

A few hours later, Sam was driving with more and more ease, high on the hills, the tractor angled way over, the big cultivator tining deep into the soil. He had learned it was necessary to continually keep his eye on the mark, guiding the tractor and the cultivator along the hillside and making sure he did not drift down. And he was beginning to enjoy it.

At lunch, he stopped on the top of the biggest hill in the system, looking out across the shimmering green or brown folds of the Palouse. Far away on distant hillsides he saw a couple of other tractors raising thin trails of dust, and farther off the dust plumes of a few more. The day was bright and clear with hundreds of cotton puff clouds floating overhead.

After lunch, Sam dove back down onto his mark and was going along as usual on an even steeper section, turning the front wheels to keep the front of the tractor pulling uphill with the rear wheels driving it along horizontally and the cultivator hanging down at another angle, when—coming around a nearly blind bulge of the hill—he very nearly drove directly off an uncultivated eyebrow where the hill went almost vertical like a cliff.

He jammed over the steering wheel, steering wildly straight up the hill to aim the tractor away from the eyebrow, feeling as he did how the cultivator slipped over the edge and was trying to drag the tractor back. Luckily, the hose connections held and he got the tines up, and drove the tractor up onto the top of the hill without losing the implement.

"Whoo boy..." Sam brought the tractor to a stop, and there caught his breath for a full minute.

He lifted the cultivator out of the ground and looked it over. He did not see any broken tines and the wheels were sitting straight and well inflated. He slapped the tractor into drive again and headed back to his mark.

"OK," he said. "Yes. I got it."

Sam slammed his car door shut, carrying the lunchbox and water jug over to the big house. All the first-floor lights were on, and he could hear laughter from what must have been the dinner table. He set the box and jug on the porch and had turned and was starting to walk toward the car when he heard the screen door bang behind him. He turned and saw Dan standing there, a napkin stuck in his shirt collar.

Dan raised his eyebrows. "Everything go all right?"

"A little lost at first, but yeah."

"It's a pretty big system. It'll take you about three full days to get it all." A big laugh came up from the house. Dan looked over his shoulder, grinned, then looked back at Sam. "You'll find your box here in the morning. If you get done early in the next few days, just leave a note in the box." He picked up Sam's lunchbox and jug and went back inside, the screen door banging again behind him. Another gale of laughter came from inside.

Sam eyed the house for a moment and then turned towards his car.

Chapter 6

ONE evening in late April, Dan called to say he wanted some help moving furniture for a couple of friends. They drove in his pickup into a heavy-treed backstreet in Gainesville. Dan pulled to a stop in front of a house, which lay barely visible through the overgrown trees and shrubbery. Before they got their doors open, a woman came running out to them.

Blonde, with dark eyes and eyebrows, she wore faded cutoffs and a white vest. She leaned in at Sam's window, speaking across to Dan.

"What are you going to do?" she said. "Carry all that shit out here from the back?"

Sam looked at the tiny gold earring in her left ear. She smelled faintly of something like orange flowers.

"How much have you got?" Dan asked.

She patted the door of the pickup. "As much as this'll hold."

"Good," Dan said, starting the truck again. "Meet you around back."

"OK," the woman said. She gave Sam a smile and then she was gone.

"Her name's Susan Palmer." Dan drove around the block towards the alley. "And her roommate is named Ruth Kirby."

"Just a couple of friends, eh?"

Dan sort of smiled, and didn't, at the same time.

At the rear of the house, Sue helped guide them across the yard. Wooden steps were built onto the exterior of the house, and they followed her up to the apartment on the top floor. On the way up, Sue introduced herself to Sam by explaining that she and her roommate were legal secretaries working over at the county seat in St. Pierre. They were moving to a house a few blocks away. Living on top of a family, she went on to say, was a little restricting. Sam could find nothing to say.

The door of the apartment next door opened, and a dark-haired woman came out. Sam thought he had seen her somewhere before.

"Hey, Danny," she said.

"Hi, Julie."

"Got a new friend?"

"This is Sam."

"Sam... Oh, right!" She gave Sam a smile. "Don't you get around."

After a second, Sam managed a grin. "I get hauled around quite a bit, it's true." Then he remembered her as well. The friend of Marilyn.

She turned to Sue. "So just leave all the pots and pans and the laundry stuff and I'll come pick them up after you're out. How long will that take, you think?"

"Should only be a couple more hours," Sue said. "Now that we have the help and the pickup."

Julie smiled, and looked at Sam again. "See what happens when you stick around? Watch that Danny doesn't wear you out like all the others."

"I don't mind giving a hand."

"That's what they all say."

"So far, not too bad."

"Maybe not," she laughed, and in a way that even made Sue laugh.

Sam could feel how there was an entire conversation going on around him.

Julie gave him another smile. "Who knows, wrangler. But be careful. You might end up liking it here."

"Already do."

"Well," she laughed. "That's your first mistake."

Dan sighed. "We've got to get busy here, you know?"

At that, Sue went into the apartment.

"Sure, sure," Julie said. "See you guys around." She grinned at Sam. "Most probably." And she turned and went back into her apartment.

Sam looked at Dan, who looked back, shaking his head and sticking out his tongue with a frustrated grin. Then they followed Sue inside.

They were standing there, looking around at all the things to be moved, when Sue's roommate came out of the back room holding several empty cardboard boxes.

Sam had been gathering some things and at her approach he stood up and found himself looking into the most striking eyes— clear green and slightly downturned on the outside edges—that he had ever seen... sultry bedroom eyes, without meaning to be. But also, right then, giving him a look of wary curiosity.

The same height as Sue, her hair, somewhere between brown and gold, was full and wavy, framing an exquisite face, with those eyes. Beneath a long, fine nose, she had a wide, even smile. The thought flashed through his mind that she was lovely where Sue was pretty. In fact, more than lovely. The word that came to mind was... impossible. She was in another league. Breathtakingly beautiful. He remembered that her name was Ruth.

"Here," she said, handing the boxes to Sue. "These are left over."

"Good. How much have you got left?"

"I'm all packed." Ruth laughed. "Have been forever. You have ten times the junk I do."

"OK." Sue took the boxes. "I've got a little more. When I'm ready, we can start hauling it down to Dan's truck."

Ruth looked around the living room at the boxes and trunks piled on and next to the furniture, and at the stripped walls, and at all the pots of plants forming a small jungle near the door, and then into the kitchen where dishes and glasses and a variety of utensils and appliances crowded across the counters. She gave it all a sour look and shook her head. Just as she turned to look at them again,

Dan sat down, finding a seat on a large trunk, with his back against a chair.

"Anything left to drink?" he asked.

She smiled. "That's what I like about guys. They know how to kill time constructively."

"A beer maybe?" Dan asked.

"You know where it is."

Dan groaned and pulled in his legs, looking as if he was getting ready to make the big effort to get up. Ruth drooped her shoulders.

"Oh, don't bother. Please. Allow me."

Dan smiled.

"Since you're up..."

She looked at Sam. "And I suppose you'd like something, too."

"I wouldn't mind, I guess."

"You guess. Well, maybe you'll help. I'll have to unpack some things."

He followed her into the kitchen. He liked the way he immediately felt comfortable with her, and he wasn't bothered at all by how she barely seemed to notice him. If he was her, he wouldn't have noticed him, either. He picked up a box she was pointing to and set it on the kitchen table.

"So you're the new hired hand," she said to him while they unpacked the box. It was full of things from the refrigerator, some still cold.

"Yep."

"Your name is Sam."

"And yours is Ruth."

"Well, we've got that all figured out now, haven't we?"

He smiled, wondering if Dan had told either of them about a night a few weekends before when he had wandered off from a bar in the next town over and got lost for most of the night.

"It's so much fun meeting new people," Ruth said, giving him a bit of a look. "Don't you think? I mean, new people are so very interesting, aren't they?"

He did not know what the look or the statement meant. Perhaps she thought he was not being very friendly, or she was saying it against herself, or it meant nothing at all. Taken all together, he felt there was nothing he could say in return.

She made a triumphant noise and pulled a sack of canned beer from the box. "And still cold," she said.

Back in the living room, Ruth tossed Dan a can. "Your Majesty," she said.

"Thanks," Dan smiled. Sam helped himself to his own and then held one out to Ruth. Taking it, she went over and plopped into the stuffed chair behind Dan, putting her feet up on some boxes. Sam found a seat for himself on the couch between piles of boxes.

Dan eyed him, then smirked. "Now... there... you look in your element."

"What?"

Dan laughed, "... like a moving item."

Ruth clicked her tongue. "How nice is that?"

Dan looked at her, grinning. "C'mon, Baby Ruth. He doesn't care. And anyway, it's true."

"Ah," Ruth said. "Thanks for filling me in. And stop calling me that." She settled back into the chair, taking a long drink. She rested the beer alongside her legs, which by then were stretched out and crossed at the ankles. "God, moving is a pain in the ass."

Sam liked her and couldn't help noticing she had nice legs. And then realized he was looking, and quickly looked away.

"You mean, moving Sue," Dan said.

Ruth looked at the boxes.

"You don't want to move?" Sam said.

"Oh. I suppose, yeah," she sighed again. "It'll be good to get a little more privacy."

"Neighbors noisy?"

"Nosy is more like it," Dan said.

"Actually," she said, ignoring him, "I'm looking forward to it. I've never lived in a whole house before."

"This sounds serious," Sam said.

"It is. I'm tired of moving from place to place like this. This is the last, I hope, and maybe we can settle in and get some good things

33

around us instead of this part-time stuff." She waved her hand at the room's contents. "It's true. Sue has most of it. But we have a lot of acquired junk that sort of belongs to no one. Sort of temporary stuff, in a way."

He followed the gesture. "For temporary, you have a lot."

"It piles up," she nodded. "You stay, and beyond a certain point things begin to accumulate until you can hardly recognize where you started."

"That's almost the exact opposite from me."

"If you don't stop moving around, at all, it doesn't accumulate. You wander around a lot, then?"

The question, which wasn't really one, startled Sam, as questions about himself always startled him. Not that he was shy. But like many people who did not have the habit of being—or felt it was in some way impolite to be—curious about and asking questions of other people, he was always caught off guard when it happened to him. He nodded. "Wander... I don't know. But it's true I've been a lot of places. Depends on the jobs, I guess." He suddenly wished he had more to say about it. But there really was nothing.

It did not seem to bother her that he did not have much to say for himself and gave him a disinterested smile. "Must be nice not really knowing what might happen next."

Sam suddenly got that familiar feeling he'd often known in these small towns, where if you stayed for any period of time people you did not know at all seemed to know everything about you, or felt they knew, anyway. It wasn't presumption. Small town people just took for granted they knew everyone. Sam had never been bothered by it, but he had never really got used to it, either. Every time he would feel this quick shock of discovering its existence. And generally he ignored it, although there could be times when he was curious about what people thought they saw in him.

He looked over at her, but whatever it was she saw in him, or thought of him, she was giving him a friendly, comfortable look. Her eyes—those amazing eyes—even had a hint of amusement.

At least, he thought, she was not looking at him like he was an outright bum. But he could see that was about all it was. When you're out of their league, he thought, you might as well be a ghost.

He cleared his throat. But before he could say anything Sue, with a flush on her face, came back in the room and set some clothes in a corner.

"Look at this scene. I'm in there working my ass off and you're all out here having a party."

"You've got more to do?" Dan asked, handing her a beer.

"Oh, Lordy..." she dropped herself onto another stuffed chair and put the beer to her lips, taking a long drink.

"Sweet, sweet Jesus," she lowered the beer at last, wiping her chin and neck with her hand. "I love beer." She looked at Sam and laughed.

"You know," Dan said to him, "some people just don't know how to relax."

Sue smiled at that, closing her eyes for a moment. For just that moment she looked as though she were sleeping, and dreaming of something wonderful in her sleep.

"So, Mr. Sam," she said. "What sorts of things do you like to do?"

She had a look on her face showing she expected a joke, or something resembling one. He looked back for a moment in silence and then he thought of actually talking about something she might want to do. Not that he actually wanted to do something with her. The person he would, in fact, like to find something to do with was looking at him with blank curiosity. And something like wounded pride kicked in.

"I like to fish," he said.

"Fish?"

He thought maybe describing it would make it sound interesting. To anyone. "If it's a nice day. Out on a lake. Take a picnic, a few beers. Get some sun and some air. Maybe catch something."

"Fish?" Sue crinkled her nose. He didn't dare look elsewhere.

Sam's mind practically emptied. "I like to water-ski, too."

Sue nodded. As for fishing, all she had pictured was the creature, wet and bloody and gasping as it came into the boat, flopping there frantically in the bottom and maybe over against her leg, and a hook that had to be pulled out.

She twisted up her mouth. "I hate fish."

"Or movies."

Sam's mind flashed to Main Street and he realized there was no such thing as a movie theater in town. He glanced at Ruth, but then quickly over at Dan, who was leaning back, watching him with eyes half closed, faintly smiling. Dan suddenly pursed his lips appreciatively.

"Maybe catch... something." He gave a hint of a wink. "Here's a man who makes his pursuits sound tempting."

Ruth pulled in one corner of her mouth. "And you do, I suppose?"

He wasn't really listening now. He saw he was caught out as a fool, and worriedly looked at Sue. But she didn't seem to care. He looked again at Dan and Ruth. Dan raised his chin at Ruth.

"Seems to me that..."

Ruth cut him off. "I like fishing," she said, and turned to look at Sam.

Sam still felt blank but managed, "you don't mind the fish?"

"Who says you have to catch fish?"

Something about the way she said it told him she wasn't just kidding him; he saw something else. A certain deep kindness in her eyes. A generosity of spirit. There was no way she could register that he found her disturbingly attractive, but she evidently saw that he was struggling. In fact, it was more than that. He was floundering and just wanting desperately to get out of there.

"Fishing opens next week," Dan said. "For anyone who'd like to know."

"It does?" Ruth said.

"Myer's would be good."

Sam did not mind being teased, as long as it wasn't the sort of teasing that was spoiling for a fight. But this particular moment seemed to have no exit for him without it getting worse. He looked at Dan, giving him an expression that most men understood. Dan decided to ignore it.

"Why don't you go? Right?" he said. "And take Ruth. She doesn't mind not catching fish."

Sam went from embarrassment to irritation. "Depends on the weather." He looked over at Sue but she, too, had a smile that could have meant anything. He looked at Ruth. "You really like to fish?"

"Love it."

The ease it was said caught him off balance. "OK, maybe we could go sometime."

He wasn't actually thinking of going. Not with her, nor for that matter anyone else. But especially not her, and he wasn't sure why. The eyes. The glint of humor in them. Or, worse, the kindness. Or especially maybe just the impossible beauty. Impossible.

"You don't have to work next weekend if you get the swathing finished. We'll be all caught up by then," Dan said.

Sam turned to look at him.

Then Sue joined in. "Too bad the nearest movie house is in Spokane."

Sam could now see it. They were having fun.

"There's never anything playing in April," Dan said.

Sam looked at them both, and then couldn't help a smile coming to his own lips. Because, in the end, it actually was pretty funny.

"Anyway, all you like are like ... The Fog ... or Mad Max."

"Better than American Gigolo. Or what was it? Coal Miner's Daughter?"

"You didn't seem to mind so much."

Sam looked over at Ruth, and she nodded. "They go to movies."

He looked back. "So, what's Myer's?"

"A private lake. But good-sized, with a resort and a bar and restaurant. And ..." she smiled, "next weekend would be fine."

After they had dropped off all the rest of the boxes and furniture at Sue and Ruth's new place, and were leaving in Dan's truck, Dan started laughing.

"Hey, how did you do that back there?"

"Do what?"

"I mean, I've tried to get something like that with one of those girls for a long time, a whole day's outing somewhere, but ... nothing. I'm impressed."

"Very funny. And, you might have told me Sue was more than just a friend."

"She's not. I mean, we've gone to a few movies, it's true. But she's keeping her distance."

"Not working out?"

"You think I'd be over there moving furniture if I thought it wasn't worth trying?"

"If you are trying with one of them, what was I along for?"

"I didn't say either of them, I said one of them. Sue. And I couldn't just go alone. Ruth, as you might have noticed, doesn't like me much."

"I didn't notice."

"Yeah, I wouldn't think you would. You not knowing anyone. Fact is, Ruth thinks no one likes me. And sometimes I think Sue thinks the same."

"So my being a new guy helped...?"

"Freshen things up. Make me seem likeable."

"Absolved of all your sins." Sam laughed. "You must be running out of friends."

"Absolved of my sins." Dan made a thoughtful face. "May ... be."

"Glad to be of help."

Dan shrugged. "Anyway, there you go, asking Ruth out so ... easy ... like you did not even mean to do it."

Sam took a breath. "How long are you going to keep this up?"

"No, I mean it, man. I'm impressed."

"OK. I get it. Fuck you."

Dan laughed again. "Well, try to have a good time... and who knows? Maybe you'll catch... something."

Sam ignored him. "You know. You might have told me, beforehand. About the rest. So I didn't just walk over the edge."

"Doesn't matter. Anyway, it's not really all like that. Like I was saying, it's more like... like ..." Dan paused, and then the pause turned into a frown and Sam saw that was where things had to end.

"I need something to eat," he said.

"Yeah," Dan finally said. "Me too."

Sam discovered that when Dan had had a few drinks, he did not let go of a joke very easily.

"No, man. I mean it. I'm impressed. You're my hero."

"And for about the tenth time, fuck you."

Dan was pleased with himself. "Oh, well. It worked."

"It worked?"

"You got what you wanted."

Sam stared off at the empty pool tables and slowly blinked. "What did I get?"

"Miss Untouchable Ruth Fucking Kirby."

Sam got up and shot some pool for a while. When he eventually sat down he found Dan had gone on to think about other things. He found that, and he found two other things as well. The first was that Dan could talk the wind right out of the air, and the second was that Dan's favorite subject was Dan and how he *handled* things. For half an hour or more he talked about a contention he had had with some equipment dealer down in St. John. A contention seemingly involving all the complications that came from dealing with what he called "settler snobs". This, Sam learned, meant descendants of people who had moved into the territory going back to the 1860s and who, "even if they didn't themselves own an acre of the original land," still treated people like the Petersens, who had settled in the late 1880s, like newcomers. A remark which then sent him into a rambling monologue about owning the land and what that meant. Dan finally gave a sigh...

"... the thing about farming is the ownership and the action. It's like a physical addiction. A man's work. For the men who like to put their hands on their work, and create and control it."

He paused there, looking out over the pool tables, and it was only after a full minute had passed that he realized Sam had only been offering up complete silence, and for how long he could not remember. He looked over at Sam. "You sure don't talk much."

Sam smiled. "I can't really talk to all that."

Dan glanced over at him for a moment, and then nodded. "I suppose not. Well, that's honest of you. A lot of people have no problems talking about things they don't know about."

Sam couldn't talk about owning land, but while Dan had been talking, he thought about the one thing he did know, about how there had been times when he had become as much bonded to the land he worked on as the people he worked for. And he had thought at times about how he might have liked to have some land of his own. The only problem, when he got to thinking in that way, was that he was never able to imagine the place where he would want to have that.

"Don't like the idea of being tied down to the land," Dan said.

"Didn't say that."

"Well, you can't do it if you don't have any goals."

"Think I don't?"

Dan looked over at Sam again, and something in his eye told Sam that Dan had a very definite thing to say to that, or ask, but he did not say it or ask it. And that was just fine for Sam, as he knew he would not have any answer, either prepared or off-the-cuff, that would sound truthful.

There are times when goals, especially those of the elaborate variety, are not readily available to people, and all they have to work with are vague yearnings and dim visions.

Most of the time Sam did not pay much attention to things like goals and large ideas, but in the week following his meeting Sue and Ruth, and for reasons he was barely aware of and that he would have probably dismissed if he had been, his mind would drift in those obscure directions, with thoughts seemingly disconnected and random, even though they could all be very easily tied together—by any objective observer who was cotton to the particulars of his circumstances—to one single, obvious and overriding condition of Sam's life.

That he was completely alone.

40

It had been a bit later, in Ruth's kitchen, when Sam had gone in to fetch the last box, that a miserable feeling of embarrassment finally came to land completely. And with no one there, he gave in to the feeling of helplessness at his own stupidity.

Staring at nothing, he let out a sigh and looked up at the ceiling, holding his hands imploringly upward. And at that, he heard a cough of mirth behind him and turned to see Ruth in the doorway.

She turned the amused smile on her face into a questioning squint. "Just wanted to check," she said. "You did want to go fishing, right?"

Chapter 7

HE was working a field half a county distant from the bulk of Harley Petersen's land. Acquired at the death of an uncle and forty miles away, the property was good land even if Harley only marginally maintained it. There was nothing exceptional about the work Sam did that week, outside of the extreme solitude.

In the morning, he would get up before dawn and make himself a breakfast of eggs and toast. Taking his coffee in a thermos, he would drive out to Harley's, arriving before anyone was up. There on the porch, he would find the lunchbox set out for him with notes about fields or equipment inside. He would then drive off towards that distant field located near a place called Cammas-Dian.

Fred had told him that Cammas-Dian, now just a relic of a town with a few empty storefronts surrounded by old locusts and maples where a few houses must have been, was named after an Indian who had done something or been something important around there at one time. Each morning, as the early sun cast pastel lights across the hilltops of the gray-brown farmland, with an indefinite bluish mist in the still and shadowed bottoms, he went through Cammas-Dian without giving a thought to it, or whoever the old Indian had been. The fields were only half a mile down the road from it.

Harley had rented out the land's old farmhouse to a man who worked over in Harrington. Sam drove past the house each morning but never saw the people, arriving too early in the morning and leaving too late at night. A few times, when he was on a near hillside at the right time in the afternoon, he would see at some distance a long yellow school bus winding along the highroad, making its way through the hills. It would stop and two small children would jump out and start up the long driveway to the house.

The first few days, his being alone out there had given him that familiar and strange feeling as though he was some sort of ghost that came and went with the rise and set of the sun. Each morning before dawn he drove up the long access road, passing the house and crossing over among the farm buildings to the equipment sheds to get the tractor out and hooked up to the implement, and spent the day circling out in the far-off hills, leaving each night near dusk. But as the newness of the place wore off, so did that feeling, and then all there was to it was the land, and he forgot about that feeling of being only a ghost.

They were beautiful hills, some of them enormous, and he loved the way his harrow sculpted smooth the gentle swells of the sides down to the valleys, feathering the differences together until all of it was the same with a rolling, unbroken coverlet of fine-sifted topsoil. With the harrow, he was healing the ground.

Twice in that past year the ground had been ripped open and left raw. The first time had been after last year's harvest, a disc having cut the stubble back into the ground so it could rot and soften through winter, the disc making deep, straw-choked wounds in the topsoil. Then, in early spring, the field had been rough cultivated to even out the disc-cut surface. But the ground still had been torn, naked beneath the sun. He was now closing it with the harrow, smoothing and protecting its moisture from the coming summer, the small tines sifting a thin skin of dirt that would crust with the first rain.

If it had been the right year, the fields would have been planted, the seed inserted through that surface to the fertile ground beneath. But there were other fields at Cammas-Dian for that. The ground he was on had been worked hard for two years and was to be rested a year as fallow.

He worked carefully to make sure he went well, and that the marks were smoothly overlapped. There was no one to talk to, and the big tractor, although it had a comfortable enough cab, pressurized to keep the dust out, had no radio for company and he was left to his thoughts for the entire day, never getting back to Gainesville until late at night, where he went straight to bed after dinner in his room. Day after day, the whole stretch of the week, he dipped and soared over the hillsides, turning the big machine, tracing the marks and following the traces around and around the hills and along the fence lines in a world of field and sky. Soon, even the dull roar of the engine became a form of silence to an emptied, trackless mind, where small thoughts appeared, then gathered to themselves and suddenly went on forever. Even the most minor and petty of them swelling bigger than they ever could have normally deserved, rushing off then in sweeping waves out across the far hills, taking him with them.

Occasionally, his thoughts bored in upon one hapless memory or idea. But it did not worry him. He knew it as the natural state of mind out there in the fields, a mild and familiar form of absorption that all farmers knew. And like all other forms of compelled states of mind, it acted as a safety valve, a form of protection, given all the possible work his mind could have been doing.

Perhaps there was a stagnant quality to that state of mind, a plodding numbness, but there was a stability as well and he accepted the state of mind with the same acceptance he applied to any other facet of farming. There was one state of mind, however, that he wished he could have completely avoided, and to push that away he would go in other directions, any directions.

But she'd come back and would hover in front of him. She danced there, and laughed there, and kissed him, and he told himself over and over that he was just going to be the recipient of pure kindness. The most awful kind of kindness imaginable. And he told himself he did not feel attracted to her. He did not. And never would.

And what he was doing almost worked, and for long stretches of time, he could hold everything like that. He would look at the pleasant way the hills folded on themselves and gaze off at distant fields and farms and even farther to a butte not far south, its rocky,

44

tree-covered flanks looking like an old battleship heaving itself upon the rolling Palouse farmland. But no matter how long that lasted, or whatever else he might be in the middle of thinking, slowly, unconsciously, those light green eyes beneath golden hair would begin rising up into his thoughts, and upward and stronger, and then full and aching, she would be there and claim him, hers for the taking. And it was on a Thursday morning, in the half-light of dawn, that his concentration went completely away, and the punishment for it was both swift and severe.

He had decided that it was time to change the oil in the tractor. It had been changed sometime in the fall but he knew there had been hundreds of hours put on since. He went into a shed and brought out a big pan and a sixteen-inch crescent wrench.

He had run the engine to warm the oil, and now, with the engine off, he crawled beneath the front axle, dragging the drip-pan and wrench along with him.

There beneath the engine, now popping as it began to cool, he sat with his back against the transmission frame, the drip-plug in front of him at eye level. Pulling the pan beneath the plug, he took up the big wrench, awkward at that level, and adjusted it to the head of the plug. The bolt was in really tight and would not break loose at the first try. He tried again, his mind wandering along other lines.

Maybe it really would rain by the weekend. The forecast said to expect showers by the following week. But the wind had freshened since that time, and he felt that it could move things along a little faster. That would make it impossible to take Sue's roommate fishing.

But then, he thought with a sense of fatality, he knew it was a waste of time to speculate. Fate said it was either going to be fishing with Sue's roommate or nothing at all. Caught up in the weather like it was, there was no way of being sure of anything until Sunday and that would make anything else he could dream up impossible.

He gave the bolt another pull. It was as if it had been welded. He damned himself for getting himself trapped for the weekend, and he also damned whoever it was who had last set that bolt.

Christ, he thought, they must have set it with their boot. He

45

strained again, putting his back into it and pushing against the tire with his legs. But it did not budge.

Fishing my ass, he thought. Let's go fishing...

Getting frustrated, he braced his foot further up inside the right wheel well and, putting both hands behind the wrench, gave it everything he had. And right there and then he discovered why the bolt had been so tight. It was one of those bolts that had been overtightened so many times, each time its threads opened up a fraction more and causing it to be overtightened the next time and the next time in a vicious circle, that there was no longer such a thing as degrees of tightness. It was either on or off. And to get it on or break it free basically meant a kick with a boot.

If he had not been so preoccupied with trying not to think of the person he didn't want to think of he would have set the wrench and given it a kick himself. Instead he put every bit of his strength into that gigantic pull on the wrench, the handle only a foot or so away from his face. Stupidly. And so the perfectly stupid thing that might happen did.

Straining with all his might, the bolt finally broke loose, and he practically knocked himself out cold, the heavy steel handle of the wrench smashing into his face just below the right eye. Too late, his reaction was to jerk his head back so that immediately after the blow from the wrench came a second crashing blow from behind as his head slammed into the unyielding axle of the front wheels. The heavy wrench dropped from his hands down into the drip-pan.

For a while, it was very simple. Shooting flashes in his eyes and in his ears, the pounding waves of the biggest ocean in the world. Then he got nauseous and he felt as though he was sitting on the edge of a towering cliff with nothing but air below, and he was dizzy trying not to fall off. Feeling that, he reached up and curled his fingers around some linkage cables, holding himself still. In that cramped area, half-inside the engine space, it was a real possibility that if he started to get faint he might make a hard, uncontrolled jerk with his head, knocking himself out for good.

He went through the worst of it just holding on and waiting for the first hard pain and dizziness to pass. He shut his eyes once, thinking that might help, but it did not, only nauseating him even more. He opened them and tried to focus on something.

He looked at one of his boots. It was on the other side of the drip-pan and it did not seem like it was part of him but just some lifeless thing. A long time passed before he could let his eyes move off his boot and travel up his leg to his shirt, to where he could see how his blood had splattered there on his chest.

"Shit."

Suddenly, all he wanted was to get out from under the tractor, but because he did not want to crawl back under there again, he tossed the wrench out of the pan, reached up and undid the bolt, now easily turned out with just his fingers, and let the hot oil begin pouring out. He then got his body turned around and crawled out from under the tractor, his head pinging and pounding while he was on his hands and knees. Getting up on all fours, and then to his feet, he walked away from the tractor.

He went to the toilet room in the shop and was annoyed the room had no mirror. He found a roll of paper towels under the sink and, wetting one, wiped at the dirty feeling on the right side of his face. When he took the towel away he saw it was covered with blood and dried blood, the dry blood beginning to dissolve on the wet towel. He threw the towel in a rag box and took another, wetting it and putting it against his face.

Mechanically, for a while he did that until he was sure that the blood there was from the bleeding itself. At that point he took a dry towel and pressed it against his cheekbone like a compress.

He sighed.

His head was clearing and only the slightest of headaches was coming on just between the temples. With his free hand he reached up and spread his fingers across his forehead, his thumb at one temple, the tip of his little finger at the other, and he massaged his head with his hand like that until the pointed thing inside delocalized into something more general.

He saw that he had stopped bleeding and knew why it had stopped so quickly. It was not because the size of it was small, but because of the fast swelling. Even without touching it he could feel the puffiness coming on big under his eye. He might have gone to ask at the house if there was any ice, but even if there had been someone there he couldn't bring himself to do it. He'd had an experience one time of breaking down, and knocking on the door of a farmhouse where a farmer's wife had let him in to make a call... and had barely been able to make a phone call before he was suddenly having to deal with the occupant of a pickup truck who had arrived in a cloud of dust.

Going out of the bathroom, he went and sat down on a chair by the shop door, watching the tractor over by the shed dripping out the last of the oil. The rest of that day he would feel like a different person.

And punished. For lying to himself the whole long week.

Two days later, it would be like having a different face.

He looked at the door, pursed his lips, and knocked. He heard steps approach and the door opened and Ruth looked out at him. It took her a moment.

"What'd you do?"

"Like it?"

He stood there while she stared at him, which, as a thing, turned out to be not as hard to undergo as he had expected.

"God. What do you do when it's like that?"

"Not much. Except maybe wear a paper bag."

The look on his face made Ruth smile. "Sorry," she said. "You just caught me by surprise. Does it hurt?"

He grinned on one side of his face and shook his head. She let him in, saying she had a few last things to get together. She went off and left him and he sat down in a chair to wait.

No, he thought, it did not hurt much. Only when it got looked at.

When Ruth returned to the front room she smiled again at the sight.

"You get in many fights?" She watched for him to smile and then went into the kitchen to get the lunch basket.

"No. This one I did all by myself."

From the kitchen, he heard her sigh and then begin to laugh, and a moment later she came out, leaning in the doorway with the basket under one arm.

"Was it difficult to do?"

"No. It's simple when you use a sixteen-inch wrench."

He could see her trying to picture what he might do with a sixteen-inch wrench.

"So, you're not a fighter."

"Not like this." He felt grateful to her for the change in direction, making it all just what it was.

She smiled at him cheerfully, and he noticed for the first time how fine she looked that morning. She was the first woman he had ever seen who looked right for going fishing and looked good at the same time. All she wore was some jeans and a sweatshirt, and in her hair a headband going across the top and underneath in the back. Her only jewelry was a necklace with a small, pearl-like stone.

"So now you're going to also have to spend the day with Frankenstein."

"I'll just look all the better by contrast," she said, putting some things in a bag.

"That would have been the case, anyway."

Her eyes quickly flicked over to look at him and then looked away. "All right... let's get out of here."

He could never tell the difference between what was careful and what was casual about the naturalness of women like Ruth, women who seemed to be natural all the time. She wasn't a type of woman he knew much about but he found that, in some ways, he was beginning to feel glad he was going fishing with her instead of Sue.

They got in his car and he followed her directions to the lake. As they drove out of town, Ruth suddenly stretched her arms up over her head, pushing them way back beneath the roof of his car, sighing comfortably.

"Oh, God! I've been looking forward to this all week."

"Me, too," he said.

Chapter 8

ON the way out from town, the fields along the road were deepening and thickening with young wheat, the bright green of it spreading across the rich soil of the hills. Turning off from the main road, they had gone down to the lake, passing through a small, cool valley filled with bitter cherry, alder and maple. The trees were full-leafed by then and the air was clean-smelling beneath them.

He had been prepared for a big crowd at the lake on opening day, but it was practically deserted. By the bait shop sat only a few boat trailers, and most of the rental boats were still tied up along the dock.

Ruth began to carry their things out to the dock while he went into the shop. He bought two bottles of bright red eggs and two dozen hellgrammites. The young dragonflies, still wingless and mud-colored, crawled around in the bottoms of the refrigerated plastic containers. As far as he could tell the woman who ran the shop never looked at his face once.

He went out the back of the shop and down to where Ruth was waiting on the dock. Their gear was piled at her feet. She pointed at the nearest boat. It was the driest and cleanest. "You're rowing, right?"

"Yes ma'am."

He took an oar and snagged a gunwale, pulling the boat alongside the dock. They climbed in and stowed the lunch and most of the gear up underneath the covered bow. Ruth settled herself on the stern seat. When they were ready, he pulled on one oar, shifting the bow out toward the lake. He glanced at her. She was looking over the side into the smooth, green water.

"OK?" he asked and she nodded. He set the oars with a full bite and began pulling out onto the lake.

He rowed slowly along a thinly wooded shore where a high rock cliff reared up behind the trees. On the far end of the lake, where the cliffs lowered to gently sloped banks, there were deeper woods, and that was where the exit stream ran out. Of the few boats on the lake, most were there around the lily pads. He did not think it really mattered where they went on such a small lake.

In the middle of the lake was another shallow place where lily pads and reeds grew thick. He rowed to it and found a place where the water lilies made a half-circle like a small bay. There they were close enough to entice the fish out, but also far enough away not to get caught up in everything. She was ready for him when he shipped the oars and as he began to lower out the bow anchor, a plastic bleach jug filled with concrete, she was doing the same with hers at the stern.

He was surprised by how far down the jug had to go. There, only twenty feet from the water lilies, the water was more than thirty feet deep. That shallow spot would have to have walls going practically straight up and down.

He looked back at Ruth tying her anchor line at the stern. He could see by the length she was using that she had gone that deep as well. They would try it at different depths. One of them would hang just off the bottom and the other would go down half-way to see what might come out from the lilies.

He picked up one of the rods and began jointing it together. The line on his reel was still clear and bluish on the spool and he knew it was strong and supple and he began threading it out through the guides. He saw her do the same thing and saw she did not throw the bail open but simply loosened the tension a little and pulled the line out as she needed it. He reached for a hook but before he could begin tying it she stopped him, holding out her own.

"Show me how," she smiled. "That's as far as anyone's ever gotten me."

He leaned toward her and tried to show her how it went, but there was something about the upside-downedness of it that made it difficult, and she told him to hold up. She moved herself next to him for a better view.

"OK. Here it goes." He showed her the simplest good knot he knew. As he trimmed the leftover leader down clean, he said, "If this were heavier line, or the fish were bigger, or if the lure were more expensive, you might want to take the end and run it back under the big loop before you snugged it down."

"Easy enough." She began doing it herself while he looked on. She went all the way through it exactly as he had shown and all he did was give it a last pull for tightness.

"Thanks," she said, and she watched as he pulled out the bait. The hellgrammites were the best, he knew, but he wanted to see how the eggs went first. She loaded her hook while he was crimping a couple of split shot on her leader about five feet away from her hook. After it was all ready, she lowered it over the side and let it go out until the line went slack when the shot touched bottom. She pulled in about six feet of line by hand and then rewound it on her spool, counting the turns of the handle as she went.

He put his shot on and lowered out a dozen feet or so on the opposite side of the boat. They sat in silence for a while until she decided to make herself more comfortable by moving one leg over the seat so she was straddling it, and then leaning back against him.

"Comfy?"

She wiggled her shoulders. "Yep. You're as good as a tree."

He felt flattered by how quickly she was so comfortable with him. It had never happened before. As time passed, the rhythm of her breathing and small movements of adjustment brought him to relax against her as well. So relaxed he barely noticed the first words she spoke into the calm silence of the lake, or how they were shockingly similar to his own thoughts.

"I hope you're not too disappointed that it's me instead of Sue you have out here."

"Yeah, I suppose that could be the impression."

"Well, you did seem to be asking her."

There was no way Sam could tell anything close to what had been going through his mind for an entire week. So he laughed. "I don't remember what I was doing. Can I play a joker here?"

"You don't need to apologize. I haven't been jealous of Sue for years. I mean, there are enough other things to deal with."

He couldn't just let that sit. "Believe me, there's nothing to be jealous about..." But that was all he could get out.

"I'm not."

He liked her for that. "You're good friends."

"We've known each other for so long, I suppose so."

"Not so close then."

"Different worlds. But, yes. Close enough. We trust each other, and confide in each other, if that's what you mean. We've known each other forever. I knew her even before we moved to Gainesville."

"You did not always live here?"

"I grew up on a farm. But I moved to town when I was fourteen. So that makes me a townie as well."

"Your parents gave up farming?"

Sam felt her take a breath. "My mother died when I was two. She was forty-five and Dad was almost fifty. They got married late but wanted kids. Before me there had been two miscarriages and they knew it was dangerous trying again. I'm lucky I'm even here."

"And then you and your father moved to town."

"No. If it had been the other way around, with Dad dying and only my mother and myself, I suppose we would have come straight in. But he kept on farming right to the end. He died when I was fourteen and that was when I came to live here in town with an aunt." She shifted her back a bit. "And you?"

Sam had long ago come up with several ways to answer questions like that, each being just a different way to say next to nothing. But he found he did not want to use those answers, neither particularly genuine nor outright dishonest, and his mind turned a bit. The real story he could not find any way to tell that he could feel comfortable with right then, and all the rest since then did not sound much better, he had to admit. And he also had to admit it was the

53

first time he had become aware of how deep this avoidance had been. As he thought about this, he did not notice that he was letting the silence build until he felt her shift and saw her glance back at him.

"Sorry," he smiled. "Bad conversation habits. Fact is, I can never find the good starting point. I guess it's the same sort of thing as you had but I didn't have a real place or much opportunity to have many friends. So I didn't stick around."

"I didn't make a lot of friends, I was always kind of more one of the farm kids even living in town, but you can't help but knowing everyone and ending up part of it."

"Maybe."

"You're not from a small town, then. Or else haven't lived anywhere for long enough to make it like that."

Sam gave out a laugh. "How do you know that?"

"Because small town folk, when they move, don't move to other small towns unless they have to." She shrugged. "Get married, or something."

"I've been in enough small towns."

"I'm saying move to, not move through."

Sam looked out across the lake. "I guess that's right enough."

Ruth laughed. "OK, I'll leave you alone."

And she did. And that was another thing he wasn't used to.

An impossible coincidence, he thought. In some ways theirs were almost the same story. But in others, though, and especially how it turned out, it could not have been more different. In her case, it fit her pretty well. The only child of a farmer in his fifties, she carried that calm of having been raised in circumstances both simple and serious. A sober little farm girl went to school in town and returned in the afternoon to the usual evening chores all farms consisted of. "And Sue was your earliest friend," he finally said.

"We had other friends, of course. Like I said, you can't help but know everyone. In a way, around here, it's just one large family."

"I don't know about the family part."

"You're really not from a small town. I'm guessing you really have moved around a lot."

"Yeah. So if I start in on it, it'll just sound like a list of places."

"What it sounds like, is nothing made you want to stay."

"Does that sound bad?"

"I don't know. Must be nice to move around. Or just have that as an option. Sue always says she wishes she had but I know she never would."

"Is that the thing that makes you different from her?"

"Yes and no. She's always been so much of what the town is and I can't imagine her anywhere else, even though things haven't been easy for her. The boys were rough, you know? And when that was over she had to deal with the fact that the cream of the crop was never going to stay around here, and college did not work out at all. And she just can't make the jump, up to Spokane or something."

It was not lost on Sam that this easy way of talking about her friend, neither judgmental nor jealous in any way, showed that she was a friend indeed, and probably more so than she realized.

"She didn't have any opportunities?"

"None, as far as I know. And she's not adventurous enough to imagine her own. I've never completely figured out why, except maybe it was because she had always known some sort of success here. For good or for bad. I mean, here at least, she knew what she had. But this is making it sound like she's unhappy. She isn't."

Coming to town, Sam had met one attractive woman and then another and, as for Ruth, there were no words he could find for how beautiful she was. What were the odds of one very small town having that? And despite how someone might think their looks alone might have taken them places, they had all resisted getting swept into the sort of world where looks, especially the type that Marilyn had, opened doors. But the town was evidently all they needed, and for some reason that made them all seem even more attractive.

"You weren't making her seem unhappy," he said. "She's lucky to have you as a friend."

"I'm lucky, too."

Sam stared out at the tip of his pole, a still black dot against the blue of the lake, the line dropping straight into the water. "So, how is it you've stayed here?"

She was silent for a moment, and then smiled. "You know? You just made me realize how some things can't be easily explained. Especially when you've never been asked to explain."

"I get asked all the time."

They both laughed at that and angled around to look at each other. And, as usual, right when it seemed that everything was going the other way a fish was on.

The tip of Ruth's pole jerked down once, then again and stayed, and she gave the pole a soft twitch upwards and set the hook. Sam had felt it from the first moment, through his back.

"God, that was fast," she said as her light pole now went over with a deep bend, the line cutting the surface of the water away from the boat in a wide arc. At the heavier tugs, Ruth loosened her spool tension to where line would click off slowly, the pole losing a little of the tightness of its curve and becoming more lively. It really was a light pole, Sam thought, and while it looked by the bend as though she had something big on, it did not take much of a fish to make it go over like that.

Before long the tip rose and Ruth began to reel in. The line, now straight down beneath the boat, made quick circles in the water. The fish fought well the whole way and at a depth of about five feet Ruth suddenly caught its glimmer in the murk below.

"There he is!" She stopped reeling for a moment, then reeled a little more, looking, and then did see it as it circled and pulled. And that seemed enough for her and she brought the fish up to the surface and alongside and, trusting both hook and leader, in one motion hoisted the fish over the side and dropped it, flopping, into the bottom of the boat.

Maybe fourteen inches, it was a fat brown trout, its spots bright greens and reds and blacks under an iridescent sheen, its belly ivory white. Ruth got the hook out and handed the trout around to Sam.

"If you don't mind...."

"So I'm the hit-man."

Holding the trout belly up, he rapped its head hard against the aluminum gunwale, its body going stiff and then relaxing quiet. Ruth let out an "ugh" and Sam set the fish down into the plastic box with the ice. He reached over the side of the boat to rinse off the blood and scales.

"It's pretty crude," he agreed. He dried his hand on his pants leg and handed Ruth the egg jar. "He's a nice one." He looked over at the sleek shape lying on the ice. "Nice and fat."

"He's beautiful."

Sam nodded. They really were the one thing that fit in perfectly where they lived. Even better than birds.

He just about said that thought to her, but then dropped it. There had been enough talk about fitting in as it was. Although, suddenly, he found himself wanting to continue talking to her about things like that. He glanced at her.

Ruth had settled herself again and concentrated on her line. Fishing, suddenly, was serious business. But she noticed him and turned her head to give him a happy smile and for the first time that day Sam felt something different wash through him. It was not long afterwards that she brought up another trout, a little smaller but fatter, and the whole scene repeated itself. After that Sam just lowered his bait to the bottom but nothing happened.

Ruth caught a third and then a fourth just before lunchtime, leaving Sam to just opening beers, killing fish, gazing across the lake, and enjoying the feel of Ruth against his back. It was only once in a while that he remembered how his face looked.

At lunchtime, just for the sake of quiet, they brought in their lines, Sam wondering if it was really necessary for him. Ruth unpacked roast beef sandwiches made with mayonnaise and sweet pickles and there were barbecue-flavored potato chips to go with the beer. If they talked about nothing in particular, it did not really seem to matter to either of them, and they were companionable in a way as though they'd known each other forever. But he did see how that was, and he also was aware of how a lot of the things he had been carrying around since Montana and Wyoming, and even before in other places farther south and west, had just slid away.

The lake was so smooth. The glassy surface like oil with only a slight heaving motion reflecting the clear blue sky and the brilliant sun above them. Most of the other boats that had been on the lake that morning had long since left.

Sam looked across the water at the nearest shoreline where high, dark banks and old, overhanging trees cast a deep shade. Lily pads floated out across the shallow waters underneath and in a few places the underbrush beneath the trees leaned out over the lake as well, hiding the shore, the dark waters floating the forest there. A dim movement in the shadows caught Sam's eye, and he discovered a heron moving slowly through the reeds and lilies. Dusky blue with black wing plumes and a dark head, it moved with slow, precise steps, sometimes hesitating, one foot poised above the water, its long bill, shining dark above and shell-white below, held just above the surface. A few times it probed slowly into the water but each time the bill slid back out and it would take another step.

For a long time, the heron fished like that, peacefully and uneventfully, and Sam became used to the quiet spectacle of the bird's seemingly futile occupation. But then the heron froze as though suddenly becoming a lifeless museum specimen. Sam waited for the plunging slash and time stretched out and just at that moment when Sam was tensed for something else, the bird took another careful step. It was incredible, that concentration, so focused the bird was not even aware of its own movements, its neck a still tension, the tip of its bill just below the surface. Then Sam was not aware of any movement at all. Again. Three heartbeats went by and the head of the heron went in neck deep and when it came out a silver flashing was caught crosswise between its bills. The heron tilted its head back and the flashing was gone, and then, with its head feathers slightly raised, it folded its neck back into an S-shape again and looked out across the lake. Satisfied with whatever it saw and shaking its head feathers down and resettling its wings, it began fishing again.

Sam turned and found that Ruth had been watching too. She smiled and he reached for a beer, handed it to her and then grabbed one for himself. She took the beer, looking back at the heron, but then handed it back.

"Don't want any more?" he asked.

"Sure, I would."

"You're pacing yourself."

"No. As a matter of fact, I wouldn't mind having another right away."

Sam stared at her and she laughed.

"I think you're forgetting. I don't have the same capacity you do."

Sam nodded. "I guess it does look like a lot."

"That's not the capacity I was talking about. I don't give a damn if you drink yourself cockeyed and fall overboard."

He got the boat over to the shore as quickly as he could, and then waited as she picked her way up into the bushes. It was no wonder, he was thinking, that women might not care much for the lethal combination of beer drinking and fishing out in small boats. But he knew there were other reasons women did not like fishing, and not just the solitude. And yet Ruth obviously liked fishing and there she was with him. Or maybe it wasn't just the fishing, he thought.

He looked back towards the bank, a sudden and relatively unfamiliar sense of expectancy coming over him as he waited for her return.

The afternoon was hot and quiet and, once in a while, a jarring, rapid, trout. By the time the sun began to fall toward a cooling evening, they had caught their limit. Sam had never in his life spent a whole day out on a lake like that. When they finally pulled anchor Ruth said she wanted to row back.

She rowed easily and he watched the dark water swirling smooth around and then away from him at the stern. Deep green into the depths, the water was fairly clear with faint organic lights. It was another world below and they were sliding over the top of it. He tried to see as far into it as he possibly could. Below them, the diminishing perspectives of filtered light shifted down in waves through that translucent medium, a liquid gemstone glimmer. And then he looked up at her and saw her looking at him, her face glowing gold with the lowering sun. Those incredible green eyes of hers were lit up with the sun's rays and maybe it was the reflection of the sky, or the water on the lake, but a sudden flash of blue mixed with the green, and it just slipped out under his breath.

"Turquoise."

She looked at him for a second. "Oh," she finally said. "You mean this." She stopped rowing and put her fingers on the small jewel on her necklace. "It's an opal. My aunt gave it to me on my eighteenth birthday when I graduated from high school."

He just nodded. The jewel was, in fact, lovely, with rainbow sheens brought out by the sun. And for her, it obviously had meanings that made it even more precious.

"You know," she said, "you don't look so bad with the sun behind you."

"You don't look so bad, period."

He saw her expression freeze, and he picked up his hand to say something, but Ruth stopped him.

"Oh, for god's sake, don't apologize! I don't get a chance to hear many real compliments, or get to feel that way."

"And how do you feel now?"

Ruth gave the oars a deep pull, her eyes suddenly brilliant again with the sun going golden in them. "I feel pretty good."

"So do I."

Ruth made several more thoughtful pulls of the oars.

"You like working for the Petersens?"

Sam smiled. "If you mean working with either Dan or Fred, it's all right."

"That means working for the Petersens, right?"

"I wouldn't know."

"What do you mean?"

"Other than Dan or Fred, I haven't met anyone else."

"You haven't met Carl? Or Dan's dad?"

"I've heard about Carl." Sam smiled. "And plenty. From Dan."

"I imagine."

"It's funny?"

"No. Just makes sense."

"What makes sense?"

She gave him a look. "Can I ask you a question about Dan?"

"Sure."

"Do you like him?"

"I've met worse."

"And that's all?"

Sam shrugged. "You know, OK, I came over with him to help you guys move and all, like I would a friend, but I don't really know him all that much.

"I was thinking you might have gotten an impression already."

"Impression?"

"I don't know. Such as, let's say, that Dan likes to be careful about things?"

Sam had a neutral look on his face, but something about it made her feel more confident.

"If you work out there for any length of time, sooner or later you'll notice that Dan likes to make sure things are just right."

"You mean he's a control freak." Sam smiled. "Yes, you could say I've noticed that."

"I wouldn't say freak. You haven't met his family?"

"You're saying I'm not going to meet anyone out there until Dan's decided what..." he paused, realizing what he was about to say.

Ruth stopped rowing. "Yes. Until he decides what he sees you as." She frowned. "He's complicated... it's complicated out there."

Sam grinned, then winced. "Ow," he touched his cheek. "It shouldn't take long for him to figure me out. I'm pretty good at being whatever it is that people see."

"You're making fun of yourself. I'd say you're one of those people who seem to be exactly what they are."

Sam found himself staring at her. Again.

For a moment she watched him looking back at her like that but then just took a breath and started rowing, and now looking out across the lake.

He turned and looked in the same direction and saw how, out at the far end of the lake, the sun had turned to a sliver just above the hard line of the cliff above the trees, and then watched how it suddenly and quickly dipped from sight and how the green shadows of the trees went black.

"What a nice day," he said.

For a long minute or so, they moved across the smooth water, the boat now gliding with the rhythm of the pulling oars. And then into the quiet of the lake Ruth said "thank you."

Later that night, the cool air flowed through his window as he drove back to the hotel. It had a cold, almost wet feeling on his forearm where he was sunburned. He was remembering how the lake had looked so flat and calm and how blue and graceful and unconscious the heron had been and even more so later when it had suddenly spread long wings and lifted itself off over the trees.

And then he thought about the best of it, and as he remembered that, it reminded him of some of the other times when he had thought he was having the best of it, but never like this. And he was able to feel good about it and even managed for quite a while to not remember about what had always happened to what he'd thought the best of it was.

Chapter 9

SAM sat in his car. With his window down he could hear the voices inside the farmhouse. After a while Dan came out of the house, nodded at him, and he got out and followed Dan into a shed by the barn where they took down some heavy haying chaps hanging on nails. Next to the shed was a flatbed truck with all the sides taken off but the front one. They got in and Dan drove towards the nearest hay fields. Five miles into the hills they turned off the main road and then bounced hard on the heavy rear springs along the rough road.

"Hope you got a good breakfast," Dan said.

"Eggs and bacon."

"Make it a steak for a while."

"How long are we going to be doing this?"

"If we can get up to around nine hundred, a thousand bales a day, about three weeks."

"Fifteen steaks."

"Twenty. Saturdays included. Actually, maybe double that. We have steaks both breakfast and dinner when we're hauling hay. So buy about fifty. We might go Sundays, too. You can never tell about the weather and we can't afford to let them get wet."

Dan's first "we" did not sit well with Sam. He not only nearly came to asking why he wasn't being fed like the other hands, but even felt belligerent enough to pointedly ask if he might get a raise. To cover, at least, the steaks. "I'm going to have to invest in half a cow," he said.

Dan half turned his head, but Sam could not tell what might

be registering, so he developed it, holding up what were a pair of tight-fitting, cowhide bucking gloves. He had bought three pairs the day before.

"As with everything else."

Dan smiled and looked back at the road. "Personal expenses."

"Right. Which I'll claim on the line for undeclared wages."

After a short pause, Dan nodded. "Noted. I'll see what I can do."

Sam suppressed a smile of his own. "Noted. Can kicked."

If Dan had heard Sam, he showed no sign of it, now looking intently at where the wheat fields were just turning, patches of gold beginning to tinge among the green. That would normally have been a subject of conversation, but neither of them felt like talking. The ripening wheat fields meant there was only so much time for this other work, and it would be hard work they were getting started on, and all of the days were going to hurt in some way, but it was the first that would be the worst.

The road skirted around the bottom of a big wheat hill until they came upon the edge of a long coulee. Its floor, dry and flat down in the cut, meandered between vertical rock ledges, the remnant of a channel carved by an immense prehistoric flood. Only a hundred and fifty or so yards wide, the coulee turned and twisted for half a mile and was planted for hay its entire length except at the edges where scrub brush and stunted pines grew. Sam could see the alfalfa grew well down there, thick and green even in its shorn condition, and he figured at least a thousand bales lay spread from one end of the coulee to the other. That would be a good day's haul even if the nearest barn was not too far away and they were in good shape. He wasn't sure at all about the first one. But when it came to the second—and here Sam instinctively hunched his shoulders—he had few doubts about what sort of shape he was in.

Down in the field Sam climbed out and fixed on his chaps. Heavy, grey leather with a belt at the waist, the chaps strapped in place with loose bands behind the thighs and knees. He pulled on the cowhide bucking gloves. They were new and stiff but he knew by evening they would be soft as deer skin.

He did the driving and bucking and most of the time it was easy, only having to swing the bales as high as the smooth steel bed of the truck. Even so he followed them with his knee, taking some of the strain off his shoulders and back and sending them with a snap over to where Dan was stacking.

Weaving five to a layer, Dan stacked six layers and then started another behind it. It was less running around than what Sam was doing, but the work got even by the high stacking he had to do when he got above chest height. For the top layers, he had to buck the bales up with his knee until they were balanced onto his fists for the last shove. He had to do it in one smooth motion, otherwise the full weight would come back on his arms. One or two could go wrong like that, but a whole day of it would have been too much.

Dan was good at it; Sam was hit and miss. Luckily, he only had to do it when the truck was almost loaded, tossing the last ones up to where Dan was standing on top of the bales. Dan said there were guys who could lay bales right into place at seven high, actually more like ten high because of the height of the bed. There were guys who could toss even higher, like his brother Carl, who had the technique of going with the bale sideways, grabbing both strings in one hand and bucking it up end first with a finish sort of like a basketball hook-shot. Sam tried one, and got it to wobble up five high.

"Not bad," Dan grinned.

"Shit," Sam said, his shoulder immediately aching.

"You'll get the rhythm after a while."

Sam slung up another bale. Every other place he had hauled hay for had used mechanized buckers. "Maybe it'd help to do a little weight-lifting, too."

"Hell, no. You know Max Carter?" Dan glanced at Sam. "He's this kid. Only about eighteen. But he would be about the biggest person you will ever meet. He could probably lift the back end of this truck. But when it comes to haying he can't buck worth shit. He's all arms and strings and whenever he tries to toss high he just blows half of them apart."

Sam had already done just that, earlier in the morning. Trying to toss one of his first bales by just the strings alone, he had been left standing in the middle of a pile of hay.

"And Carl can go all day," Dan went on. "Carter's dead by noon."

"He might not be alone," Sam said to himself as he reached for another bale. With only the first load of the day on the truck he was beginning to feel it in his legs and shoulders and even across his stomach muscles. Only by using a swinging momentum would he be able to get through the hauling, not only for that first day but for all the rest.

With the truck stacked high, Dan climbed down and they headed back to the barn at Harley's, taking that time to renew their strength for the stacking they would have to do there. At the barn they threw the first bales in, laying them flat across the wide floor. They made two trips back and forth from the field like that and on their third trip out, the Petersens' farm dog, a massive yellow Labrador called Buster, ran out with them and then proceeded to chase down the mice that had hidden beneath the bales. By noon they'd taken in four loads, and they took a break in the field to eat their lunches. By evening they'd made five more runs. Nearly nine hundred bales.

"Pretty good," Dan said on the drive back to the farm. "I guess we're both in better shape than we thought."

Sam nodded. "I'm not going to lie. I'm sore."

After a moment Dan said, "yeah, me too."

Sam watched the hills going by, his mind wandering toward going home, and a sudden thought crossed through and he said for no particular reason, "I think I'll drop over and say hello to the girls."

Dan frowned. "You're kidding."

"Didn't think I was."

"You mean, straight over?"

"Yeah?"

"Have you got any idea what you smell like? What we smell like?"

"Mostly hay, I'd think."

"Think again."

66

Sam looked down at his dusty clothes and saw how wet and sweaty his shirt was. Practically dripping. With the dust congealing into all that. "Right, right. Don't know why I said that."

"Neither do I, but it doesn't matter. Just don't do that. Don't do that and don't even think about it." Dan laughed.

From the farm Sam drove straight home. Back at the hotel he drew a bathtub and lowered himself into it with a groan.

As he lay there, soaking in the warm water, letting the kinks and knots loosen, he remembered how Dan had ignored something Sam had joked about which was not really a joke.

He had worked for a lot of outfits, some paid well, others less, but there had always been something reasonably straight up about the pay. Here, though, Dan would just hand him a check on Friday. True, it covered what he needed for the hotel, food, gas... personal expenses... but it was just that. Since he had arrived there, he had not accumulated much of anything. He could not even buy a new pair of boots, or a shirt for that matter, if he wanted.

He knew that wasn't right, but also knew it was now partially his own fault. You go too long accepting something, after a while you don't have the right to expect any different. He was going to have to say something, and not by joking but asking flat out what the wages were out there. And a few other questions he had not considered before, like what he might expect over time. Because if a Friday night paycheck was all he could reckon on, he would need to find something else.

Even if it was just to be able to get out of town. If he wanted to. Or had to.

In the morning he went out to the farm and worked in the same way as the day before, and having cleared the first coulee he and Dan went into another where two thousand bales awaited. And a few days later another after that. And then another. And after a while the world just became field after field with afternoons of heat and effort, the sweat running down their bodies, while the hard packed dirt shimmered beneath the sun and the bales were piled and unpiled and piled again. And every night Sam would have the same thoughts occur to him and he would make the same resolutions, and in the mornings he would always forget them again because it was the sort of work where the things you thought about at night did not come back to you during the day. It was only the other way around.

Days went by, then nearly two weeks, and it became as monotonous as the tractor driving, with the exception of having someone to talk to. Although they did not talk much about anything other than what they were doing.

They filled Harley's closest barns with most of the first cutting and by the time they finished they had to turn around and start into the same fields again for the second cutting that Fred had already swathed and baled. The bales seemed to never finish and with each passing day the air got hotter as they drove further and further into the depths of summer, eventually working the Sundays as well. The work, with the increased heat, seemed continually heavier, and nights became dreamless blackouts of exhaustion. But as time passed the muscles grew strong and a good day began to see well over twelve hundred bales layered into a barn somewhere, and working without their shirts they soon darkened to a color as golden brown as the rich Palouse dirt.

But if it was hard work it could also be peaceful there in those fields cropped close to the ground like huge lawns. Because of how Harley's hay fields followed down in the gullies and coulees of the ice age scours, those places too intricate or small to be useful for wheat farming, there was an estate-like feeling around them. Finished with one series of fields they could look back and see an elegant park, like some landscape artist's dream of terraced gardens and towering rock ledges. Sam had mentioned that to Dan, but Dan made little sign that it meant anything to him, and after that Sam kept those sorts of thoughts to himself, and after a while he did not find himself thinking those thoughts either.

But it was not just the day thoughts he began to stop thinking, but the night thoughts as well. Those more involved thoughts that ran in directions well beyond those of the day. Because those night thoughts had also included more than just questions about how he was being paid and how that might continue. For a while those other thoughts had made him feel uncomfortable but as the days went by, the fatigue increased to a level where nights were no longer favorable to complicated things but were just a time to regain strength in dreamless sleep. And soon, and easily enough, he was not only not thinking about much of anything at all but he came to have an instinctive feeling that it was maybe better that way, anyway.

Sam, tired and sore as usual, a can of coffee and some biscuits under his arm, was in the meat section holding and staring at a large package of steaks. Buying in bulk was way cheaper than buying just three or four at a time. But he did not have much of a freezer in his fridge, which was just a small thing meant to keep a day or two of groceries and drinks. The package, holding easily a week's worth of steaks, represented a small irritation, but it built on a larger one that was becoming ever-present as a thought he kept forgetting about that was suddenly there and very present. "Yeah," he mumbled, "see what you can do..."

A voice came from behind him. "What are you doing moaning about steaks for?"

He turned to see Ruth. "Oh, hi!" He looked quickly away from her. "Yeah, I'm supposedly... uh... supposed to eat steaks." He looked up at her again but saw no sign of humor. A lot of impossibly fast thoughts went through his mind, and beginnings of things that had any meaning at all, but all he continued with was "and it's true, in fact."

"Man's been working."

"You could say that." He was suddenly conscious of his dusty, sweat-stained shirt. And where before Dan had made him feel worried about that, he was suddenly glad for it.

"And I just did," she said. "Two weeks. Or something. You were going to call?"

He had planned on doing so. At first. And if he had not because of reasons like not having had much of an idea what he might talk about, or just honest exhaustion, he now wished he had anyway and had spared himself a situation where he had even less he could think to say. "I was..."

She waited but not too long. "You were...," she shook her head, "... what? Going to? And then, not?"

For a moment he thought she was going to walk off, but when she did not his thoughts came back to him. "No, it's not like that. You remember what I told you? How it was going out there? The thing is, none of that has changed. For weeks now I've been trying to find out and...," he frowned, realizing he was not being truthful, "and then as far as you were concerned..."

"As far as I was concerned?"

"Remember? How we talked about all that? How you're here. And I'm not really. You see?"

She gave him a long look. "I do, now."

Out in the fields, if Sam had ever imagined himself having a conversation with Ruth about his presence there in that town, he probably would have been pragmatic about it, told her it was all for the best probably that they did not see each other. But with her there in front of him he did not feel pragmatic at all and whatever it was he might say to her, that wasn't the thing he wanted to say. But he knew he was in no position to go the other way, either, and so he just began talking around it in a way that, just maybe, she could understand. "I mean, I'm living in a hotel. I'm being paid cash. And beyond one job behind another I don't feel I've really got a job, you know? It was like that two weeks ago, and it's like that today. Tomorrow, or maybe not tomorrow but in a few weeks, I could be flat out of a job."

"So everything is the job."

He hated how the only thing that came to mind that he might have said was how they seemed to be having an awfully serious conversation for two people who had only spent one day together out in a boat.

Ruth took a breath. "I love how you talk. Letting everyone fill in the blanks. You mean like you did me a favor by not calling because you think you'll lose your job?"

Whatever it was Sam was feeling fell out of him. There was a long moment where Ruth looked at him and it was in a way that she had not looked at him even out on the lake. He wasn't sure what the

70

look meant but it did not seem to have anything to do with phone calls. And then he saw her expression change to something else.

"You're really bad at this, aren't you?"

"Bad?"

"Yeah," she said. "You know, out there on the lake, I was pretty surprised, too."

And there it was. The thing a few phone calls, or maybe just one, would have made clear. He had been surprised that day fishing, maybe more than her, and what it came down to was that he had not spent any time trying to imagine how to tell her that. But now, right there in the frozen foods aisle, she had got there first, and there was no need to imagine anything.

He nodded. "Me, too."

That was all she needed. "Right," she reached out and took the steaks out of his hand, "let's go get these cooked up."

He put his hand on his shirt. "I'm pretty dusty."

"Yes," she said. "So go get a fresh shirt so you don't make our place smell like a hay barn."

"You're being nice. You mean not like a sweaty pig."

She leaned in. "No. You just smell like a pile of fresh hay."

The field went to the edge of the cliffs, where a long, narrow lake fifty feet below reflected the blue sky from its smooth surface. At noon it made for a pleasant place to scramble down to where they could sit with their feet in cool water, eating in the deep shade of the willows and birches growing along the scanty banks.

One day, so hot that even by noon the field shimmered beneath them, they found themselves alongside a place where the cliff had no bank below and the rock wall dropped forty feet to the water and then continued straight down into dark green depths. In fact, the lake was just another coulee, but this one so deep it had filled with water. They had the truck standing a ways back from the edge and Sam walked over to look over. Dan watched him from on top of the bales on the truck.

"How deep is it?" Sam said.

"Goes down as deep as the cliff above."

Before Dan had managed to hop down Sam had already got off his chaps, boots and socks and had launched himself out into the air.

A whistling trip down, instantly cut and shockingly cold, all deep green with bubbles white in his face. Then he was up and breathing. He shook the water from his eyes and looked up at the cliff, watching for where Dan would come flying off.

Later, they sat in the shadow of the truck eating their lunches.

"This is a pretty big lake for the coulees," Sam said.

"William's Lake." Dan pointed with his sandwich. "It's over two miles long, just like that. Except it widens out up at the other end."

All Sam could see were the high cliff walls and the narrow slit of water barely three hundred yards wide twisting off out of sight.

"At the far end there's a resort. With a sand beach."

Sam looked at the flinty-looking cliffs. "Sand?"

"They bring it in on trucks."

"Any fishing?"

"No," Dan shook his head, but then shrugged. "Well, maybe, I guess. Somebody, maybe it was Fred, said there are native rainbows and something they call tiger trout. But you can see for yourself nobody's down there. If we do anything, we water ski up at the other end."

"We?"

"Carl's got a boat. Hey! You know... if you want, we can take Ruth and Sue."

"I haven't done it much."

"Yeah, I know. You like to fish." Dan smiled, but then squinted. "As for that... how's it going with Ruth?"

"Going?"

"C'mon. I'm responsible after all. I set up the whole fishing thing."

"You did not."

"And cleared you from making a fool out of yourself with Sue. Which, by the way, is also something you should thank me for."

"What do you mean?"

"Nothing. Just... Sue is Sue."

"You don't like her?"

"She's plenty nice. But not nice like Ruth, eh?"

Sam tilted his head.

Dan opened his mouth and breathed out: "Ah, OK, we're talking serious."

"Far as I can tell, you're the one doing the talking. But if you want, we can do that. Want to talk serious?"

Dan smiled, his eyes narrowing in a sly way. "Sure."

Sam nodded. "Fine. If you want to talk serious about something, let's talk about harvest."

Dan's face changed. "Don't worry about that."

"I'm not worried. I'm asking a serious question."

"Yeah, yeah, yeah. OK. But, I mean, I haven't even put out a notice yet for drivers or operators. And anyway, you're here, right?"

"You tell me."

Dan took a bite of his sandwich and looked over and gave Sam a smile with his cheek muscles, and said between chews: "Let's take Carl's boat and take the girls tomorrow."

"I thought we were working tomorrow."

Dan cocked his head. "Sunday."

"When did that make a difference?"

"C'mon. We deserve a break. I need a break."

"OK. But like I said, I'm not very good."

"Who is?"

"You have no idea."

"Don't worry. We'll go easy."

Sam looked at Dan's grinning face. "I'm sure."

"I'll call if I can get it set up. So," Dan nudged him with his elbow, "anyway. Admit it. I am responsible. I mean, you might have ended up with Sue."

"We're back there again? OK. First of all, that wasn't in the cards, at all. And you know it. So drop that. And, anyway, what's so wrong with Sue?"

"What's wrong with Ruth?"

"Nothing at all," Sam said. "But what's wrong with Sue?"

"Nothing either, but..."

Sam waited, and then said: "But what?"

"But... past her looks, I mean...."

Sam laughed. "What do you mean by, her looks? Anyway, you're the one who told me you'd been trying to get things going there for yourself."

"I never said that."

"Oh, Christ..."

"I didn't. Never did."

"You ever listen to yourself?"

"I would remember."

"I don't think you can remember what you said five minutes ago."

The smile never left Dan's face.

"Well, if I did say something like that, and I wouldn't have, I was just bullshitting you."

"Didn't sound like it," Sam said, looking out at the lake. "So you really don't think much of Sue?"

"Oh," Dan grinned. "I think about her. And anyway, what about you?"

"Just going along, man. What do you want to hear?"

"So, you have been seeing each other. I knew it."

"Why do I get a feeling you already know all this?"

"Bothers you, eh?" Dan grinned. "There it is. You see? You're finished. You know it. Halfway to pussy-whipped."

Sam waved his hand in frustration.

"OK..."

"Pussy-whipped! What a word!"

Sam looked away from Dan, out towards the lake, contemplating a few things he would very much like to say to the only identifiable employer he had, and then decided he might as well. Keeping a job was one thing, but it was not everything.

"Maybe," he turned to look back at Dan. "But better that than jealous."

Dan's face froze. "Hey, wait now. I'm just joking."

The look of genuine surprise on Dan's face made Sam wonder just how often it was that Dan got actual pushback. From anyone.

Let alone employees. But Sam wasn't going to make of it any more than just that and he reached for his boots.

"Sure," he said.

They worked hard for the rest of the day and went home. Sam did not hear anything from anyone that night and, with no alarm clock set, slept far into Sunday morning.

The phone rang just before noon.

"Hey," Ruth said. "Seriously?"

"What?"

"Listen. I don't care. But having Dan grousing on and on for the past hour about this is getting to be too much, especially since you're the one who wanted to do this so much. I mean, he did get all organized for you and went and got Carl's boat and got over here and all. The least you could do is show up on time so Sue and I don't have to listen to all this."

"Hey, wait..."

"I don't want to hear it. It's bad enough having Dan drop in here every other night and telling us how you're always complaining about being too tired and all that. But then getting him all lit up and then not showing up? No way. You get things started all the time and then just let them die on the vine? But, anyway, Dan said you insisted, so I'm going to insist, just for the sake of Sue, who really wants to go to the lake. Me, I could give a shit. But that's it, and Sue and Dan expect you to come along as a foursome. So get it in gear, Sam."

"I'm not that tired," Sam said quietly. "And what do you mean by getting him all..." He stared at the rug. Then frowned. "He comes there every other night?"

A moment's silence.

Sam started again: "You said that..."

"We'll be out front in half an hour."

Chapter 10

A DEWY June morning, a feathery blue and purple mist clung low between the grey hills. Far off, the sky was going blood red in the east with the approaching sunrise. Early, Sam was already out on the road driving a swather toward a distant hay field. He had no trouble seeing where he was going as he ran the hay-cutting machine along through the light fog and each time the road climbed in elevation enough to break out of it, he saw that strangely scarlet sky.

He did not believe in the old warning for sailors, and especially not in a country where the winds moved from west to east. A red sky morning meant the storm was already blown out beyond the eastern horizon. When he looked around the expanse of sky in all the other directions he saw nothing else, and when the sun finally did rise it was as though to completely take over that end of the world. For Sam, then, all the rest of his world was just the swather.

The swather's engine, almost unmuffled, blasted away in his ears as he drove down the road. Sam had never driven a swather quite like the one he was sitting on. Built like a tricycle in reverse, the big traction wheels were fixed up on either side of the cabless driving platform, leaving a swiveling crazy-wheel to trail in the back. Two hand clutches accomplished the steering. In the straights he did not need to touch anything and in the corners he would gently dog the inside lever as he went. An easy machine, and even with the roar of the swather it was a pleasant drive, and he looked forward to an easy day. All he would do was cut down the last standing hay into swaths to dry in the sun. He understood it was not a very big field and he would be done before noon, which was important because that afternoon he was going with Dan to Union City to collect a new combine that had come in on the train. No word had yet been said about whether he would be hired for harvest, but he was now assuming it, even though hiring was practically an institution, with the same people being hired year after year and little room for others.

Sam was even thinking he might not only get hired but might actually get a combine. They now knew he had driven combines, although only flatland machines. But the fact that Dan had told his father he wanted Sam to help unload and drive the combine back up to the farm, while he would be driving escort out front, meant he was trusted to at least run the new machine. It was for that reason Sam had volunteered to run down and swath this last pasture, a job it seemed no one else had wanted to do. Being a handyman meant being just that.

When he came upon the field, he stopped for a moment and looked it over from the road. The field was long and slightly inclined from one end to the other, and was bisected its entire length by an irrigation channel. Sam could see how a number of culverts crossed the channel so machines could get from one side to the other without having to run down the whole distance, and along that channel the heavy grass was thick, tall and lush.

He stepped down and undid the gate to the field, just a wired fence section to be unhitched and pulled out of the way. Before he climbed back on the swather, he looked at the cutting header once more.

Built like a combine header, a line of slicing teeth ran along the bottom edge of the wide, ground-skimming cutting platform, above which a big reel with wooden slats would beat the cut hay back onto augers feeding it into the maw of the machine. Unlike some swathers that just dumped the hay out behind, this machine had a sort of conditioning process as well. Two heavy rubber rollers pressed the hay into a tighter mass, and then pushed it through a narrow chute, where it ended up lying neatly in a line on the ground. Later, when the grass of the windrow was dry, Fred would drive a baler down the line, making yet more bales for Dan and Sam to haul.

If there was one thing farmers could never get enough of, it was hay.

He looked over all the attachments and gears, pulling and pushing. Satisfied, he climbed back up, threw open the header lever putting all the workings in motion, ran the motor up to power, and started into the field.

He made the first swath all the way around the edge of the field, the grass cutting easily into the header and going out behind in an orderly row. On the next swath around, he saw he could only make a few more circles before he ran out of culvert at both ends and would be forced to run down along the irrigation channel, doing out half a field at a time.

He continued the big circles, and the sun came up higher and warmed the air fast, the light around him yellowing as the morning fog went away and was replaced by the faint, hazy dust of a field being worked. At the horizon the crimson skyline became nothing but a fluffy bank of harmless clouds trailing north and south and swiftly disappearing in the direction of Idaho.

Each time he passed near the culvert area, the grass slowed him down. Seven feet tall in some places, it made for a good-sized swather bite and he listened to how the engine's note deepened as he went into it and how the machine seemed to work smoother as the grass filled its workings tight. It was a good, full feeling and when he swung the machine away from the last big circle into the first cut down the center where the grass was exceptionally abundant he expected things to become even more so.

The grass was thicker than it had looked. He slowed his ground speed even more to keep the engine from working too hard. Glancing back he saw a satisfyingly fat, dark green windrow lying behind. In fact, it was so fat he couldn't even guess how many bales were going to be made there.

Halfway down the field, with the grass suddenly even thicker, the engine's noise deepened. He watched the grass going in and he looked behind and saw a good, thick windrow. But then the engine nearly stalled and a thumping noise began under his seat and he immediately pulled the header clutch out.

Stopped from turning machinery the engine resumed a reassuring, normal roar. Sam pulled the lever rolling the header workings on and off and that was also normal. Thinking something had plugged the intake, like combines sometimes did, he got down and looked into the header but he saw nothing.

He got back up in the seat and set the header in motion again and ran it at full speed. Thinking that had taken care of things, he pushed the wheel clutches in and it was then that he could feel where the noise was coming from. He shut down the workings again, climbed off the machine and crawled beneath the swather from the rear. There, inside the hay chute, he could make out the big mess of grass wrapped tight around and fouling the conditioning rollers. If he had not shut it down, the belts would have burned up.

"Oh, shit," he said softly, crawling in past the hay chutes and putting his hand on the hot grass. He tried to pull some of it out, but the thick green stems were too strong and too tightly bound to move. He needed a knife to cut them loose. He did not have one. He tried pulling again, digging his fingernails into the stems. He might as well have been trying to scratch the bark off a tree.

"Fucking hell."

If only he had something like a sharp rock or nail to break the stubborn fibers. He crawled out from under the swather and climbed up to look in the toolbox. Even a screwdriver would work. Or a claw hammer. But the box held nothing but plastic grease cartridge caps and odd nuts and bolts.

He sat back in the seat and looked down the field. He was in a real jam. If he was back at the farm he could fix all this in two minutes but he couldn't get back there. The conditioning rollers went in gear when the wheels were running. He could not go twenty yards, let alone five miles, without ruining the bearings or maybe even setting fire to the grass. He had no radio.

Five miles. And most of it on back roads that only saw maybe one or two vehicles a day.

His eyes wandered some more and then he saw, high on a far rock bank, an old hay barn. It was a ways off, but maybe there he could find a nail. He shut the swather down, the sudden silence of the field ringing in his ears, and got down and set off across the shorn grass.

Not really much more than a long high shed with big piles of old hay crumbling and falling about, the hay barn was dark and musty inside like an old church, sunlight floating in thin streams through the dust-laden air.

He made his way across the uneven floor of broken bales and old haying equipment. The hay was rotting in there and it was evident no one had much use for the place anymore. He could see where roof shingles were beginning to shift and he knew that it would only be a few more winters before this was all on the ground.

He looked along the walls and beams for nails or pieces of metal but there were none. He could not find any nails in any of the posts or crossbeams either. It was a haying barn, or had been one, and nails for hanging items up were at best a nuisance.

He went outside the barn and looked along its sides, but could not find anything he could pull off except one very rusty shingle nail that did not look as if it would take much work to destroy.

He looked out across the field to the swather, at that distance insignificant seeming compared to the sweeping hills beyond. He was not going to walk all that way with one rusty, lousy nail in his fist to show for his efforts.

The sun continued to climb, the morning half over, and he began to feel frustrated, knowing he would not now be able to say the field was done before going off with Dan that afternoon. If he could even get back, that was.

Going along the barn, he spotted another nail behind a board and pulled on it, but it did not move and he could not get a grip on it. He pulled out his old green bandana and gave it a few turns. That gave him a better hold, but instead of coming out the nail bent and snapped in two, rusted through and through. Another piece-of-shit nail, he thought, and his anger rose up within him in a hot, blind wave and he flung everything into the rocks alongside the barn.

"Fuck this," he breathed out.

He went around the barn twice and then back into the barn again and kicked hay away from the sides. But always nothing and all the time it built on him until he felt like breaking something. He kicked some more hay around but it was more just for the feel of it than anything else.

Walking back out into the sunlight, he took a deep breath. Oh, come on, he thought. Just one nail. Give me anything, I don't care. He smiled suddenly. "Give me a nail and I'll believe."

And with those thoughts he could see it was all over. He was in for that long walk back to the farm, and maybe the whole goddamn way if someone did not come along. Five fucking miles.

He gazed around slowly, letting the pressure go out of himself. A pile of rusted equipment lay over by some rocks across the way, and he walked over to it. Behind the equipment was a large pile of old barn boards. Actually, not a pile, but another small barn that had indeed completely fallen down like a tired old cow gone down on its knees to die. In one board there was a fat, six-inch nail resting loose in the shrunken wood. In fact, there were a lot of other nails there too and he pulled out four, just because, and put them in his pocket.

As he went down off the rocks into the field towards the swather, he sort of smiled, but not too much. Even without a cloud in the sky, red or otherwise, he felt eerily as though he might get struck by lightning.

The grass tore apart quickly under the nail and he had it down to the rubber in no time. Then he began to yank out strands. Probably he could have just gone up and spun the rollers but it was satisfying pulling all this shit out. But if it felt good cleaning all that out, it was also tight work in there between the sheet-steel hay chutes, and uncomfortable. Years of flowing hay had put a fine edge on the guides, and he had to take care that he did not tear his shirt or jeans on them. He pulled at strand after strand, and shortly he felt things giving a little easier. Not so bad after all, he thought. Nearly there.

He reached for another strand and braced himself again, pulling with a hard tug at first, as was still necessary. The grass came slowly and then stopped for some reason. He set himself and gave a huge pull. The grass held still for a moment, and then for the second time since he had started working for Harley, something bad happened. The strand basically broke and his arm flew back violently against the edge of one of the chutes in a sliding motion. In that split second Sam knew he had cut himself badly. He looked down.

Across the top of his wrist the skin was wide open, and also open was the thin cutaneous layer over the muscles below, shining there dark and bluish purple. Only two thoughts went through Sam's mind before the bleeding started. One was that he could see he was really going to bleed that time, and the other was how amazing it was that he had not sliced his whole goddamn hand off.

It went bloody fast and there was a lot of it just as he had expected, but he was still surprised by how much was pouring out onto his forearm. He reached for his bandana but the pocket he carried it in was empty.

"Damn it," he remembered.

He got his dusty shirt off and then his clean undershirt, and wrapped that a few times tight around his wrist. While it had not taken long he could see how much blood had splattered onto his jeans and the grass around him. He even felt a little dizzy but he knew it wasn't the blood doing that so much as his nerves.

The undershirt tucked tight, he pulled his shirt back over his other arm, just sticking the shoulder of his injured arm inside, and then began to crawl out from underneath. Using one hand, it was not easy to back out, and he cursed at the nails in his pants pocket, jabbing sharp at him each time he bent back on his leg.

Well, he thought when he got out, so much for swathing. A little wave of heat went through him and he laughed.

He got up on the swather and started it up. At the first touch of the clutches all the grass plugging the conditioners blew out behind him. He drove out of the field and headed back to Harley's. It was lunchtime anyway, he thought, and almost laughed again, but did not and any sense of humor for the situation fell out of him completely.

He looked down at his undershirt and saw the stain spreading. He could feel his wrist throbbing and he knew he was still bleeding good.

Goddamn it, he thought. He might as well have set the inside of his wrist against the razor-edged chute and ripped it out. It would have had nearly the same effect.

He concentrated on the swather. And the dirt road. And the turns in the road. And the endless seeming hills he was going around. And he did now feel faint.

It was not long before it seemed like he had never been on a road for such a long time. He was driving and driving and he was not getting anywhere. He could feel the swather vibrating, and he knew he was jerkily steering it along, even trying to keep it basically to one side of the road. He was aware of a pain in his arm and that his undershirt there was red and that there were brown stains on his legs. But it was the sun that was more of something than anything else. It beat on him as he drove, and he could not hear things very well. The motor was loud, but he could not register anything in his ears except a great, thumping vacuum that also sometimes buzzed in an endless nightmare of unfamiliar noise.

And then there was something suddenly wrong with his eyes but not so much that he couldn't see but that he did not understand what he was seeing. Sometimes, when he passed something, a road or clump of trees maybe, he felt oddly that he no longer had any connection there, no connection to any of it, and he went on by as though it did not matter. As though he also did not care. But it scared him not to care. What would happen if he went past the place where he had to go, the place he needed to go, the place that had something for him, without noticing or caring and drove on and on and did not even know that he had missed it until suddenly everything no longer looked right or like a place he could go, and he would be lost for good and for forever. And strangely enough, what scared him about that also seemed familiar, like a déjà vu.

A wave of dizziness went over him. "Oh, baby," he said. He said it to fill his ears with something of his own for just a moment, and he said it to make the other thoughts go away.

He looked at his arm. It was all right, he told himself. The undershirt was a mess but he was fairly certain he had finally clotted up. He looked at his jeans, and at what looked like but was not dried mud on his dusty boots. He had bled like a stuck pig for sure. He tried to think about other things. Of Ruth. Which did not seem at all out of place. But even as that was, the thought had a strange quality to it. She seemed so far away from where he was there on that road and yet he found that when he thought of her all he could imagine was that she was observing him as if all he was was what he was right there at that moment, and he was ashamed and after just a short while of thinking that he did not want to think of her any more, nor of how she was looking at him.

It was very hard to make the thought of her like that go away though, and he felt like he was in a fishbowl of something like noise and something like heat and it was hard to hide. But if it all seemed like a fishbowl then, and everyone and not just Ruth could see him there like that, then it was also a real enough thing because he could still feel it as well as think about it. And if everything was real, then none of it was surprising anymore, not even when he saw Ruth standing along the road waving for him to stop. And then his eyes really did go bad.

Colors were not right. Everything was hazy and gray. Or maybe not gray. The gray might have been caused by the haze and it was also as if he was looking through a screen of gray squares where every other square was colored in or hazy and he had to try to look through the open squares.

And there, he knew his worst moment. In his eyes and out in the air he watched as the open squares began to get smaller and the gray ones bigger. The roar of the other something also began to get louder and louder in his ears and it got to be almost as bad as the sun that was sitting on his back squashing his breath from his chest. Then the road that never stopped, simply disappeared.

He knew if he fainted dead away he would go right off the high road into a big ditch with bushes and rocks and posts and barbed wire and God knew what else and when he did he was going to be fucked for good and maybe ending on top of but just as easily beside or even beneath the swather.

He fumbled in the darkness to get the clutches in, reaching out with his injured arm as well so he could pull both levers at the same time. He missed completely and thrashed his feet towards the brakes and he knew it was all over and his guts hardened for the disaster. He now lived through a different sort of moment but it was no longer strange. Not even when he saw how he was going there, as if from above, as though watching himself from the outside, because it was really happening and that meant what was to follow was also going to be very real, and his breath stopped while the engine roared and the heat crushed him and the tension of waiting for it damn near exploded him.

But nothing happened, and all that energy suddenly brought back his vision. He was very close to the edge with one tire running half off and it was obvious that any second then he would be down in it.

He gave the roadside lever a hard pull and the swather then was powered only on the ditch side. For a moment it ran like a tightrope walker on one foot, balancing itself there, and then with a bounce the machine jumped up on the roadbed, and from there on out his vision was perfectly clear, and he ran on down the road in utter clarity and lucidity.

He felt better just seeing the house. But suddenly, feeling more normal except maybe a little nauseated, he also began to feel embarrassed. He looked at the awful looking thing wrapped around his wrist and hoped he could find something else to put there before anyone saw him. There was nothing he could do about his pants though.

Christ, he suddenly thought in frustration, just do what you can.

He drove the swather over to the shop and shut it down, leaving it there popping in the sun. Inside the shop he found a bag of clean rags.

He pulled out handfuls, finally finding the remains of what looked to have been a long white dress of some sort. He bit the edge and tore a wide strip from it. Unwrapping his undershirt, he found that it was all dried at the lowest layer onto his skin. He went out to the spigot beside the door and ran water onto the sodden wrap until it soaked off. He did not try to wash the whole clot off but just the patches on his hand and forearm, and then he wrapped the dress cloth onto it. It looked a million times better.

He let the water run on his undershirt and melted the biggest clots off and then he filled a bucket and threw the shirt in to soak. The water there began immediately to turn brown, and he picked up the bucket and placed it out of sight back in the shop. He went out of the shop and went over to the swather. He tried his hand and found he could use it, if a little stiffly, and he pulled the grease gun out of the tool box and began going around greasing points on the header. It was just before noon and he was nearly finished when a couple of pickups pulled into the yard. Fred and Dan got out of one, and out of the other got two men that Sam assumed were Harley Petersen and his oldest son, Carl. They were both strongly built and blond haired. Carl looked very nearly like a copy of his father, except on a larger scale.

All four men walked over to where Sam was finishing up and Sam turned to look at them. For a moment nobody said anything. Then Fred growled, "Harley, this is Sam. Sam, this is Harley, your boss."

At the word "boss," Dan glanced sideways at Fred, but Fred ignored him.

"Hello," Sam said.

"And this," Fred went on, "is Carl."

"Sam," Harley nodded. "What field are you in?"

Dan cleared his throat. "I sent him down to do the old Rose field."

"So you're finished up?" Harley said.

"Only about half done," Sam said.

"It's a good field," Carl said. "But it never takes more than half a day to swath."

"I'd normally be finished. But grass got in the roller, and then..." he held up his arm showing the wrapping.

Carl looked at his father and then back at Sam. "Cut yourself on the guides. I've done that. I've always said we should take them off. Time I did it, I needed stitches. Do you?"

Sam felt Dan looking at him. "Don't think so."

"Let's go have lunch," Harley said. "And while we're doing that we'll take a look."

Sam saw Dan's face and he was about to decline when he felt Carl's hand on his back, urging him towards the house.

Sam stepped through the front door into a large foyer with a big staircase going up at the back and he felt suddenly shy. All around the foyer doorways went off to other rooms, and in the one to the dining room stood a solid, pleasant looking woman, her hair as black as her husband's was blonde. He nodded at her. "Ma'am."

"Sally," she said. "So, you're Sam. The man Fred hired last Spring."

Almost everyone laughed and Harley nodded towards the doorway. "Let's take a look at that."

They filed through the dining room and into the kitchen where they crowded around him at the sink while he peeled off the strips and washed the clot off. There in the kitchen, the wound looked uglier than out in the shed and began to seep again. Sally pulled a bottle out of a cabinet and handed him some paper towels.

"Here's some mercurochrome. Dry that off and then dab that good before you bandage it up again."

"Pretty good," Harley said. "Did you clean it before you tied it up?"

"Not in the field, but later, yes."

"Ten stitches, easy," said Carl.

Sally handed him a bandage roll. She had a cabinet in the kitchen that looked like it came straight out of an infirmary.

"After lunch go straight in to Doc Bennet's office. It's next to the post office," Harley said. "Tell him you're out here with us and to put you on our tab."

"I'm OK. It'll tape up."

"Like hell it will. You go in there and you get not only antibiotics but a tetanus shot if you don't have one already. Get one anyway. You're covered. We have full insurance for everyone. Us, employees and seasonals." He turned to Sally. "Did you say he was hired last spring?"

"He started off with me on the fences," Fred said.

"All this time? What've you been doing?"

"After the fences," Sam had to think back, "I was then farming for a while. And then hauling hay with Dan, and this and other things."

"Where did you farm?"

"Endicott, and the other side of Williams Lake, over by Sprague," Sam looked at Fred, "and Cammas-Dian?"

Fred nodded.

"Endicott," Carl said. "I wondered who'd done the Waukon fields. Beautiful. Where else?"

"Dan started him off by Hole-in-the-Ground," Fred said.

"Oh?" Carl pursed his lips. "So you've driven hillside tractors then."

"Not up 'til then. But now I have, for sure." Sam smiled.

"You're telling me your first field on a hillside tractor was over there by Larson's?"

Sam nodded. "Yes. I think that's what they called it."

Harley gave Fred a look. "That was your idea?"

Fred shook his head. "Hell, no."

"Trial by fire," Dan said.

"Trial by fire, with the second most expensive piece of equipment we own?"

"It's not that bad out there."

"You did not go up on that one until your second full year," Carl said. "You've forgot or something?"

"Nobody forgets," Fred said.

Harley grinned and looked at Dan. "What were you trying to do, scare him off?" He looked back at Sam. "You came through OK. That's the main thing. But I'll bet it got exciting."

"Truth be told," Sam said, "I did wonder at one point if I was going to find out if tractors can fly."

Harley laughed out hard. "I'll bet." He looked at Carl. "You said something almost exactly like that yourself, first time you went."

Sam was looking at Dan for no particular reason, and saw a fleeting, but an unmistakable, shocked widening of the eyes, which was then swiftly hidden under half closed eyelids. As well, he heard

88

Fred say, under his breath, something like "oh no...."

Something in the air felt like a family argument was about to break out, and Sam found himself examining his wrist. Then Sally said, "OK, all right. Come on. Lunch is ready."

Harley looked at Dan. "Has he done the paperwork?"

Dan shrugged. "I don't know."

Harley turned to Sam. "How have you been paid?"

"A check on Friday."

"Cash, eh?" Harley glanced at Dan and then back at Sam. "Before you go in to the doctor I want your social security number and your address."

"Wait," Dan said. "He was going to go with me to get the new combine off the train over in Union City. I had it all planned out. After we got the combine off the train and set up, Fred was going to convoy him back up here with a pickup, and then I was going to go on down to Colfax and pick up that header we bought from the Harris brothers."

"That's what happens to plans, Daniel."

"Shit. Now Fred's going to have to convoy me, and I'll have to drive to Colfax tomorrow...."

While the others went into the dining room, Dan stayed behind, watching Sam finish his bandaging. Sam had the feeling Dan wasn't there just to watch, and after a minute or so found out he was right. "Well," Dan finally said. "You might as well take a day or two off to heal up."

"I'll be all right. I can get back tomorrow morning and finish the field."

"Doesn't matter. We probably have all the hay we needed, anyway. I'll give you a call."

Dan walked off towards the dining room.

After lunch Sam was walking over to his car when he saw Dan coming out of the shop holding Sam's dripping undershirt. When he saw Sam he held it out to him. "This yours?" he said. "I need the bucket."

"Sure," Sam took the shirt. "Sorry I screwed up your plans."

Dan looked off across the yard and then shrugged. "No big deal. We'll figure something out."

"Right. OK. So I'll see you later."

"Yep," Dan said, going back into the shop. "I'll call."

Sam nodded, the unwrung undershirt dripping from his hand making a small puddle next to his left shoe.

Sam was tired that night as he lay in bed, the balcony doors open and the cool, sweet air flowing in. But he could not sleep and it was not because of the low pain in his wrist. That morning he had avoided having the biggest accident he had ever had. Just thinking about it made him sweat, as he pictured the ditch and the posts and the barbed-wire fence line and how the swather and he would have made an extremely complete accident in the dirt right there, him probably going over the front into the slats of the header and then the swather itself going God knew where and maybe right on top of him. Survivability an open question. But the irony was that the main disaster of the day had been something else.

As the next day went by with no call, and then the next day, Sam did not get angry, and then another day went by and he began finding himself angrier than he had felt in a long time, even more than he had felt in other places where, if something along these lines was happening, he would have already been long gone.

There was no way of knowing, of course, and it was always worse to be on the outside. For all he knew, there had been many conversations, or maybe just one, and then he found a check had been delivered to the hotel one evening with no note inside. It covered everything up to and including the swather accident. Literally paid off, if that was what it was.

Early morning mid-week, he thought maybe it was a Tuesday, he was sitting in the practically empty Country Kitchen having breakfast, a plate of little pigs and hash browns with a cup of coffee. And Dan walked in.

Dan actually came to a stop when he saw Sam, and then walked over. "Hey, man."

"Hey, yourself." Sam went back to his breakfast. "Day off?"

"Nah," Dan took a seat. "Picking up some things we ordered. Opens at eight. So just bummed over here to wait. What've you been doing?"

Sam picked up his coffee. "Ain't been working, for one."

Dan waved at the waitress. "Hey-oh, Cathy! The place isn't exactly full up."

The waitress, setting plates back by the short order counter, turned. "I saw you, Dan. Half a second and I'll bring the coffee. Anything else?"

"One of your bear claws."

He looked back at Sam, seemed to hesitate, and then said, "so... yeah... got all the rest of the hay in, and we got that new combine set up and everything. And... oh yeah... we got that field you were doing all in. Dad said can't let such a good crop go, eh?" There was something surprisingly flat in Dan's voice.

"Sounds good," Sam said, and he was not at all surprised by the flatness in his own.

Dan took a sip of his coffee, staring over the cup at something on the counter. "How's your arm?"

"It's been fine ever since it got stitched up. A while back."

"Is that right?" Dan looked down the counter, seeming to be interested in something there. And then he turned back. "Yeah, anyway. So... right... came to try to find you. I tried to call your room. Figured you'd be here."

"If I was still here."

Dan sort of laughed. "Well, that's always a possibility, eh? Sue said you'd disappeared again."

Sam's eyebrows moved together for a second. "What's this about trying to call me? Before six? And as for the rest, if anyone wants to find me, it isn't hard. At all."

"OK, OK. So maybe we should have called. Carl, in fact, was going to, but then I told him... I had some shit..." Dan went into a long pause, his face going blank.

"Some shit..."

Dan finally just nodded. "Anyway, whatever. And here you are."

91

Sam nodded back. "And here I certainly am."

They finished their coffee together and Dan his bear claw, and Dan said he would give a call to start getting things set up and Sam said that was fine.

Two brilliant, sunny days passed, and then a day went by that was so dark and wild and rainy that by afternoon he found he had to turn on the light it was so dark outside, with a wild storm raging. But the morning after that, the sunrise came streaming in. He got up early, got coffee and fried up some eggs in toast, and waited for the phone call he had decided he should expect. And not make.

There was just no way, he thought, he was going to call when he had been told he would get a call. How many days, how many times, had he sat here like this thinking these exact thoughts, in the same sequence?

But after what would normally have been breakfast out there, he suddenly thought to hell with it. He went over to the bed and sat down, and reached for the phone, picking up the receiver, and then setting it down again. He knew the hardness he felt would be unavoidably clear in his voice. He looked at the bandage on his wrist and unwrapped it. There was no blood and it looked like it was well knitted together. He picked up a pair of nail scissors and snipped out the stitches, and that was it.

He got up and went down to the lobby. The deskman was sitting there, watching a small TV he had set up back of the counter.

"Any messages?"

The deskman barely looked at him. Sam went out the door.

Chapter 11

THE best drink on earth for getting drunk, he was thinking, was whiskey, and there was no better whiskey than a Kentucky bourbon that evaporated off the back of the tongue like the hot kiss of a lover baby.

He took another sip and then smiled sourly. Lover baby indeed, he thought, because like all good lover babies she could make the knees go weak.

Like those of a man in love.

Sitting alone there in the cocktail lounge he was no longer thinking about the swather accident, or Dan. But he was thinking about another sort of accident.

"I know," he said to himself. But the fact was, it just was not working. And even though it was nice pretending it could, he was more sure things were leading in a direction where getting rolled over by a swather seemed nearly preferable in comparison.

No, he had not called, neither them nor her, because there was nothing he could talk about.

He picked up the glass and finished it off. Enough of this shit, he thought, and he started to pull himself up and away from the bar.

Lonni, having seen from the moment he had come through the door that he had a mood all over him like a heavy overcoat, had been keeping her distance, even though there was next to nobody in there except a couple of old gentlemen who lived in the rooms above the old restaurant and who liked to have their morning coffee in there. But now seeing him obviously moving to go, she thought she could attempt a semblance of conversation. Lonni was well practiced at seeing off customers. Or friends. And she wasn't going to let him go without having at least acknowledged his presence. "Now I'm sure I know what you've been doing in here," she said, coming up to him.

"It happens."

"Maybe. But not at 11:30 in the morning." She picked up his glass and looked at it.

He nodded. "You're right. And it don't. Not even for me." He looked at her, and then decided to just let go of it. "I've sort of been out of work."

"Ah," she smiled. "So that explains that. You're either bored or commiserating with yourself."

He smiled back. "In turns."

"Normally, I'd imagine you wouldn't stick around long in such a case," she continued, seeming just to be bantering. Her eyes, though, had something else about them. "But you haven't left," she said lightly. "You must like it here for some reason, then."

"I like a lot of places."

"Oh yeah? What's the longest time you've been anywhere?"

"About two years."

"And the shortest?"

"A week."

"And which did you like better?"

"The week."

"You make it sound like it's a matter of barely getting out alive."

"That's happened too."

She looked down the bar for a second. "It's certainly a different way of doing things. I don't know if I'd like it."

"I'm not sure I do, either."

"Just asking, but... you got plans?"

"I haven't needed any up to now."

"Just waiting until something right comes along."

"I've never looked at things that way. But maybe you're right. And nothing's struck me in any way."

"You just must be real picky. I don't mean to be personal, but it's sort of interesting in a way."

Sam had never got used to the way some people had for talking to him as though they were talking about someone else. Not everyone was like that. But quite a few. And Lonni was one of them. Mostly, he knew, it wasn't a personal particularity but more like a professional habit, or deformation. In her case, that of being a bartender, where sooner or later observations became first a habit and then, over time, a hobby. He did not mind. But he also was not going to get into a discussion. At least not from the angle she was hinting around at.

"And so, you haven't moved around much."

"When I got married, a bit," Lonni said, and then twisted her mouth. "And then divorced."

Although it had nothing to do with the conversation, he felt the whiskey drop out from under him. "Here. Why don't you bring me some coffee?"

"Am I taking the fine edge off your morning?"

"I was doing that, myself."

She went over to the bar and filled a mug of coffee and brought it back. And this time she sat down.

"So tell me about Sam's Life."

He laughed. "Most of it isn't worth hearing, much less the telling."

"I'll be the judge."

"What's there to say? I've liked it in some places, liked it really well as a matter of fact. But then would come the time when there wasn't much left. And, no, not what you might be thinking. No matter what, you can't sit around for a season waiting."

"Is that what's happening?"

"I don't know yet. But I do know that when you wait for too long, by the time it comes around again you find you don't want it anymore. So better just to go. Start fresh."

Lonni nodded. "It's true. Waiting can ruin everything for everybody."

For half a second, it seemed a bland remark, but then suddenly for Sam a thought hit him from an unexpected direction.

Lonni, though, had no idea of the small commotion she had

set off, and into Sam's silence said: "So the first time you came in here, you really were just right off the road with no plan at all."

"None at all," he said. "Except I was just about broke. I pulled off because I needed something to eat. I do remember that. The rest, I don't know. But there wasn't much about how it started up that was different from other places, or I would remember."

"Never sad on leaving?"

"Not once the decision is made. Then it's just doing it. In fact, it often feels good. Feels great. Turning the car out onto the open road and just going. There are some parts of the country you wouldn't believe if you'd never driven through them."

"So, you've got no attachments to anywhere."

"A bit."

"Let me guess. For one thing, your way of talking, you sound like you're from here, but you're not. And the only other part of the country that sounds the same is west Texas."

"I noticed the way people talked, around here, too. Almost like coming home." He laughed. "And you're close enough. But anyway, I'm really more just from all over the place now. You know something? You can set out sometimes in the morning and by afternoon it's like you've driven into a completely different world. So...," he paused for a second, "...so when I say sometimes it just gets to be too much of a wait, that isn't completely true. Because there's not just a push to it, but also a pull, also there waiting on the other end of it."

Lonni was gazing at him as he spoke, and he could see that regardless of what she thought of it, she could certainly see it. He took a sip of coffee.

"God," she said finally. "I wish I were a man."

"No, you don't."

"Yes, I do. You can go where you want, and when, and the only responsibility you have is to yourself."

"I was talking for myself."

"Yeah. But you're a man."

"Oh, hell. Everybody makes choices."

"Do you ever go back anywhere?"

"Not really."

"But you have."

"A few times."

"So," she said, "you don't go back. Don't? Or can't."

"There's never been can't, Lonni. But more like, shouldn't."

"You must be running out of places."

He smiled at her smile. "There are a lot of places."

"You trying to set some sort of record? Most places gone to? Or is it most places left from?"

"Good point."

"You don't know, do you?" It wasn't a question. She reached out and put a hand on his good arm and gave it a squeeze. "Except that you clean yourself up and work hard, the way you're so outside of it all, you're the closest thing to a bum I've ever met."

He closed his eyes for a moment, but it only poked him a little and he smiled again. "Maybe. But it isn't always up to me."

A gravel road went off from the highway about a mile south of town and ran back to the river. There, it settled in and followed the winding course up into the hills.

He drove for half an hour, barely glancing at the river slipping past. Finally, though, feeling the solitude of a few miles of river behind him, he began looking more carefully at it. By that time the river had diminished in size and was broken as it fell through more frequent rock gullies. For another mile it was like that, and then he went around a bend where the road had to go up and over a small bluff and he suddenly found himself looking down into a box canyon where the river was cascading in small falls among big rocks.

It was a fast glance, though, the road going quick around a corner, and he slowed to a stop and then backed up. It really did look good down there. Plenty of trees and bushes overhung the pools and the water was neither very high nor fast. He let out the clutch and half a mile farther on he found a fence line road heading in the direction of the river and he turned the car onto the two dusty tire tracks and joggled slowly down towards the canyon until he could drive no farther. Switching his engine off, he heard nothing at first, and then he had it: a soft rustling and gurgling coming up out of the trees.

The canyon was not straight up and down; there were plenty of easy ways to get below, so he walked along the top until he found a place that looked good. The pools at that spot did not look too deep or big, some big rocks breaking surface, and the high cottonwoods and lower chokecherries hung long branches across the water. Using one hand to brace himself, he scrambled down a steep cow path, the trail smashed and beaten by countless hoofs. From the looks of things, none of the animals had been there for quite some time.

At the bottom of the path he stood on a wide bank, the gravel scoured by the springtime flooding. Unlike mountain streams left piled with timber and brush after waters receded, that river just swept itself clean—almost too clean. He looked back up the trail for a second but then thought that since he was there he might at least give it a try. He started up the river to get at the pools. Most of the way he could go along the bank, but from time to time he was forced to climb onto rocks in the river until he could get back on the bank again. On the bank there was sometimes hawthorn making things difficult and sometimes a patch of nettles, but mostly it was tall grass and easy going.

Finally, under some tall cottonwoods, he found his stretch of river. The banks were grass with some flat rocks and the birch and alder were back away from the water. The heavy foliage overhead shaded the river from both sides. It was only down the center where the sunlight reflected off the big rocks and the stones in the bottoms of the shallower pools that a sparkling stream of light danced brightly.

He put his pole together and threaded a sinking line out through his guides, clasping on a fly that looked like a bug. He had no idea what was flying around but in any case the fish wouldn't be rising yet and he needed to entice them out.

He made one small back cast and flicked the bug out above the nearest pool, and let it drift in. The water there, just off the center of the stream, was fed by a small, sideways tumbling rivulet. The color of the water graduated from a deep blue and green-black at the head to a dark gold at the other end where a big rock tilted yellow towards the surface. Clear throughout, the water rolled across the length of the pool and then disappeared beneath a line of flat rocks to rejoin the river.

He let the bug drift with the slow boil of the current. When he got no nibbles there, he shifted to another pool, and then another. He fished steadily right through the heat of the afternoon and tried hard to enjoy it, even though once in a while he felt the whiskey and the conversation come back to him. At those times he made himself just set to working the pools in the river, moving from one to the other, knowing it was doubtful he could get anything to come out but maintaining a stubborn optimism that was determined to ignore what he knew only too well about rivers and pools in rivers and how once you'd been through them and nothing came up there wasn't much sense in continually going back unless circumstances... a shift in the sky, the hour of day, something swarming... changed.

As evening came on, the canyon went quickly into shadows. At that he switched to a dry line and tied on a short-winged fly and began casting out onto the surface of the pools. It was early yet for that but it was a little lazier as well and he felt like getting a little lazy. He cast and recast the fly out onto smooth water, and each time watched as the fly made its way across the surface of the pools and then down small cascades. And finally, he thought he saw a shadow move where no shadow had moved before.

He popped the fly up from the bottom of the pool and flicked it back to just above where the shadow had been, and it only went a couple of yards before there was a swirling and the fly disappeared and his line tugged tight down the pole. It was a small pool strike where the fish just took the line straight beneath a rock and fought from there. Of all the types of fishing Sam had known, these small pools were where it was possible to have both the best and the worst types of luck, if luck was what it was called.

He managed to tire the trout out of the hole and work it over to the bank to a shallow bit of sand between two stones. He wet his hand and set it over the trout, pinning it down in the shallow water.

It was a good-sized trout. Maybe a pound and a half and a full eighteen inches, it had the blunt nose and heavy belly of a pregnant female and he worked the fly out of the corner of her mouth and pushed her back into the channel. There wouldn't be many fish like that in this stream, he thought, and he felt fine about leaving her in peace there in that small pool where she could do more good. At that he stopped fishing and sat down. He had brought a sandwich and he ate that and rested as the day went dead before the approaching evening. As he chewed he barely tasted the sandwich or noticed it was a little dry. Neither did he feel how the evening was rapidly cooling the air nor see the sky turning a blue of endless depths, streaked here and there with a pink-tinged waste of cloud. The rock beneath his thighs was cold and there were suddenly swallows and nighthawks out sailing over the tree tops, chasing the insects out of the fading day. But he hardly paid any attention to them either. It was only after a long time like that, with the river bubbling cheerfully over the rocks in the stream beside him, that he finally let himself go into exactly how awful he felt.

At first he did not think about it and just let whatever it was get pushed out as though it was breaking loose or breaking up. And it wasn't just Dan, and it wasn't just Ruth, but now something else was there too. The old thing. Which normally had nothing in connection to the thing Lonni had said, but now suddenly did because it made things entangle with the way he was. He had never considered that before, but in a way it made things worse, because he could not see how any of it could be different. Always losing everything, eventually. Like a question of fate. And it was sad to see it that way, and the more he thought about it the more the sadness of it became very insistent, and began to grow, looking for that place it could feed on him the worst. And then of course it found it. Ruth.

"Jesus," he said angrily. Angry at himself for letting things get this stupid.

There was no escaping the pain of it though. Above him, in the last rays of the setting sun, a sudden flash of turquoise blue caught his eye. He stretched back his head and saw a small mountain bluebird land, long enough to preen itself on a high branch. And then it flew away. He stared at the sky, looking at the first stars appearing there. The cool air fell on his face and he breathed it in deep as things came and went in him like waves, and sitting like that, keeping himself very still, he finally felt those things go away. For a while after that, in the silence of the evening, he just stared at the river.

In the failing light he gathered up his gear and made his way back out the way he had come in, going over the rocks and along the banks beneath the blackening shapes of the trees. Finding a path, he made his way up on top and went along the edge of the canyon towards the field where he had left his car. As he walked along he looked out towards the place in the west where the sun had just set, bright colors painting the sky a gaudy farewell of orange and red. He had just missed watching the sun go down, and he was sorry for that. He liked summer sunsets. Unlike in the winter when it plummeted straight in and everything went black, the summer sun took a long run at the horizon, finally coming down close, red and comfortable, skipping there fat above the surface and then sliding along just below, and at the moment it touched that movement became visible, making it almost possible to feel how the earth was turning away from it and the immensity of everything that was out there.

As he drove out along the tracks, he left his lights off. The colors of the evening were still with him and he could see the path clear enough there with the sky's deep blue hanging over the dark hills to the west.

Back on the highway though, with the lights on, everything went black and then all he had was the road.

Chapter 12

THINGS could very easily drift any way they wanted at that point, and he knew it finally and completely. More than a week had gone by without a call. Haying was done, or nearly so, whatever being left being finished by others, and whatever preparations were being made for harvest, setting up machines and vehicles, he was no part of. He was now living in a thing he knew well. But he was also holding off on what he normally did in those times, and not just because he needed a few more paychecks. He knew he had to deal with the other thing head on as soon as things became clear.

He had got a call, and it was not at all what he had been hoping for, or needed. But he had gone along with it, as usual.

A drizzly morning, barely beyond dawn, he and Dan were cleaning out those grain bins which had been sitting empty for weeks or even months, the grain stored in them from the previous year now having all been sold and shipped out. It was his first job back out there, and it was not really farming but just cleaning up, with no word included about harvest, not even when Sam asked directly. Every time, the subject meandered off into something else, and that was now all there was to it.

The work was not hard and to be inside the bins was pleasant with the soft rain pinging at the steel walls as they dug loose the old clumps of mildewed wheat clinging at the edges and swept clean the smooth concrete floor. With only the inspection port open, it was dark and musty inside, the air hanging lightly with old grain dust tingling both sweetly and sourly in their nostrils from the malathion used the year before for red weevils. At first that air had felt heavy, but it became nice to be dry inside listening to the sound of the rain outside. Later that morning, though, when they were out in the fields gathering up the remnants of a fence Fred had taken apart and they had to pick up the posts and the coiled wire and boxes of clips out in the drizzle, it was not nice. Sometimes the rain came down hard as though it was going to stay, but then it did not, and the unpleasantness was not in the rain but in how they would go back and forth with thinking about packing it in or not.

At lunchtime, they ate in the pickup as the rain fell. The cab was humid with their wet clothes and they had the windows down so they could breathe. They were not looking forward to the afternoon. But then the skies went really dark, and the rain made up its mind to come down for good. They decided to go to town and shoot some pool.

Bob's was quiet: just a few men along the bar. Bob had the doors at both ends open, and the only sound was the hissing of the rain and the occasional slash as a car passed by. Sam went to the bar and got a rack of balls and a pitcher of beer while Dan switched on a hanging light above one of the tables. He looked around and finally found a rack and some chalk underneath another table. Having done that, he went and sat down, leaning back in a chair with his legs stretched out, pulling his hat down low over his eyes.

Sam came back and sat down, and they remained there like that looking across the bright green felt of the table toward the open back door where a pale gray light from the alley filtered in. At one point Bob walked by carrying some boxes.

"New way to play pool?"

Dan picked up a shot glass of whiskey. "We're warming up."

Bob set the boxes in the back, picked up a broom and started sweeping back by the rear door, working slowly and steadily around the place.

"I couldn't work in here unless I owned it," Dan said after a while.

"Neither would Bob."

"It makes a hell of a difference, employer and employee."

Sam stared out the back door at the rain coming down.

Dan looked over at Sam's shot glass. "You haven't touched that."

Sam shrugged and Dan picked it up and drank it off.

"You know," Sam said. "I've known a lot of guys who don't stay on the farm. Head out the first chance they get."

"That's right. But not me. Carl tried. He went down to school. Made the football team and everything. We thought for a long time he'd be long gone. Up into Spokane, or just off wherever things took him. Marry some gal in Boise or, God only knows, Portland or something. But in the end," he looked over at Sam. "In the end..."

"I guess if it's in your blood."

"Yeah. Blood."

Sam regretted bringing the subject up. He had only wanted to move away from the other thing. But this was family stuff, and it was no conversation he wanted any part of. He looked at his watch.

"I don't give a shit," Dan said. "I suppose every fucking bastard in town has it all figured out by now. Figured us... figured everything out. The succession. Down the line. They can figure things out pretty fucking easily around here. Can see it and can figure it out. Like we're living on a glass farm."

"Glass house."

Sam looked off at the back door again. When they had come into town they had first stopped to pick up Sam's car and it was sitting in the back parking lot just out of sight.

"Fact is, it's true. With Carl coming back and all and me always here..." Dan shifted around in his chair. "I was always here. Always fucking here."

Dan looked off at the bar room, nodding to different points as though he was talking to a room full of people. "But he'll fucking have to get into it full time now, though. And that's fucking right." His eyelids narrowed and his mouth twisted. "Damn right. And especially considering who he's marrying."

Sam very nearly stood up. If he had, though, he would have had to fight the impulse to walk away. He would not have wanted to make any statement like that, and he would have probably just gone off to the men's room for a few minutes. But as it was, he brought his boot down off his knee onto the floor, and reached for his beer, hoping the movement, and his silence, would be enough.

It was not.

"Jesus Fucking Christ," Dan grabbed towards his own beer glass. "Marilyn Fucking Sutton."

"Marilyn. The friend of Lonni's, right? You know, I think I met her the first day I came to town."

Dan did not pretend to believe Sam's pretending. "You wouldn't forget it." He took a drink. "And imagine that. First day in town."

"Coincidence."

"Yeah, right. Anyway. Who would have guessed it? Carl coming back, and then... the Queen of the Nile. But, hey! You get to thinking about it, it makes all sorts of sense. Although in other ways not. I mean... Marilyn. Of all people." He shook his head. "But it makes sense."

Sam had no idea what to say. "She doesn't like farming or something?"

Dan's face went hard. "I have no idea what the fuck Marilyn likes or doesn't like. What it comes down to is who's entitled to what. And I've worked my ass off..."

Sam grabbed a pool cue and stood up, going over to the table. He spotted the cue ball and sent it hard to break the racked balls, but nothing dropped. He held out the cue to Dan, but Dan sat there looking at him.

"I know," he said finally. "I know. You don't give a fuck."

Sam smiled. "What's there to give a fuck about? It's not my farm. Although it would be nice to know how much I've been hired for out there. For example, with harvest coming..."

Dan's hand waved tiredly.

"It's just that when Dad retires, it's hard to say what will happen."

"With your folks?"

"No, no. They'll just move to town. I mean the farm."

"You're telling me you don't know what will happen with the farm?"

"Course I do. Me and Carl will get it. What do you think? But... yeah, yeah. It's going to have to get bigger."

"It seems big enough."

"Not for both of us. Especially if Carl gets into it full time."

"Seems pretty full time to me."

"You wouldn't know." Dan looked out at the rain, something hard going across his face again. "Just like you don't know anything about who he's marrying."

That was enough for Sam. "I suppose dividing up the land is getting harder for everyone."

"Yeah. And it's one of the reasons why families are smaller."

"And the farms get bigger."

"Yep. The ones that move away sell off to the ones that stay. That's the way it goes."

"So you'll be a big farmer someday."

Dan grinned. "Bigger than Dad. But how much bigger there's no way of knowing. That'll be another thing."

Sam nodded and Dan got to his feet, took the cue out of Sam's hand, and started to line up a shot.

Sam, glad the conversation seemed over, felt the earlier irritation come back.

Employers and employees. Dan, with his usual disregard, talking out loud like that with one of the help. As if he was not even there. But setting aside Dan's bad manners Sam could admit that even if he was just an employee and might never own any land himself, at least he did not have to worry about the garbage that went with it. And evidently, there was quite a bit.

He did not know Harley well, but he had had the impression the man was thoughtful and would never have left things to chance or misunderstanding. At least, not where it came to his two sons. But maybe it was just that, Sam thought.

Because Harley saw things so straight ahead and clear, he figured everything was like that everywhere else. Sam had seen that before, and especially in the people who had grown up during the Great Depression. They did not fuss around with things, saw what needed to be done, and did it. Shared, and worked, and everything else was just jawing. And the ideas of who got what, who married whom, and whose ego got damaged, were just a waste of time and nonsense. And they did not pay attention to how a younger, more privileged generation that had time to develop grudges and ambitions, jostled each other and occasionally rubbed each other raw.

They played pool for a couple of hours, and they drank beer, and all the time it rained hard outside. The fields would be completely soaked, Dan said, and there was going to be no way, even if it stopped right then, that anyone could do any farming for a day and a half. And where that, in itself, would have fed even more into Sam's doubts about his situation, Dan's not giving Sam the slightest idea of when or if he might be working again created a final, ominous feel.

On his way home he drove past Ruth and Sue's but saw no cars or lights on, and he drove back to the hotel. He thought he might try to call her later, but he fell asleep and it continued to rain that night and then into Friday and then it rained all Friday and everything came to a dead stop and Sam decided to quit thinking about anything, anymore. There had been just too much of that, and so much that it had begun turning itself into a bad habit. And the worst thing about bad habits, he thought, was how comfortable they could become.

Chapter 13

IT rained all Saturday and into the evening as well, and Sam, having spent most of the day washing all his clothes and bedding at the laundry and then reading cheap western novels, finally gave up and went down to Main Street for dinner and then onward to the Fireside. He went in through the back door and stood there for a moment, looking around, water dripping off his wide-brimmed hat as the rain pounded down behind him.

Despite the crowd, even the atmosphere in the Fireside seemed less dense than usual, with Lonni leaving the back door open to let the sound of the clouds bursting outside wash over everyone's conversations.

He shook his hat off and walked to the bar and got a beer from the bartender. Lonni coming back from somewhere with a tray of empty glasses spotted Sam, put the glasses on the counter, and put her arm around Sam's shoulder. She was in a good mood and Sam guessed that she welcomed anything that seemed like a change, even if it came in the form of a torrential downpour.

Sam smiled. "At least someone's enjoying this."

"Someone should, no?"

He liked Lonni. She was good people. And he put his arm around her waist, her back feeling firm inside his forearm. When he finally let his arm drop she did not move away and rested one hand on his shoulder.

"You know," she said, "you really are a nice guy."

"Uh oh."

Lonni laughed. "I knew it. That would bother you."

"What?"

She smiled and leaned in. "Never mind. I just like fooling around."

And at that she gave him a pat on the shoulder and ran away. The immediate effect was as though he was left hanging in the air. But then she came back carrying a tray of empty glasses and as she went by she said in a low voice: "You think I'm always just kidding around, don't you?"

She set the glasses onto the black counter, Sam turned to look at her, but she ignored him and picked up a tray and then was fast gone again.

Good technique, he admitted. Like a hit-and-run driver but then coming back to see the effect.

A three-man combo began to play some mournful country song, and then another. Up to then the dancefloor had been nearly empty, but the slow dance numbers had now filled it, and the band knew better than to break the mood. When they started on a third one he felt himself get restless, downed the rest of his beer, and headed for the back door. He was just out the door onto the porch, buttoning his jacket and setting his hat, when he heard his name called. He turned and saw Lonni standing there.

"Hey," he said.

"You mad at me?"

"No," he said. "Why would you say that?"

"I mean... it's just the way things are tonight. I just fool around. And you may not know it but you really are a nice guy."

He saw how she was studying his eyes. It was clear she was owning it but when he did not say anything she gave him a nod, only slightly questioning, and then a smile and disappeared back into the bar. He went down the steps and out into the downpour, pulling his collar up under the back brim of his hat.

It was only about six blocks, and when he got there he found the house dark. So he turned and jogged back to Main Street. He did not go back to the lounge though but went down the alley behind the buildings on the other side of the street to Bob's, the downspouts in back spurting water at his feet.

He hopped up the back steps and went in past the pool tables towards the bar. Nobody he knew was in there, which was good, and when Bob raised his eyebrows, he pointed at a whiskey bottle.

With the shot glass in front of him, he was in turn thinking and not thinking about things but also enjoying the quiet in there with the rain out on the street falling in a white spray across the surface, capturing the unnatural luminescence of the street lights. Then Dan came in.

"And once again," he said, "wherever I go these days, there you are."

"Could say the same."

"Ain't a big enough town."

"Can seem that way."

"You're drinking whiskey."

"Not really."

Dan nodded at Bob. "The same and him another." He pulled out a bill.

Sam did not have much to say because most of what he wanted to say, or what he had asked, had already been said and asked too many times. That left the field open to Dan, who, as always, was only too glad to have the floor to himself.

"... and the only way to keep from going under," Dan was saying a while later, at the moment when Sam began to listen to him again, "is to keep changing with it. If that means getting bigger, then we'll get fucking bigger."

It was obvious that Dan had been thinking a lot about that conversation they had had, and it was interesting how what the crux of the problem seemed to be, with Carl and him both farming, was the size of the farm. Sam could understand why Dan might feel defensive about his position. The Petersen farm was one of the bigger ones in the county, and a lot of people could wonder why it would be so difficult to share, and would be left wondering what the real problem was.

And it was no wonder Dan was going around in circles about all this, Sam thought. Because no matter how much Dan discussed and explained, the one thing he could not explain to anyone, or at least just say it out loud, was what was at the bottom of it all.

Sam felt a sense of déjà vu wash over him.

At one of the tables to the front, Dan's name was called. Several men and women were over there, and there were some empty chairs. Dan looked back at Sam.

"You might find this interesting."

Sam looked over at them and found himself looking directly into the eyes of one of the women who was looking.

"You mean the dark-haired one?"

Dan grinned.

Sam did not.

"OK," Dan said. "Never mind. Man, sometimes... Well, let's do something. I get tired of just sitting around with all this talking."

That did make Sam smile. "What do you suggest?"

"I don't know. Just get out. Go around the block. Or go over to Harrington."

Harrington was something like twenty miles away.

"Harrington?"

"Goddamn, are you coming or not?"

Sam looked around. "Sure. But not to Harrington. Not with you driving. And not with me driving."

"OK. Fuck Harrington."

They got to their feet and went out onto main, standing under the awning for only a second until Dan set off across the street and Sam found himself back at the Fireside again.

Lonni spotted them coming in, but was too busy to give them more than a wink.

"A pitcher," Dan said to someone, and next thing Sam knew he was sitting at a table with a pitcher of beer in front of him and Dan nodding happily.

At some point since he'd last been in there, and maybe because of the muggy heat in the bar, Lonni had changed into a cream-colored dress. She was sexy like that, and looked like a black-jack dealer at some Las Vegas casino. She was smiling at everyone but now even more at Sam.

"Lonni's in a good mood tonight," Sam said.

"Yeah, you can say that. Especially when she's all ready to jump someone's bones." Dan reached past Sam and poured himself a sloppy glass.

"What are you... drinking or drowning?"

There was a second where they looked at each other for what must have been the first time in hours, and laughed. And Lonni was suddenly there.

"I can see this isn't your first stop," she said. "Am I going to have to shovel you two out at last call?"

"Might," Sam said.

"We're just catching our second wind." Dan took a long drink.

"Looks more like three sheets to it." Lonni gave him a long look. "And that might not be such a good idea. You know, I thought you might be in here earlier."

Dan grinned at Sam. "She meant hoping. She's always had a thing for me."

"Marilyn was here."

"And Carl?"

"No, just her and some of the girls."

"Perfect."

"I thought you or Carl would be in."

"And here I am."

"No, I mean earlier."

"This isn't the only place in town."

Lonni contemplated Dan for a second and then gave Sam a look and walked off.

"Did you see Carl tonight?" Dan said after she had left.

"I would have at the same time as you."

"No, earlier, before I found you."

"Were you expecting to?"

"Not really."

"That solves that then."

"Never mind. It's complicated."

Sam smiled.

"When Dan Petersen uses that word, it only means two things. Farming and women."

112

"It isn't what you think. And it ain't funny." Dan took a drink. "But luckily, I ain't in it."

That was not what Lonni had seemed to be getting at, Sam thought.

He could feel it. The thing in the air that seemed to float around these people he'd met there in Gainesville. There was Lonni, then Dan. And this thing about Marilyn, and Carl. And people being here or not here.

It was exactly the sort of thing about small towns that he liked the least... that sooner or later a guy ended up knowing about things he did not need or want to know. And this was no longer even getting close to that. He was already beyond it.

Normally he would have walked away at this point. And not just where this evening was concerned. But he had no other choice. There was no other harvest there in Eastern Washington he could now hook up with where he might get a combine job rather than just driving truck. And, of course, there was the other thing. And with that thought, two different thoughts suddenly aligned themselves and he found himself now wondering what else was out there among the things he did not need or want to know. God, he thought, being around these people felt like picking at a scab.

"There's no big deal to women going out on their own," he threw out, thinking he might be addressing some worry of Dan's, but even as he said it he knew he was partly addressing one of his own.

"Did not say there was."

"You should see your face."

"I don't give a shit about Marilyn. That's Carl's problem."

"That's not what it looks like."

Dan tilted his head back for a second, and then let out a sigh. "Listen. For me, I don't give a damn. For a guy like Carl, it matters though. I look at it that you have to choose. Someone like Marilyn... you have to make up your mind that that's the type of woman you're getting and there's no sense in trying to look at her any other way than how she is. Women have got to do the same thing, you know. It's just choice." Dan paused, as though contemplating what he had just said. "Don't get me wrong. I like Marilyn all right. I don't know, maybe she'd do all right if she was married again, this time to Carl. But I just think the only type of guy she wouldn't drive crazy is someone who doesn't give a fuck about it. The problem is, my shit-for-brains brother gives a fuck about absolutely everything."

All of this, Sam could now see, was about Carl. Whatever the subject, it had Carl in it. Whether it was the farm, or here with Marilyn, and Sam could see that, when it came to Dan, it would always be about Carl, and Carl and something. For all Sam knew, it was maybe even tied up with his own situation, with Dan wondering on which side Sam would come down on.

Why that would matter at all made no sense. But somehow, with Dan, Sam thought, you could almost think these sorts of things did matter. Some people were like that, being more worried about things that did not matter, than the important things.

But, regardless of whether it mattered or not, Sam also knew that even if the easiest thing was just to go along with Dan's humor, it might not be the best thing in the long run. "Carl seems all right."

"He is mostly," Dan said after a moment, his voice flattening into something that sounded more sober. "Except when it comes to Marilyn."

So that was now clear. Dan could absolve Carl of whatever faults he might have, but his girlfriend wasn't included.

Seeing the look in Sam's eyes, Dan went on: "You don't know her. But I know. Everyone knows. She says she loves him. But she's not..." Dan paused, and then frowned. "The thing is, sometimes a guy has to keep a bit of distance, even when a woman says that. Some kinds of women. Who, when they do that, they've got you too much."

"I'm not sure you can really know about other people's stuff."

"Doesn't matter. I just can't figure Carl out. He's probably home watching TV right now, and either he's stupid, or else he knows damn well he can't keep her from fucking around all over the place all the time."

Sam had always hated this sort of talk. "You don't know what Carl's doing."

"But... I know Marilyn."

"Do you really? And do you know Marilyn and your brother, together?"

"I know Marilyn."

Sam looked across the room and saw Lonni looking at him. He shook his head slightly and he saw her shrug. "Sounds pretty bad."

"Yeah, it's bad," Dan spat out. "It's pretty bad. And I can see some real shit coming and there isn't a goddamn thing I can do about it."

"I don't know a damn thing about any of this. But I know one thing: with the things you can't do anything about, it's best to just stay clear."

Dan sat back in his chair.

"Keep clear?"

"Maybe you'd be better off talking to Carl." Instead of me, Sam thought.

"Keep clear?"

"Other people's shit."

"That's just it. This isn't just other people's shit. It's going to end up being my shit."

For a long moment the conversation seemed to die and Sam was glad of it. When the beer was finished he said, "Hey, let's get out of here and get something to eat."

Dan seemed to come up out of the depths.

"You don't like it here?"

Sam smiled. "It's not a question of here. It's a question of us."

"You've got a hell of an attitude."

"I've barely got an attitude at all."

"That's what I meant." He gave Sam a long look. "You know something? I don't think I've ever seen you and Ruth out together. How's that going?"

"Fine."

Dan, despite his condition, noticed what the question had caused. "Oh sorry. You know, I did sort of notice, but wasn't saying anything."

"About what?"

"About how thorny you've been all evening. I'd sort of guessed."

"Guessed what?"

Dan shrugged. "That there was a problem. I mean, you know, I wasn't going to say anything."

"And so, of course, you did not."

"So there is a problem."

"No," Sam said, nearly wanting to laugh. "There's no problem. But if there is a problem... You want to hear the problem? Here I am, sitting here and listening to all the inner workings of this town, and about the farm, and your brother and future sister-in-law or whatever, and then you go asking me if I've got personal problems going on... and I don't give a royal fuck because... you know why? Because I don't even know if I've got a fucking job."

It took a moment, and then Dan stuck out his jaw. "Oh, is that it?"

"Yeah, oh, that is it."

"Did not seem to bother you before."

"If I did not know better, I'd think you were just pulling my chain. Look, your Dad... and you were standing right there when he said it... said I was going to get a contract, or at least paperwork, to cover my work with the farm. And you were going to do that. And I haven't seen that. I haven't seen one bit of that. So what am I supposed to think? And what am I supposed to give a shit about anything else?"

Dan's jaw was still stuck out, but something in his eye seemed furtive. "I never said you weren't hired."

"I'm serious here."

Dan waved his hand. "Shit. I can't believe this. Listen. Fuck it. For what it's worth, just consider yourself hired now. So just drive out and don't come up with these nobody-called excuses. Dad says you should just come out for fucking breakfast and get going with whoever. OK? But... anyway... that's not what I was talking about. Not. At. All."

"Excuses?"

Sam felt the anger rise in him.

Dan looked back at the bar. "God," he said. "I've got to do everything, it seems."

Sam had a vision, and it was a very real, very red one. But he wasn't ready for that. "OK," he said. "I'll be out there, bright and early. You've now just said it, and that's what I'll do."

"Fine. Fine."

"And I'll have the tax paperwork."

"Right. Of course."

"No, of course. It'll be done."

"Fine. Fine."

And there it was, and for Sam nothing else mattered about anything else he had heard or seen that evening. Or, at least, that was what he felt right at that moment.

It seemed to be raining even more heavily when he walked out of the bar, and it felt like a weight on him. When he got up on the hotel porch and as he was standing there shaking his hat, he patted his pocket, and an immediate bad feeling came over him that was not sickness but of something more like hopelessness. And it had nothing to do with Dan or Ruth or anything else.

He knew exactly where he had left his keys but he felt through all his pockets anyway, and then slumped. Goddamn fucking slam shut self-locking doors.

The deskman was gone at that hour. After hours he left the front door open, but otherwise just went home. Sam looked around at the hard wooden furniture in the dark lobby and considered it. Then he stuck his hat back on.

Ten minutes later, he stood on the corner beneath the streetlight with the white rain coming down on him, looking at the house. Except for a very dim light in the living room, it was still all dark. Cars were parked up and down the street, and their cars were in the driveway, but there were also other cars parked along there in front by the curb and looking at those cars, he suddenly did not want to be out there in the rain standing under the streetlight.

He backed out of it and walked back to the hotel and around back to his car. The one thing he was never locked out of.

He had to get in the front because the back was cluttered with tools.

Lying down with his head on a blanket, his knees bent and crammed beneath the steering wheel, he was thinking how, from then on, if worse came to worse, he knew it would just be a matter of pretending nothing mattered, and then pretending to believe it. And how sooner or later it could be forgotten, as he would be forgotten, and then there wouldn't be any need to pretend anymore. He thought for a moment of how Lonni, of all the people he had met there, had already figured that out about him and did not care, but just had the common sense and practicality to keep everything very, very simple. And see where things went from there.

Chapter 14

AS the hot, long days passed into August, they readied the combines and harvest trucks. Although everything was late that year because of all the rain, the wheat had turned golden and they began hearing how harvests had started in the counties farther south in the Palouse and even earlier in the Big Bend and down below that in Oregon. From there on out, it was like going down a slide. Or more like harvests were coming up a slide, all the time hearing about this farm and that farm, each time coming closer, and they then heard harvest had gotten as far north as Adams and Whitman Counties, just below.

Each day Harley went out and tested. Sam would often be the only one around after breakfast, so he would drive Harley up into the fields and then watch as Harley walked out into the golden wheat. Harley was so much shorter than either Dan or Carl, so heavily built and close to the ground that when he went into a field he looked, out there in the high standing grain, the hills rolling off away and the sky huge overhead, like a part of the land itself.

At first Harley only broke off heads and rolled them in his hands, seeing how easily they came apart in his hard palms, and then chewing on the kernels. It was not long before he found them dry most of the way through and he began to use a moisture tester, pouring a cup of wheat over an electronic meter. One morning, Harley had Sam run a combine fifty yards into a flatland field between two hills where the wheat was the last to ripen, and then climbed up and scooped the cleaned wheat into the cap of his tester and poured it over the moisture sensor.

"Fourteen percent. We're good. By the time it's harvested and hauled, it'll be dry enough."

"I heard last night they were already almost halfway finished in Umatilla County."

"That's nearly Oregon, which is always done before us. Whitman and Adams are just barely going. Everything ready?"

"Headers are all on. Belts. Bins. I heard Carl say most of the elevators have their crews."

Harley reached into the cab, picked up the CB and punched the button.

"Dan?... Carl?..."

A long pause, and then the scratchy voice of Carl: "Here..."

"Call everyone. We'll start the day after tomorrow, six o'clock sharp for breakfast."

"We start by the house?"

Harley thumbed the button again, grinning at Sam. "We start right here where I'm standing."

"Where's right here?"

"By Ole's. We'll convoy tomorrow morning."

"OK. Out."

Harley hung up the mic and looked out across the field. "We might only be able to cut in the afternoons for a couple of days." Harley's eyes squinted with whatever he was thinking. "But it's going to be a good one."

"Good one?"

"Harvest."

"How do you know?"

"The good ones you can feel in the bones."

Dan leaned back in his chair. "Here we go." Nobody said anything, but everyone was thinking the same thing. It had begun, and for thirty days there was going to be nothing but harvest. All day long it would go and then all night long when it got to the point they were dreaming about it. Sam looked around the lunch table. It was Sally, sightlessly pursing her lips in concentration, who caught his attention. She caught her husband's as well.

Harley grinned, his white teeth shining in his darkly tanned face. "What's the matter, Ma?"

She brought her focus back and looked at him. "I guess I'd better be calling my helper."

"I guess you'd better, too."

For Sally, harvest meant thirty days of cooking and cleaning, just like always, except for the amount which made it almost as continuous as the field work. She smiled, and Sam had a sudden thought that he was seeing the same smile that had appeared on her face at that moment for thirty years.

The dinner went along with normal talk of things to be done, a discussion of the order of fields, and who'd be doing what. But when the blackberry and rhubarb pies finally came Carl held up his hands. "Good a time as ever, I guess. Just to let you know. When it's over we'll all be going to Coeur d'Alene."

Harley had starting cutting out a wedge from the blackberry pie. He and Sally had gathered the berries from below the barn the evening before. "We are?" He worked the knife under the wedge. "How come?"

"Because that's where Marilyn and I are getting married. And that's when. And next year, Mom, you won't have to be calling in anyone."

It sounded like good news to Sam but glancing around the table he did not see much that looked like happiness. Instead of looking at Carl, Sally was looking at Harley. And Harley, who anyone might have expected to have been looking at Carl, was instead giving Dan a studious look. Sam looked at Sally again and just momentarily saw a look of private pain go across her face. But also something more than pain. And maybe it was only the look of a mother but he could see there truly was turmoil somewhere. Dan had not been just talking through his hat. Carl and Marilyn were causing worries for the Petersen family. Or maybe it was just Marilyn, as Dan implied. In any case it was something serious.

Carl, who did not seem surprised by the reception of his announcement and who had been looking stubbornly around the table, now turned and stared straight at Dan.

There was a grunt from Fred. "Now, what the hell would make you want to do a stupid thing like that for?"

At that a slight smile came to Harley's face.

Carl turned to look at Fred, who was squinting back, and then looked back at everyone else, finally giving them a big smile.

It was all pretty awful, Sam thought, and especially awful was the look on Dan's face, all red and a little wild in the eyes. But what was worse was the look Carl then gave Dan, smiling but staring and staring, as though daring him to say anything at all.

Harley dumped the wedge of pie he had cut onto a plate and handed it across the table to Sam, who took up his fork and fell into it, heart and soul. He knew very little about Marilyn but suddenly he felt an enormous amount of sympathy for her.

Sam and Fred were working under a big, tandem-axle wheat truck, lubing joints, or taking up wrenches to tighten nuts.

"So there you got to see some of the family... conundrums. I was wondering how long it would be before you had the pleasure."

"All families have their problems. But this Marilyn, I mean, if Carl's OK with her, she must be OK. No? I don't get the impression Carl makes many mistakes."

"It's sometimes a pain, knowing way too damn much."

"So she's a problem."

"I didn't say that. I agree with you about Carl, and I agree with you about her."

"You've known the family a long time."

"Yeah, Coeur d'Alene folk. Moved here when she was little. Good people. But you know how it goes. Even the best of families get complicated now and again. But when you don't know them..."

"Ah... no, no," Sam shook his head. "I'm not judging or saying anything."

Fred turned his face towards Sam.

"I know you're not. It's not her fault. She's just someone who causes others to talk about her way too much. She has that thing. Some people have that thing where they get talked about whether they've done anything or not."

Sam hesitated, and then just decided he might as well just ask the question. "Has she done something?"

"Yes...," Fred said. "Yes, she has. What she's done is that she grew up to be, just flat out, a too good-looking woman for such a small town."

"You like her."

"I do. If you ever get to know her, you will too. She's one damn good girl. I knew her parents and one of her grandfathers. Good people, all of them."

"That's not what you made it sound like to Carl."

"What I said," Fred said as he picked up a big wrench and started off for the other side of the truck, "wasn't for Carl."

It was later that afternoon, tightening wires on some fence lines up in the hills, that he started really thinking about what had gone on that morning. The Petersens were as good a family as anyone could expect and went easier on each other, and on other people, than a lot of people he'd known. But Marilyn was definitely going to be a thing to absorb.

Sam did not know her at all. But he had come to see that she had a tough, almost defiant way of handling herself. But at the same time her smile was always wide and genuine. And she was charming, humorous, sympathetic, and friendly. And it made no sense to him at all why Dan seemed to have a problem with her.

One time, he had mentioned her to Ruth, saying how uncomfortable it could be sometimes in small towns to know things about someone despite not really knowing them at all. Ruth had just shrugged, and then had said people can't help talking.

The thought of Ruth made him stop what he was doing for a moment, straightening up and looking across the golden hills. Harley had said this year was going to be one of the good ones, that he could feel it in his bones. But when it came to that, as far as Sam was concerned, there was no telling what this harvest was going to be like. Except for how he had never found himself so deep inside of one as he was finding himself suddenly in this one.

Chapter 15

IN no hurry, he ate in town the first morning of harvest and then drove out to the farm. The truck drivers, high school boys, were busy servicing their trucks and the field mechanic was running the fuel truck along behind the line of combines and trucks fuelling each in turn. It all had the air of a well-practiced drill, even on the first day.

He parked his car by the house and went in through the back porch to the service room, and pulled a frozen jug out of the freezer there.

He was screwing on a plastic cap when Sally came in behind him and got a couple of frozen pies out. Her face looked warm and a strand of hair had fallen across her forehead.

With the pies balanced on one hand she pushed the strand back in place with the back of her other hand. He had liked Sally right from the start. He liked her practicality and did not mind at all her good-natured view that sooner or later everyone would end up more or less like Harley and herself, with a house, a family, steady work, and hopefully not too much trouble after retirement, and as long as she could maintain that belief towards a person, then that person shared the same world she was in and they were understandable. Being understandable then was what Sam was determined to be with her. Regardless.

"How're you doing?"

"Done," she answered. "Finished."

"You or the lunch?"

She smiled, her hand going instinctively to her hair again. "I suppose I do look a little frazzled. First day is always like that. A big shock."

He saw a girl with dark hair go down the hallway on the other side of the kitchen carrying some things. "How's your help?"

"Oh." She paused to give him an idea of what that first morning might have been like. "We're going to do just fine."

The girl, pleasant-looking with large, dark eyes, reappeared there in the hallway, giving him a half smile. Really, she was not a girl at all, just timid. Her face was as flushed as Sally's but he could see it was not from overexertion. There were a lot of reasons women went out to work as harvest cooks each summer, generally unmarried women, and the money was not always the main one.

He gave her a smile, and she disappeared with it back into the kitchen. Sally leaned closer to him and spoke in a lower voice. "She really is a very good cook, Sam. Just isn't used to the proportions."

"Good. Nothing more miserable than a bad harvest cook, is there?" He winked at her.

"Oh! I'd forgotten you already had one of those." She gave him a sideways glance and despite it being a subject she had evidently learned about from Dan, and therefore imperfectly, he had to laugh at how she did it.

"That's right," he said. "And you do a damn fine job."

"I wasn't talking about me."

"You weren't?"

"Not at all."

"Nobody's doing my cooking for me."

"That's not what I've been hearing."

"What you've been hearing?"

"Yes. From what I heard, you're really getting yourself settled in over there in Gainesville."

"You heard that, huh?" He felt for a second a pinch of annoyance for Dan, but then another pain went through him. He could only make to joke about it.

"You heard that I was getting all... settled?"

She smiled. "You make it sound like something terrible."

"I don't mean to. I don't have anything against it particularly."

"Nothing... particular?"

"No." He shrugged. "There's nothing particularly wrong with settling down." It was getting hard to keep his face from hardening with the thought of the ways Dan would have rambled on about him, joking probably, an amusing subject of dinner conversation.

She looked at him steadily for a moment, and then she put both arms around her pies and threw back her head with a laugh.

"Oh!" she cried. "As I live and breathe!" She eyed him again for a second and let out another laugh. "Nothing particular... just everything in general, right?" At the look on his face she cocked an eyebrow at him. "Sam. Who do you think you're fooling? As if you could fool anybody."

"I did not mean that. Exactly."

She smiled sympathetically. "Never mind. It's just terrible the way people go on, isn't it?"

"Oh, I don't care...," he started to mumble.

"Of course not," Sally said with a remarkable depth of sympathy, and she saw a genuine look of confusion or maybe even worry on Sam's face and her humor became reflective. "You've moved around a lot, haven't you? Lots of small towns."

"You can say that."

She nodded. "Dan told us that. But I'm thinking you really haven't lived in any for long. Or not enough."

"Enough?"

"To know how people talk." Sally gave him a shrug. "It's not bad, Sam. Talk's just talk. And I was just kidding because I thought you already would have known that."

"Known what?" Sam couldn't keep back the bit of irritation he felt, thinking of himself as a subject of conversation. She was right. He wasn't used to it. "That I'm also an item? Like Marilyn?"

The smile remained on Sally's face, but the look changed and he could see she was somewhere else. He suddenly felt ashamed of himself but even as he struggled with that Sally's face suddenly cleared and she looked back at him with a smile.

"That's something else," she said easily. "And anyway, it's all not going to matter, is it?"

At that she reached out and gave him a pat on the arm and walked off with her pies.

Sam stared after her. At first he thought she had meant that last thing for Marilyn, but then he realized that it could very easily have been meant for him. If it was for Marilyn, he had to admire her pragmatic acceptance of whatever life presented. But if it was for him, he suddenly felt caught off guard by how much Sally could figure out.

And then he realized it was probably both.

That night after dinner, Harley, his face high with color from the good company and several bottles of beer, said it was one of the best starts to a harvest that he had ever known. They had gone out onto the front porch and had stood there talking quietly, the living room lights behind them glowing warm and yellow through the curtains. Above the far hills shone the full moon, and from the high-flung branches of the cottonwoods black shadows were cast down across the lawn where crickets sent out the smooth and softly rolling crescendos of their song.

The still, warm air of the evening and the low sound of the crickets near the house took Sam a long way back, and the evening became another. But the other had been hot and sweaty, and, unable to sleep, a barefoot boy in bib overalls had crept down the stairs of a strange house and had gone out on that house's front porch, walking carefully to make no noise.

But it had been no cooler out there with the smell of magnolias and something like oranges—recalling the smells almost more than the place—and he could remember how, other than the low chirping of the crickets that had been alongside the house in those bushes, it had seemed as though the whole world had died.

He sat down on the steps of the big covered porch, wiping at his neck with his hand and drying it on his shirt. There were other houses on the street and other porches but there had been no lights or movement, just darkness out there made all the more so with only the dim light of a single lamp at the end of the block.

In that house slept an old woman. He knew her as his

grandmother but little more than that, just like he did not know that house or the street of that town or for that matter the town. But that was not supposed to have been important. It was supposed to be right for him to be there and that was all that mattered. He could barely remember anything else but he did remember how he had trouble, later that night, going back inside... as though he did not feel like he could, as though he was stuck outside, there on that porch.

The boy stared at the street with a lost, frightened look on his face. He did not know much but he knew things were wrong.

He pulled from the pocket of the bib a picture of a couple with a baby. Earlier that day his grandmother had given it to him. "Here. It's the only one there is. You can have it if you want it and think you can take care of it. You want it?"

The boy nodded.

She pursed her lips. "You'll stay here through the end of the month and then you'll go with George. He and your dad got along fine and you'll do your school over there."

Even at his young age the boy knew when something was final and nothing to be discussed. "Yes ma'am," he said.

Later that night on the porch he stared at the photo for a moment and then put it away. He wiped his face with his hand, the sweat running down it like tears as though he was crying, which he had also done, and he took a long breath and looked up at the moon riding full and shining down like polished ivory from the blackness of the sky.

He did not remember how long he had stayed there in that house, or how he had arrived there, and he had not been afraid at the time. The fear had only come later when he had learned how it happened, how he had got lucky about what people called the tragedy, if it could be put that way. But at the time he had not been able to think about things that way and he had just been a boy living in a house on a street with a forgotten name. Years later, and for a while, it had almost been a sad thing to remember that boy who had gone down those stairs to be away from the terrible sweltering stickiness of old sheets wrapping around hot legs and arms, only then to have found it no cooler on that porch. It had almost seemed sad, because that was what might have been expected when it came to thinking about children who are all but alone. But then that changed and he did not think like that, with the memory reverting to how it had really been at the time: just a little boy on a porch in the dark, who maybe had felt a bit lost and frightened but it was nothing to be sad about because that little boy, while not happy, had not been sad either. Of all the things he could do about it, he knew he could not be deciding later to make the boy be some way he had never been. What was left for him then from that time was simply the feeling that he had not been in the right place and that he wasn't sure anymore that there would ever again be a place where the houses and the people were not strange to him, and he was more than just a little boy who was not sad. All he had left of it was that it was the first time he had really known what it was like to be alone.

Of all the places and all the times he had known since, he had never found a better way of defining the feeling. Not so much lonely as just alone and on the outside of what might have been. But then, too, not in the right place either. It was that last thing, perhaps, that had made being alone an easier thing to have to put up with. It made being alone just a matter of circumstance and not the general condition.

Standing next to Harley, Sam looked up at the bright moon above, seeing how clear it was there in the starless sky. Harley, leaning against the porch railing, suddenly flicked into the garden below the butt of a cigarette he had been smoking in the dark. Harley did not smoke much and usually only in the evening and if so always out on the porch. Sally would not allow it inside. He looked at Sam and gave him a smile. Sam could see that wherever Harley had been, it had been a long way away, too. It might have been interesting to know where Harley had been, to know what remote period—hidden deep in the folds of the history of his people out there—would capture the silent attentions of the farmer's imagination on a warm summer evening. But as it was with people everywhere when it came to their silent thoughts, unless they told you, you could never ask.

"Time to roll in," Harley said. "And you've got a ways to go to get back to town. Why don't you just bunk out here?"

"Thanks." Sam nearly smiled.

Harley grinned. "We fumigate the bunkhouse every year."

"I've been told I snore."

"We all do."

"Exactly."

Harley looked up at the big moon again. "We'll be seeing him again before harvest is over."

"Supposed to be good luck, isn't it?"

"Supposed to be," Harley nodded. "But you know what I think?"

"What?"

"I think it's just the moon." Harley gave him a wink and for a second Sam had the strange impression he had seen a wink like that somewhere lately, and then he remembered where. Evidently both Harley and Sally had come to share the same form of pragmatism. Whether they had come by it naturally or had grown into it over the years together was another question, and Sam wondered whether people came together because they were fundamentally alike, or whether they just evolve into seeming that way?

"Maybe so."

"You never know. Whatever happens is bound to happen. But one way or the other, it won't make any difference in a hundred years." Harley turned. "I'll see you in the morning."

Sam looked back out across the lawn again and then stepped off the porch. Oddly, a sense of peace came over him and he found himself repeating quietly as he walked in the moonlight toward his car, "whatever happens is bound to happen..."

Chapter 16

HARVEST went without any snags for two straight weeks, but the weather did not hold and one day the clouds came up fat and white to the west and began clumping. The weather report out of Spokane said that a wet system was piling in off the Pacific and neither the Olympics nor the Cascades would do much to stop it. There was no rain that night and they started the next day as usual, but by noon the clouds closed together and went grey and the first drops made black streaks through the dust on windshields. Even before Harley called on the radio, everyone in the field was engulfed with the rain falling heavily and steadily. Combines dumped what they had, and trucks raced off with their last loads to the elevator.

As Sam approached the farmhouse he saw the Petersens and most of the crew standing on the porch.

"Shit," he heard Dan say as he came up the steps. "Can you believe this summer?" There was a dark look on Dan's face and his voice was more irritated than mere bad weather seemed to call for.

Harley turned to the crew. "That's it, fellas. Everyone's on standby. If we're lucky, only about two days."

The harvest mechanic, Pete, a dark, heavy-set man with a southern accent of some sort, grinned. "This would be a good opportunity," he said, looking at some of the dustier truck drivers, "for a few of the people in the bunkhouse to do some laundry in town. As for myself, I'm going to go play some pool."

Dan smiled. "I might join you."

"Make sure everything's greased up and put away," Carl said.

"Everybody knows to do that," Dan said.

131

"I'm sure they do," Carl said, without looking at him. "Anyway, boys, get your rigs put to right before you go anywhere."

"They know what to do."

"No doubt. But it has to be said."

Sam saw Harley turn quick on his heel. A quicker movement than Harley normally made. Sam followed Harley into the house for the lunch Sally had set out.

They were sitting at a table toward the front of Bob's, and through the front window and door they could see the canvas awnings across the street stretch and flap with the gusting wind, the rain itself being blown against the sides of the buildings and then away down the street.

When the glasses and the pitcher of beer were brought over, Pete poured out the first round with the flourish of a man on liberty. He had been in the navy and it was obvious he still liked to give in to the instincts of a sailor in port. He drank off his first glass in one go and then rapped his glass down first, laces of foam drooping slowly towards the bottom. Then he poured another and gave a contented sigh. "When you're thirsty, you're thirsty. That's how to make it better."

Carl lifted his glass. "Well, what's it to?"

When nobody said anything, Sam raised his glass. "To a heat wave?"

"Careful what you wish for," Dan said.

"Whatever gets us through the rest of harvest then, either a heat wave or otherwise."

"Sounds good to me," Pete said, and another round disappeared. He began pouring again. "I can see that you old boys like to drink a little beer."

"An we kin see," Dan said, "that yall've drawnk a bit yoseff."

Sam saw Carl's eyebrows twitch and how Pete looked down at the table for a moment. "I guess that's so," Pete said finally, his accent somehow not quite as pronounced. "And I imagine there'll be a lot more to come."

When the second pitcher was gone, Pete threw a wad of money

on the table for the next one and stalked over to the jukebox. Carl went away towards the toilets. Sam looked out the windows at the weather for a second.

"God," he said. "Blown around like that, it's almost like being under water. We'll need to grow gills."

He turned back and found Dan staring at him intensely.

"What?" he said.

Dan, seemingly startled out of something, shook his head and then stretched his arms out wide, like he was crucified. "Nothing."

"You weren't giving me a nothing look."

Dan snorted. "Don't go getting sideways."

"Something's bugging you?"

"No."

"Could have fooled me."

Pete had the first few bars of a song pounding out of the jukebox. Bob brought over another pitcher and Dan filled Sam's glass and pushed it at him. "Drink up, shithead. Learn to be happy. Like me."

Sam reached for his beer. "Where's this going?"

"Nowhere," Dan said, not looking at him. "I'm not the one that's always going or not going."

Sam could see Dan was in a strange mood, but had no idea how really bad of a mood it was. He was to find out quickly. But for the moment he just went along with things as they seemed to be. "I see. To avoid talking about what's making you so uptight and irritated, you divert it all by getting me all uptight and irritated. And, yeah, to answer what you didn't ask, all I've done since the beginning of harvest is just cut wheat, eat, and crawl home to bed. No, I haven't gone over there. And no, it hasn't been on purpose. So, we'll just stop there."

Dan either should have been amused by that, or not care, but for some odd reason a dogged, almost mean look had come over his face. "It's OK," he said. "None of my business, in fact. But it must be nice to have the freedom to be a total asshole whenever you feel like it."

"And you're saying you aren't ever?"

"I'm a goddamn knight in shining armor in comparison."

Sam was nowhere in the same sort of mood as Dan was, but let some irritation come up, just as a defense. He looked at Dan carefully, trying to judge where things were going.

"I don't pretend to be one."

"You say I'm pretending?"

"Damn, man." Sam felt real anger now come up. Dan felt like needling him, he could return it in full. "It must be sweet to have all your wet-dreams come true."

Surprisingly, Dan did not take that as an insult, and his face changed.

"You know," he said. "She really isn't all that bad."

"Oh, really."

"No, asshole. I really mean it. I mean, she's pretty nice."

"Did not say she wasn't."

"Yeah, yeah. But you know how we used to talk about her."

"We?"

"But really, I was wrong about her. And I don't care what anyone says. Just fuck it."

"What people say?"

"You know."

Sam did not, but did not care to, either. "Glad to hear things are fine."

"But you know," Dan leaned in. "Sue's good friends with Ruth."

"Yeah?"

"Just saying."

"Saying what?"

"Well, you should know, I mean, no, Sue and I talk about stuff. Ruth never does. But Sue, you know, is one of those people who can't help just talking and talking. She doesn't mean harm, I mean. But sometimes she says things that make sense, and she said she thinks you're in love with Ruth, but you either don't know it or are scared shitless."

Sam sat flat back into his chair and stared. "How the fuck did we get into this?" Sam stared at Dan for about three seconds and then looked out across the bar, saying to himself, "Who could not love this?"

"Anyway," Dan shrugged, "maybe Ruth doesn't know herself?"

"Sounds like only one person around here does."

"Maybe so." Dan nodded.

Sam's mouth formed a silent fucking hell but after a second he turned back around, eyeing Dan. "Anything I should know?"

Dan's eyes narrowed. "Actually," he said, "No. Ruth just told Sue that no, she hasn't heard from you. From the way she acts, you'd think she'd never heard of you, which made Sue think there's more there."

"Sue said that..."

"Yeah."

"Those exact words."

"Well, no."

"So, it was you talking about it and she was responding..."

"I didn't mean that."

"What did you mean, Dan?"

Dan lifted his shoulders and might have continued talking but they were suddenly no longer alone. Sam had seen Carl, earlier, use the phone in back and then slip out the door, and now saw him coming back, and with a hard look on his face.

Sam went on guard.

"What'd you do?" Dan said as Carl sat down. "Go puke somewhere?"

"Just stepped out."

"To give yourself a quickie?"

Carl glanced at Sam, and then turned to his brother. "Where's this bullshit coming from?"

"Wow," Dan said. "Can't even joke around. Not in the mood, eh?"

"Maybe, maybe not. But certainly not for this shit."

Sam could see that regardless of whatever had Carl riled up, Dan was not only making things worse, but knew it, and was doing it deliberately. And probably, Sam thought, Dan also knew what had Carl going like this.

"Oh well, fuck me." Dan jerked his head back. "And fuck you, too."

"Say one more thing."

It came out so low and steady that Sam knew it was more than just a thing to say. He had never witnessed Carl's anger but he could tell it was of the big and dangerous sort. The sort that Sam knew had to be dealt with seriously if you were going to mess around with it at all.

Dan picked up his glass, taking a sip of beer and then held the glass there, half full.

Sam's back stiffened.

He could see that when it happened it was not going to be an easy one to stop. And help was far away. Bob was all the way down the bar watching television, and Pete was over by the jukebox where some women had a table.

Dan, though, seemed relaxed. In fact, he looked in a better mood than he had all day long. "I hope you're going to be a stupid shithead like this all afternoon," he said. "We all really enjoy how you come in and ruin everyone's good time."

Sam very nearly laughed. As it was, he had to raise his hand and cough into it.

Carl lifted his head. "And you must also enjoy being a fucking asshole since you're one most of the time."

Dan grinned.

That grin, Sam thought, was maybe something only a brother knew he could do. But he was far from sure it was the right thing to do.

"Listen, headfuck," Dan said. "You're the one who started it all."

Carl lifted his chin. "How far back do you want to take that?"

"Far as you want."

"Why don't we go discuss that outside? Because you're so goddamn drunk, I'll let you take the first shot. No, I'll let you take the first two. And then I'll take the pleasure of beating the ever living shit out of you. Something I should have done before."

Sam felt himself uncoil. Regardless of what Carl had just said, the hard edge had gone from his voice.

Sam looked between the two brothers. Dan evidently really did know his brother. But Sam could not help feeling that he did not like much the way he knew him. And he liked even less having been a witness to that.

"No," Dan said. "It's raining."

"You afraid I might get carried away?"

"Times like this I'd like to break a chair over your stupid head."

"Don't let fear stop you."

"I'm not afraid of you."

Carl got to his feet.

"Where're you going?" Dan said.

"You want to come outside?"

"Sit down."

"What's the matter?"

"I said, sit down," Dan repeated, only that time loud enough to cause a few heads to turn.

Carl took a deep breath. "I don't know who the fuck you think you are. I'm going whether you come or not, and you can tell someone the fuck else to sit down. I've got no reason to stay and drink with you. But let me tell you this. Before this summer is over, you really need to be understanding some things."

"Like what?"

"I'm tired of your games." Carl picked up his coat and hat. "You know fucking well what." He turned and walked straight out the back door.

Sam watched him go and then turned to see Dan smiling at him. "What'd you think of that?" Dan said.

"You two are just what every party needs."

"We're not always like that."

"I'm glad."

"He'll be back."

"I don't know about that."

"He always comes back."

There was something contemptuous in Dan's tone and Sam felt himself getting irritated. Again. "Then he's really not angry?"

"No. He'll just go off and have a beer and we'll see him later."

"Hope so. You know, this is one of our last chances to have a beer like this before he gets married."

Dan stared down at the table. "Jesus," he said finally. "I'll be glad when they really do get married."

"Yeah," Sam said. "Maybe it's getting to him."

"Hell," Pete said, having heard the remark as he came back to sit down and having seen enough to know there were some bad feelings in the air, "it gets to everyone. Family. Friends. Ex-friends..." He winked. "Of the ex-girlfriend sort, I mean. My wife Darla, she says about exes that..."

"Whatever," Dan said hard and fast. Really hard.

Pete, his mouth having been stopped mid-word, pursed his lips and nodded.

For a moment the three of them looked at each other warily and then Dan's face settled back into something neutral.

"All I know is that he's been a pure shithead lately. I mean, worse than usual."

By dinnertime, the table was littered with empty pitchers and the even more empty conversation of men who were now tired of relaxing, and that was when Marilyn walked in, Lonni and another woman behind her.

Sam saw them first and fell back into his chair. Dan and Pete followed his gaze.

"Ah," Marilyn said. "There you are."

Marilyn had a gleam in her eyes. The other woman was looking over their table with its mess of spilt beer, empty and full glasses, and a sopping bar rag donated by Bob for the night. Lonni smiled at Sam.

Dan rocked back. "Pull up a chair, ladies." He swung his hand up, smacking Marilyn up behind.

She stepped away.

"Always the gentleman." She said.

Pete moved his chair to make room.

Marilyn pulled a chair between Dan and Sam. Lonni sat down

on the other side of Sam, and the other woman took the remaining seat between Dan and Pete.

"Isn't this cozy," Lonni said.

Pete waved at Bob for some more glasses and then looked back at the three women. "Just what the party needed."

Marilyn smiled at him. "How nice to be wanted." She turned and gave Dan the same big smile but he just reached for his beer. She looked back at Pete. "Thank you. Whoever you are."

Pete introduced himself and Sam thought he heard the other woman say her name was Debby. Because of her hard eyes and how she did not look as though she wanted to be there, it was hard to tell if she could be an attractive woman or not.

"What're you all doing down here?" he said.

"We came looking for you," Lonni said.

"It's true," Marilyn said. "Where's Carl? He said everybody was down here."

It was the first time in hours that anyone had mentioned Carl. For a moment there was an odd silence and then Sam said "He stepped out a while back."

Dan laughed.

Sam looked at him and then looked at Pete, who took his eyes off Marilyn and now looked stonily out at the rain in the lights of the street.

Marilyn looked from one to the other.

"Hmmm," she hummed. "I seem to have missed something."

"Not really." Dan gave Sam a quick glance.

"I'm sorry we didn't get down here earlier," she said. "Lonni couldn't get away and...," she laughed, "I wouldn't want to come alone."

"No, of course not," Dan said.

"Carl had to go do something," Sam said. "He'll be back as soon as he can."

Dan made a low sound.

Marilyn shook her hair back. "Well, good. Meanwhile, we have three here." She gave Lonni a look. "Or maybe it's only two."

Lonni tilted her head at Pete. "And maybe it's only one."

"That's a lot of maybes," Marilyn said, "but on the other hand, and I mean literally, that looks an awful lot like a ring there on his finger."

"Oh!" Lonni lifted her eyebrows. "What'll we do now?"

"What we always do. Hope the cavalry shows up."

Dan looked at Sam and Pete. "Anyone else feel like dead meat?"

Marilyn made a sympathetic sound and patted him on the shoulder. "What's the matter, Danny?" She looked at Lonni again. "I don't see Suzy here, do you?" Lonni shook her head and Marilyn shrugged. "I hope there isn't something wrong."

"Glad you're so concerned."

"And I'm glad you're glad I'm concerned. Of course, I can't imagine how there could ever be anything wrong."

"For sure," Lonni agreed. Sam caught her eye and gave her a little frown.

"What?" she said to him, and then looked at Marilyn. "Uh oh, I think we're getting onto thin ice!"

"I don't think so," Marilyn turned to Dan. "We're not on thin ice, are we?"

"I wouldn't know."

"See? It doesn't matter. We're not on thin ice." She lifted her glass. "Hey! This could be like a bachelor's party, couldn't it? A celebration?"

"Yeah," Pete said. "That was sort of the idea. Except that the man of honor is missing."

"The man of honor," the woman named Debby said, "is always missing."

It was the first time she had said anything at all and once it was out she was instantly and obviously embarrassed. Sam couldn't help smiling. "Women are from Venus," he said. "Men are from hell."

Marilyn and Lonni laughed.

"Sorry," Debby said. But she also smiled gratefully at Sam. She could indeed look attractive.

"Don't be sorry," Marilyn said. "It's mostly true, you know."

"I don't know," Lonni said. "Sam here isn't so hellish. In fact, I'd say he's an honorable man."

Marilyn turned towards Sam. "Is that right?"

"I wouldn't know."

"That immediately makes you one. So, Sam, you are officially named an honorable man. And that deserves an award." She put her arm behind his neck and pulled him toward her. For a second he was convinced she was going to kiss him flat on the mouth, and maybe she did too, but then she just as quickly let him go, almost pushing him away. She looked out across the room.

Sam looked over at Dan and saw Dan looking back at him with a slight smile, his eyes half hooded.

"I'll take it as a compliment," Sam said.

"Ah," she smiled, "a gallant man as well. Who doesn't expect any prizes for it. Pretty rare hereabouts."

Sam felt Lonni lean towards him. "This is where you take notes," she said in his ear and her hand suddenly stretched lightly across his thigh. Dan and Pete couldn't see it but Marilyn did.

"Oh," she said. "But we're leaving Danny out. We can't do that! Danny's honorable, too! Only for him, the whole world has to be honorable his way."

"You really are drunk," he said.

Marilyn smiled.

"Too much," she agreed. "And out comes the truth a-poppin'..."

Dan looked at Sam and now did notice the angle of Lonni's arm. "Well, well. Someone's sure popular tonight," he said. "Must be by default."

Sam felt Lonni's hand slide away.

"Don't be such an ass," she said.

"Me? All night long I'm just sitting here, and everyone's throwing rocks at me."

"Never mind," Marilyn smiled. "But it's true, you know. Danny's sense of honor. I mean," she nodded at him, "you're sort of like an ideal then, right?" She laughed. "Suzy's so lucky. But, in a way, that makes her unlucky. I'm sure she'll do all right, though. Suzy's sort of an ideal, herself, isn't she?"

"Her name is Sue."

She put her hand up to her mouth. "Oh my God, Danny. Sorry. It's true. I don't know her all that well."

"No problem."

She pushed her hair back again with her hand. "I hope not. I mean, I hope there are no problems."

"Is that what you meant?"

"Sure. I hope you never have any problems with anything. I know how difficult it can be to have standards." She glanced around. "See what a mess they've made out of me?"

Sam felt shocked, but not because of what she'd said, but by the momentary look that came over Dan's face. It was not fear, or a haunted look, but all the humor or any of the other things he had shown all evening, seemed to drain right out of him.

Dan stood up.

"I'll be right back."

They watched him go out the door, then Pete said to Debby. "I feel like dancing. Darling, do me a favor."

She did not seem to want to but got up anyway and went with him over to the jukebox. After a minute a waltz-like country song came on and Pete began steering them through the whining pedal-steel flourishes and the stricken, yodeling lyrics. When Sam turned back to the table, he found Marilyn and Lonni talking quietly to each other as though he wasn't there.

"I love Carl," Marilyn said. "And I don't care if the whole goddamn town doesn't believe it. Maybe you don't either. But it's truer than anything else you might think."

"I never said I did not believe it. I just don't know how you're going to manage it. You've got more guts than I do, that's for sure."

"It's not that bad."

"It'd drive me nuts."

"It almost did me, at first."

"But not anymore?"

"Not a fucking goddamn bit."

"And Carl?"

"Carl? Are you kidding...?" Marilyn's face went red. "Good grief. Doesn't anyone around here know what Carl's all about? I

142

swear. This whole town gets everything completely fucking backwards. How many times have I told you this?"

Lonni nodded. "Just a sec, be right back," she said, and got up.

There was no way Sam could not have heard every word of it although he had been trying to seem like he was elsewhere. But now, Marilyn suddenly looked at him and smiled at him with that gorgeous, wonderful smile, her eyes with lights dancing in their depths, and Sam found himself wondering how anyone could not have loved her if they knew her at all. He did not know much of anything about Carl but he had to admire the man for having won this woman's love.

"Quit looking at me like that," he said. "You're making me feel sober."

"You know what, Sam? Sam-I-am?"

"No. What?"

"I'm just one husband away from happiness."

"I know. And a month from now, you'll be... just one husband away from happiness. It's a pretty lousy joke, you know."

"It is. But I wanted to get it out of the way." She sighed. "You must think we're all nuts."

"No. I'm just not sure who likes who right now."

"From what I understand, someone sure likes you."

Sam frowned. "Yeah, well, as for that..."

"I'm not talking about Lonni."

"Man," Sam complained. "Is there anyone who doesn't know everything around here? Or who feels they don't? And as for that, what... we're going to tick off all the boxes tonight? First Sue, and now...?"

"Sue's a different story. We all know that one."

"Story?"

"Never mind. Just... watch yourself. And, by the way, Lonni is a good person, you know?"

"Of course she is."

"Just so as you know. You put out signs..." She shrugged.

"Am I putting out signs?"

"Maybe not. But I'm not in it."

143

"In what?"

Marilyn rolled her eyes. "Oh, brother!"

"Oh, brother, yourself." Sam slumped in his chair, contemplating what he wanted to do. Where before the evening had been what it was, it was now sliding into something he did not want to be a part of anymore.

He looked over and saw Pete, Lonni and Debby talking over by the jukebox, and they were smiling and laughing and seemed to be talking about things in a way he wished they could have been talking about before.

He turned around again, thinking of saying something interesting and funny, or at least normal, but now Marilyn was just watching the door. And he was watching her.

"Kind of sad, isn't it?" Lonni said softly into his ear. She had come out of nowhere.

"Sad?"

"Well, maybe not sad. But you know."

"No, I don't."

"I just wish there was something I could do."

"Like what?"

"I don't know. Just something."

"God," he said, but not angrily. If he did get angry, he thought, he might get angry for Marilyn. But he could not do that. You can't get angry for people you don't know. "I hate this shit."

"Me, too. But what can you do?"

"What you can do is nothing."

"Nothing?"

"That's right."

"Ah... so that's the Sam Lawrence method. Just say nothing's wrong and it isn't? You know something? I think sometimes that you don't give a shit about anything. Or about any of us."

And that was enough for Sam, and for the entire evening.

"Oh, Christ, Lonni. C'mon. What I can't give a damn about is what people do to themselves. I honestly don't know what the past hour and a half has been about but I do know one thing. I'm pretty sure she'll do just fine, despite all our goddamn sympathy."

Now it was Lonni seeming to struggle with some sort of anger. "You don't really like it here, do you?"

It seemed darker in the bar by then. The little light there was, red or blue from the neon beer signs, was thick with smoke and faded into blackness as it went into the depths of the tavern. Over the voices came the sound of the jukebox again and Sam looked over at where Pete and Debby were dancing. The song Pete had now selected from the jukebox had a plaintive thrust that would have been almost obscene if it were listened to sober the way it was listened to drunk—or danced to the way Pete and Debby were now dancing to it.

Sam felt like he was bleeding to death, right there, and that it was going out of him and onto the floor for all the world to see. Putting out signs... fucking hell.

"I've got to go," he said to Lonni.

Lonni had also turned to watch Pete and Debby. She raised her eyebrows a little, her eyes not completely focused. "Don't go," she said.

"I'll be back in a little while."

She nodded, almost as though it was the truth.

Out the back door and away up the alley, he moved quickly along, going with the first side street that came. Going anywhere. Sometime earlier it had stopped raining and what with all the latent heat in the ground and the buildings the streets were almost dry and a warm breeze was shifting through town.

It was not all that late. He walked along the back streets past the houses, most still brightly lit on the ground floors. Once in a while, though, a bedroom light, and at one house on a small, dark street, a girl was brushing her hair in a mirror.

Not long after, he found himself standing there in front, like he had once before, just looking. It was dark there, black inside. Both the cars were gone. The weeks gone by, and it had been several, suddenly seemed like a form of forever, as though a life of time separated the present from the past.

The air, warm and gentle, meant that they would probably be

able to cut in the morning. He looked at the sky and saw it thick with stars. It would be a cloudless sky in the morning.

He turned and headed away.

The hotel was deserted. He went across the dim lobby and up the stairs to the third floor and then down the hallway to his room, feeling, by the time he got there, a little sick.

When he got inside he felt very sick and went into the bathroom for a while. At first he turned on the light, but that made things seem worse, and he switched it back off and continued to wait, but the bar and everything else went away, and nothing happened to him.

Out in the room, he opened the door to the balcony and stood there breathing deeply, his thoughts drifting back downtown to where he knew no one had gone home. Back downtown, in this small, small town. No, not small. This goddamn *little* town.

Staring into the night, his mind whipped bitterly in the direction he did not want it to go but it went anyway and stayed there until he used all that up. And once he felt all that was done he finally went and lay down, sinking into the mattress and feeling how tired he was. But he did not go to sleep for a very long time, although it probably wasn't long at all.

Chapter 17

In the morning, he walked out onto the balcony with a cup of coffee and looked at where a brilliant band along the horizon showed the sun would soon be up. Already, he could see the sky was cloudless. Birdsong chirped from trees far and near, and faint smells of breakfast drifted over from the restaurant on Main Street. He took a careful sip of his fresh coffee, hot and strong, looked down to the street, and saw a pair of bare feet sticking out the back window of his car.

Sam finished his coffee and went down.

The mechanic was unconscious on the back seat, wearing only his jeans, his shirt and boots down on the floor. Sam got in and drove around to the restaurant to get a bite to eat. Pete never moved.

At the restaurant, Sam called Harley and was told that yes, they would be going, and was also asked if he had any idea where Carl and Dan were. Sam did not know. Harley said he hoped they did not have any more days like the one before.

Back to the car, carrying cups of coffee, he set the cups on the top, opened his door a foot or so, and then slammed it shut. At that, Pete's eyes flickered open and focused and he frowned, raising his arm to look at his watch. He let out a groan.

"Good morning," Sam said, handing Pete one of the coffees. He got in the car with his own, started the motor, and headed out of town.

Pete moved himself upright.

"I died."

Sam turned on the radio low and let the car carry him along

with a cool breeze on his arm. In the mirror, he saw a struggle with a shirt.

"What a fuuucking night," Pete mumbled, his drawl sprawled out as much as he was.

"It did go... ways."

Pete looked up sharp and caught Sam's eye in the mirror. He nodded. "You're probably wondering how I'm still married to the same woman after ten years."

"Not at all."

"Nah, man. I was just fucking around."

"I just said not at all."

"I don't need that shit."

"Nobody's giving you any shit."

"Not you. I mean last night. I'm past that sort of thing. And anyway, that woman was a head-case."

"That...," Sam began, but stopped himself.

Pete coughed. "If I had not been so goddamn fucking drunk..."

Sam looked out his window. When he looked back he noticed Pete suddenly bending over. Sam glanced back. But Pete was just lacing on his boots.

"How did you end up in my car?"

"Darla wouldn't let me in."

The beginning of a smile crossed Sam's face.

"But it's OK. All it is is making choices, man, and hope to Christ you don't make some stupid, fucking mistake."

Sam made a noise that sounded like agreement.

"What a fucking night," Pete sighed. "Even before the shit flew, it was fucked."

"Yeah, I was getting that impression," Sam agreed, barely listening. Despite the coffee and the conversation, he did not feel completely awake. Everything felt like cotton balls. And then Pete's comment hit him.

"What did you say?"

"How the shit flew. At first, I actually thought it had something to do with you, you know. The way you got up and left. I thought it was because of it. But that just shows I wasn't paying attention."

"Thought... what?"

"God, I don't know how those guys can work together. I mean, they hate each other."

"Who?"

"And the girls sure did not help."

Sam gave up. "OK, whatever." He smiled.

"You think it's funny?"

"I don't know what you're talking about."

Pete looked up at the roof of the car. "Oh, right, I remember now. You were gone when Dan and Carl got back."

Sam felt the morning turn. "They came back..."

"Certainly did."

"And something happened..."

"Could say that."

"Another argument, I suppose."

"Yeah. Pretty good argument. Broke a chair, knocked over a couple of tables, broke all that glass and got us thrown out." Pete blew out a sigh. "Jesus, it went up fast. You should have been there. You could have maybe stopped things when your girlfriend went nuts, yelling at Dan, and Carl got pissed off at her, too, and then at Marilyn."

"My girlfriend was there?" For half a second a vision of Ruth... but that was impossible.

"Maybe that's why she went nuts. The way you were all over each other. She must have been pissed off one thing royal when you left."

Sam got it. "Lonni... I wasn't all over her."

"Man, she just lost it."

Sam felt the irritation creep over him. "Lonni went nuts...," he deadpanned.

"Yeah. Wow was she pissed off."

"She's not my girlfriend."

"Just fucking nuts," Pete went on. "Yelling shit at Dan, and Carl got pissed off at her, too, and then at Marilyn. And right in the middle of all of that shit Dan threw a goddamn glass. I mean, not really at anyone, although maybe he meant to and changed direction with it. But anyway he just threw that fucker down and I think it was just to stop Lonni because, well, you should have seen it. But she just kept telling Dan to shut up and then Dan started this shit with Carl, going over and over, am I right? am I right? And—shit, I don't know—Carl just let go and hit him in the head!"

"Oh, no." Sam's eyes closed for a second.

"I mean, I really thought he was coldcocked the way he went down. But then he was up fast and they started beating the living shit out of each other. Or at least swinging that way, before the others could pull them off each other."

Sam stared at the road. As always, hearing about it was worse than having actually been there.

"And then?"

"Bob got some guys over and got one tossed out the back, and the other out the front. We all had to leave then or Bob was going to call the Sheriff, so we went over to the cocktail lounge."

"What? All of you?"

"Well, no. But there was Marilyn, there at the lounge, and she got to crying... with Lonni and Debby and all."

Harley's road appeared at the next bend, and Sam turned off the highway onto it.

"And you."

"And me."

"And Carl and Dan?"

"Fuck knows where they went. Or you, for that matter."

As Sam pulled to a stop by the barn he heard Pete mumble, "Shit oh shit oh dear..."

Sam nodded and pushed open his door.

He was greasing his combine when he noticed Dan appear on the next machine over. He looked surprisingly normal there, wiping down the rear window with a rag.

Dan saw him and a grin flashed on his face. "I heard you went tits up last night."

"You want to hear what I heard?"

Dan kept smiling, but a little differently. "That's OK."

"How's Carl?"

Dan shrugged and then jerked his head behind him. Sam looked past him and saw Carl working on a piece of equipment on the other side of the yard. "I've got to tell you," he said, looking back at Dan. "You two are too much."

Dan gave Sam a careful look, but then looked down at the rag in his hand. "So you really have heard all about it."

"Pete came out with me."

"What'd he say?"

Sam stared at Dan. "Is this going to get worse?"

"No. Oh hell no." Dan shook his head. And then he eyed Sam again. "And you? So what'd you do? The way Lonni was moping, I figured you'd dumped her to go looking for the others. You should know they don't go downtown much. And especially middle of the week when..."

Sam cut in. "I didn't dump anybody. I just needed air."

"I mean, I thought you did, because of the way you were wanting to talk about her all the time."

"I don't fucking believe it...," he began, but Dan went on:

"So, hey, anyway, you want to see if they want to do something this weekend? We can all do something."

Sam let out what might have been a laugh.

"OK," Dan said. "I'll call you about it. I'll get it all set up."

While everyone else milled around and talked, Sam climbed into his cab and slouched onto the seat. He left the doors to his cab open, but with the fan turning he couldn't hear anything outside and he could shut out the world just by closing his eyes. And then it was not long before the day got started and the morning's blur drifted away.

It would have been good if the day had remained simple like that but on farms, if it wasn't people it was the machines.

"Jesus Christ," Fred was saying. "I've got to quit one of these days."

Sam was not listening. He was completely dead in the field and was standing next to one of the big drive wheels, his head and shoulders halfway up inside the machine. He grabbed with both hands the pulley he had loosened and yanked it off the shaft. Of course, it wasn't the pulley so much as the belt, but it was the third time the same belt had broken and this time he was going to find out what was making it go all haywire.

"Damn it," he muttered. He could feel a dull anger at himself for not having just done this before instead of following all the advice. He set the pulley aside and reached for a wrench by where Fred was standing.

"What was that?" he said, selecting the wrong-sized open-end.

Fred handed him the right wrench. "I said this is a hell of a way to make a living."

Sam struggled with the bolt.

"It's what I thought. It's bent. We have to take it back to the shop."

The best thing to do, he said to himself, was to replace the whole unit. Whether he could talk Harley into doing that was the question. Harley was as familiar with the problem as he was and might suggest just buying a bunch of spare belts. There was no getting around the fact that even if he changed a half dozen more belts the expense, even counting work time, it would still be less than if he changed the warped mount. But what a pain in the ass to have to do that all the time, he thought. He got the bolt off and started on another.

"And I'll tell you another thing," Fred went on. "You could take me forty miles in any direction in these hills, blindfold me and tell me where you wanted me to go, and I could get there."

"I don't doubt it."

"And you know what else?"

"No, what?"

"Five years after they stick me in the ground, you won't even know I'd been here."

Sam jiggled the side of the bearing plate a little, and the whole thing slid easily off. It should, he thought, the goddamn thing had been worked on enough. He handed it to Fred.

"Well, that's how we're all going to end up, and that's the fuck of it."

"God damn it to hell, don't I know it."

Sam looked up into where all the other belts and pulleys were and stuck his arm behind another pulley. After a little groping and with some effort he drew out a piece of burnt belt about a yard long. He handed that to Fred as well.

"Shit," Fred went on, shaking his head. "I know these hills as good as any old Indian ever did. Maybe better." He pulled out a cigarette pack and started digging his finger in it, but then he looked around at the field and put it back.

"Well, look at how much good that did for them," Sam said, "not much, neither." He stepped back to consider what to do next. Maybe, he was thinking, he could weld an extension onto the swing arm and take some of the slack out of it that way.

"Well, it should've."

"Yes," Sam headed for the ladder on the side of the combine. "It should've, shouldn't it."

He talked to Harley on the radio and was told to get the whole unit, but that he would have to do the work himself. Pete was hamstrung at the moment with a truck that had lost its clutch.

Sam and Fred walked down off the hill and found a truck-road in the flat, and they followed that, looking for one of the trucks to come along headed for the highway. Finally, they saw a big tandem axle truck come around a hill back up the flat. Even at a distance they could hear how its diesel motor was full throated with the heavy load of wheat it had on and when it got to them they stopped it and climbed up into the cab, joining its driver, a high school boy named Tyler.

Once they were settled, Tyler let the clutch out and began taking the heavily laden truck through the gears, only using the clutch once at the start, after that just shifting when the engine came up to its governor.

Out on the highway he upshifted the transfer case to the second range and they ran along fast and smooth for a few miles until they found one of the pickups beside some grain bins. He brought the truck to a stop and Sam and Fred got out and walked over to the pickup.

"Good kid," Fred said.

"He seems to like the work."

"That's how it starts."

Sam gave the ignition a flick and they drove off towards Gainesville. The two of them were silent as they drove, and the silence was normal and they were both spinning along in their own thoughts until after a while Sam got tired of his own and said, for no particular reason at all:

"You ever been married?"

"Of course."

"Kids?"

"Not enough time."

"Ah...," Sam said. "Sorry."

"Why's that?"

"I don't know." Sam thought to change the subject. "Never mind."

"Nothing bad happened. It was OK. Still is for that matter."

"What? You ain't married." Sam glanced at him. "You're married?"

"Oh, hell no. Not really. Haven't lived with her for almost fifty years."

"And you still remember it as being OK." Sam nodded. "I get it now."

"No. I'm saying it's still OK. We see each other from time to time."

"I see, friends. That's nice. She remarry?"

"How could she? We're still married as far as the county is concerned. I've never checked. And as far as remarrying, there was never anyone else for either one of us."

"But you said it did not last long."

"Not long at all. Maybe all of three months in nineteen thirty-seven, three months of being married married, I mean."

"Too young or...," Sam shook his head. "No... sorry."

"Nothing to be sorry about. Actually, we weren't all that young.

I was in my late twenties. She was thirty. So, you see? I'd known her for years and then one day we went over to Moses Lake and got married. After that we came back, and I dropped her off at her folks' house and I went back out to the bunk house I was living at. That was no place for her. And we were like that for three months, and it was really hard to be married. Her living with her parents, and me over here, and for a while nobody really knew anyway."

"Her parents did though. Right?"

"Well, I'd think so."

"You don't know."

"I never told them. I know that."

"And at the end of three months, that was it?"

"Yeah. She suddenly up and got a job in Spokane with a telephone company, so we did not really have much to do with each other for quite a while after that."

"So you never really got past the honeymoon."

"It was just how things worked out. Things aren't always like what people think things should be. And in those days, people took things as they came. You can't imagine the way a girl might have been brought up around here back in those days. And, anyway, because of the way things were, we did not change much of the way we'd been before and, you see, she'd always liked living with her folks. They needed her quite a bit, and in those days that counted a lot. Not how kids go running off these days. After the war, when I got back, I found she'd moved back in with them because that's the way things had been, and it was easier for her."

"I guess it's always easier to do what you've always done."

"That's right."

Thoughts passed through Sam's mind. "But you kept seeing her after that?"

"Sometimes every other weekend."

"You dated your wife?" Sam laughed. "You could never get her to move in?"

"She just stayed on with her folks until one and then the other died, and by then she'd been there so long...."

"You did not mind?"

"We were used to it." Fred gave Sam a look. "People get used to things and then that's how they are."

"I haven't ever heard of anything like it."

"I guess it sounds strange, but you know, by the time she came back things had changed. We'd thought about having a family but in the end we did not need one. People had kids in those days to help keep everything going. Big farms and all. But we did not need any of that, and it would have meant too many changes."

Fred pulled a cigarette out of the pocket on the bib of his overalls and started searching for his lighter.

"And you never wanted to marry anyone else?"

"Why?"

"Never got lonely?"

"No. We had each other. We just did not live together."

"I guess if it works, it works."

Fred took a pull on his cigarette. "It works." And then he gave Sam a look. "You'll see. Seems you've found one that'll work."

Sam's eyes widened, and he glanced over at Fred. "Oh no. Not you, too."

Fred shrugged. "The Kirby's were good folks, and Ruthy was such a great kid. Helping her aunt, and everyone else. Always pitching in. You couldn't do better, to be honest."

Sam, feeling the irritation well up within, wanted to say something back to all that, but looking again at Fred and seeing the honest earnestness in the old man's eyes, he let it slide. And then just looked out his side window and, letting it go, said to himself. "Probably not." And what's more, he suddenly thought, he probably never would, the way things were going.

The rest of the drive into town, for Sam, was a sour affair.

They got to town and ordered the pieces. Initially, they thought they would have to wait a day or so, and had expected to just get more belts and cobble things together. But the store said they could get the unit that day, the main distribution point for the county being over in St. Pierre, if they were willing to wait a couple of hours. They were, and they went to the restaurant for some coffee. With the hot sun coming in through the glass and the solitude of empty booths surrounding them, time seemed to stretch on forever.

"Yeah," Fred said at last. "I've got to quit this shit."

Sam looked at him over the Spokane paper he was thumbing through. "You're not that old."

"Yeah, I am. I'm ten years past when most fellas retire. I should be just taking care of a garden."

"Shit. You're still getting around as good as anyone."

"Maybe," Fred said. "But maybe it's time for someone else to step in."

"Oh," Sam said. "So that's why you've been saying this all afternoon."

"Well, why not?"

"I haven't been angling to take your job."

"You couldn't if you tried. Not as long as I wanted it. But I'm thinking now it could work for both of us. I'd get free, and Harley would get a good hand. And, just maybe, that might help you with a few of your own things." Fred glanced at Sam and saw Sam now staring back, and Fred looked away. "Maybe... or whatever..."

"Or whatever?" Sam smiled. "I did not know you were also part of the grapevine."

Fred made a movement with his hand as though shooing a fly away. "Anyway," he said, "you know that boy Tyler. He's not like the others, I should tell you. Just looking for summer work. He was talking to Harley this morning. Good kid, you know? You said it yourself. And... it's about time for someone to step in."

Sam couldn't help smile. He had spent most of the spring and summer wondering if he was going to work the next week, let alone the next month, and now here he was listening to the possibility of working for the rest of however long he wanted. Of all the things he had expected, the possibility of a permanent position opening up had never occurred to him.

But where that would have helped, as Fred put it, with some things, it opened up whole new cans of worms.

But there it was, and Sam could see how it changed everything, including maybe why things had been going like they had up until then with Dan, and his on and off work accommodations.

He looked at Fred. Big, heavy shoulders and a beaten face and beaten hands. Like a fighter. And fifty years more, like he had pretty much said himself, no one would know the difference.

Sam did not know what to say. He was being openly questioned, and it was not a polite thing to leave it hanging. Sam did not know if any of this, if he, had been part of an open discussion back at the farm.

But if it had, and Fred was now letting him know, Sam knew he would have to reply at some point.

Of course, there was still a big hang up. And not just Dan. Sam still did not have the slightest idea what wages were. It did not seem possible that Fred had worked all these years only making living wages.

"Can I ask you something?" he said.

"What?"

"Do you own your own house?"

"Of course I do."

"So you've saved up."

"Yeah. Still do."

"You can save money out here."

"Anyone can, if they aren't some goddamn idiot like you boys. Yes."

Sam nodded. So real wages must be something other than what he was seeing. The problem was not in that, though. It was in whether he could really even get hired in the first place, despite what Fred might think.

He could find reasons for wanting the job, and even quite badly. But he could also find reasons for being careful, considering how unsure he was of other things. He needed to now know so that, if he had to, he could also easily go the other way and just clear out of there fast, quitting after harvest. Before any questions were asked.

Fifty years of work, Sam thought, looking back at Fred. Just like that. So easy, and all he had to do maybe was nothing, not even think about it, and the job would be his, as though that was just how it was all supposed to be. One stepped out, another stepped in, and in fifty years someone could blindfold him, too, and he could walk all over those hills like he had made them himself. Just like Fred. And it would not make a damn bit of difference, and in a hundred years even less.

And what did that matter? As Fred had said, nothing was really so strange about anything when it all worked.

"Oh, Christ," Sam said, setting the newspaper aside and reaching for his coffee. "They're probably going to have to pry you off a tractor twenty years from now. All stiff and dry."

"Like cow shit in a pasture?"

"Or bullshit in a restaurant."

Fred let out a chuckle. But then his eyes went serious and he reached for his own coffee. "You know, Sam," he said. "It ain't always."

And Sam suddenly thought it was time to find out if that was true.

Chapter 18

THE door opened. "She isn't here."

"Ah," Sam said to Sue, glancing at Ruth's car in the driveway. "Just thought I'd swing by."

She stepped out onto the porch, letting the screen door slam shut behind her. "Been really busy, eh?"

"Yeah."

"I guess that explains things."

"Explains?"

Her chin came up. "You know? Dan comes by all the time."

He had not been prepared for how hard and blunt her reception was, and he knew instantly this had been waiting for him and that he should not have been surprised.

"Yeah, I know."

"He's busy, too."

"It's not the same thing."

"It isn't?" Sue gave him a long look and then finally shook her head back. "Oh, you mean me and Dan?"

"No. I was meaning the work."

"What's different?"

Sam wanted to explain. For a while now he had been wanting to talk about everything, and nearly from the start. But there was no way to do it, talking about work and Ruth at the same time. He had not been seeing Ruth, in the way Dan and Sue had been seeing each other. But not because he did not want to, but because he couldn't.

He looked at Sue. He liked her and he had thought she liked him and he might have hoped she understood a few things about him. But right then and there he could imagine that neither she nor Ruth cared about how he might feel about things, let alone whether he was going to be there in town for any length of time.

"I guess I could have called," he said under his breath.

"What?"

He saw the way she was looking at him and, despite it all, felt anger. He wasn't about to make any declaration there to Sue. There on the porch. Like he was in some sort of tribunal. But he could see he was at a tipping point with all this.

Sue was looking at his face and after a moment turned her own to look down the street. "Can I say something to you?"

"Sure."

"No. I mean really say something to you."

"I wish someone would."

"Ruth is my friend, OK?"

Sam nodded.

"And you're not." Sue nodded back. "I don't know what you think you're doing. For all I can see you don't either. But you need to know that Ruth hasn't really had someone that she liked, and..."

She frowned and Sam could see it was now her finding it hard to sort out words. He thought of something. "Hey... did Dan say anything about this coming weekend?"

"No? But anyway, why is it every time he asks you to come over here you say you're busy?"

"He says... what...?"

"Can I ask you another thing?"

Sam, still processing what she had said, just looked at her.

"How'd you end up here?"

"I wanted to see Ruth."

"No, I mean this town."

Sam tried to smile. "Ruth didn't tell you?"

"Tell me."

"I was either almost out of gas or hungry. Both, I think." He nodded to himself. "And I was nearly broke, which explains staying on."

"At least you're consistent in your story."

"You sound disappointed."

Sue shook her head. "It just doesn't sound like much."

"Should there be?"

"Shouldn't there?"

"I don't think so. I think most of the time there's not much in how we go along."

"That seems to be the case for you."

She was right. Sam could feel it all the way through how, from her point of view, that was right. "Not completely."

"How would anyone know?"

Sam could not argue with that but also knew this was getting to be way too much for a conversation on a porch. And with the wrong person, if anyone.

"Listen," he said. "I have to go pick up something Dan wanted. I only wanted to stop by to check about the weekend. But now I want to come back by."

"Nobody's stopping you."

"I want to come back by."

"I get it."

"Will she be here in a couple of hours? Will that be a good time?"

"You want her office number?"

"Will she be here?"

Sue sighed out. "I don't know. They've been keeping her late at the office over there, and... she wouldn't be expecting company anyway."

Sam said nothing.

"OK, you might try later. Just not too late."

Sam turned to go down off the porch. "You make it sound like it already is."

"And you make it seem like it doesn't really matter," she said behind him.

"Jesus," Sam said under his breath.

"Don't go to the bars to pass the time."

He strode away down the sidewalk. He had not actually had anything to do, but had just wanted to get away from Sue. He figured he would go back just a bit after what might be dinner time. He went for a long walk all the way around town, and over the foot bridge at the park to where a path went along the river for nearly two miles along some cow pastures and scabland outcrops. By the time he came back he felt hungry and walked down Main Street and then past the equipment store to the burger place.

"Hey, Sam," said the cook as he came through the door.

"Hey, Daryl," Sam said. "Can I get a cheeseburger with some fries?"

"A double?"

"No."

"And just water," the cook nodded, and then looked up at the clock. "Or do you want coffee?"

"Just a big cup of water."

The cook dropped a couple of patties onto the grill, opened a bun and placed the halves face down on the heat. "Haven't seen you in a while. How's harvest?"

"Nearly there."

"That's what I hear. The crews from over at Miller's, and at the Olafsons and the Harrises, they all are saying the same thing."

"It's about time we got done. Really time."

"That's what I heard."

Sam glanced at the cook.

"What have you heard?"

"It's never a surprise. But, don't get me wrong. It's not all the time. But sometimes crews just get sick and tired of each other, is all. Really tired."

"You heard that, eh?"

"Who hasn't?"

Sam let out a half laugh.

"I see."

"It happens, for a lot of reasons. It isn't always the crew." The cook lifted the edge of a patty, and let it back down. "I imagine you're all pretty beat."

"We're not tired of each other. But it's been a long one..."

"Every year, you guys looking so ready to go mid-July but by the end of August," the cook laughed, "you all look whacked to shit."

"Is that what I look like?"

The cook looked over at him and nodded. "More or less. Anyone looking at you would think you could use about twenty hours of sleep."

"Yeah," Sam said. "And you'd think anyone who saw that might understand that."

"Course they would."

Sam looked out the window. "Course they would," he breathed out.

"So what are you going to do?" the cook went on, pulling the buns off the grill and beginning to load the condiments. "Going to go for Fall work... Winter?"

"We'll see. Nobody's said anything."

"Yeah, the work falls off fast after harvest. Things go pretty flat for the seasonals. Between now and the time everything freezes over there's just some tilling to do and the winter wheat seeding."

"Yeah. That's about it."

"You're with the Petersens..."

"Nobody else since I got here."

"You know I went to school with their oldest? Carl?"

"Is that right?" Sam looked at the cook, who was overweight and balding and looked easily ten years older than Carl Petersen.

The cook grinned. "We were on the basketball team together. I was a forward, he was a guard. We went to State, even."

"You did, eh?"

"We got creamed by Omak."

Sam laughed.

"Good guy, Carl," the cook said. "And good folk for the most part."

"I'd say so, for the most part."

The cook lifted the edge of the patty again and then flipped both. And then he grinned.

"For the most part."

"Oh," Sam held up his hand. "I didn't mean that."

"Sure you did. But that's OK. There isn't anyone who wouldn't say the same thing."

"I don't know," Sam smiled. "You'd know better than me."

The cook looked over at him. "I think you've been here long enough."

"I don't know, Daryl. Seriously."

"Oh, no. Course you don't." The cook smiled but then gave Sam a look. "Don't go getting all diplomatic and shit with me. I've been here all my life and there's no way you can be working out there half a year without getting a feel for the land. I mean, they are a good bunch. But I know one that can be a handful."

Sam couldn't help a smile pulling at his mouth. "And who would that be?"

The cook laughed outright. "And who would that be? Who would that be? No... don't answer."

"Thanks."

"If you stay on, would you stay with them?"

"I don't know anyone else."

"There are plenty of farms around here. You might have noticed."

"I haven't got to know any of them. A few guys. But no conversations like that."

"Want me to put around a word? They come in often enough, and more so these days."

"I don't care. But if you feel like it, OK."

"Doesn't take much more than a word."

"OK."

"And you might find it...," the cook put the burger together and wrapped it up and then scooped some fries onto a waxed sheet and folded it, "...you might find it a bit easier."

Sam pulled out his wallet and began fiddling with the bills. "It's easy enough."

The cook brought everything over in a sack and rang up the sale. "Did not say it wasn't. Just said... easier."

"If anyone wants, they can drop off a note at the hotel."

"You're still there?"

"Of course."

"Of course. Of course you are."

Sam looked at the cook and saw even more humor in the man's eyes. Sam squinted at him. God, he thought, not really. That too?

The cook smiled. "C'mon, man. You couldn't be in a smaller town."

"I'm beginning to realize that."

"It's OK. You're fine. In case you're wondering."

"I haven't been up to now."

The cook shrugged, and went back to scrape at the grill. "See you round, Sam."

"See ya, Daryl," Sam swung around and headed for the door.

Sam headed back into town and walked over to the park, feeling the dead heat of the late afternoon sinking deep into the evening. The park was empty and he took a seat at a picnic table, eating his dinner and looking at the slow-moving river.

Beyond the river, beyond the pasture land, he looked at how the wheat hills out there, now shaved close to the ground, were nearly white where the last rays of the sun fell upon them but gold going to brown in their shadowed folds. Other than the distant muffler of a pickup back on Main Street there was nearly no sound there in the park except an occasional ripple along the shore of the river or an inquisitive fly or long-tailed bluebottle.

She still wasn't there when he went back, but this time Sue invited him in and went to get him a beer. He took a seat on the couch. The television was on and there was an old movie playing. Sue spent a long time getting the beer from the kitchen. Sam knew that was where the phone was, too. Sam stared at the movie, waiting, and time dragged on so long that whatever he was watching seemed to Sam like the oldest movie in the world.

Sue finally came into the living room, handing him a beer, and then they both watched the movie. Sam could see Sue wasn't uncomfortable with him being there and that made him feel better. He figured if she was like that he wasn't going to see anything worse than what he had already seen.

Wherever Ruth was, though, it was long past dinner time, let alone office hours, and as time went by the sky outside began to darken into the dusky hues of a mid-summer evening and he watched as the streetlight on the corner began to come on, dim orange at first and then brightening.

The car stopped outside, a door slammed, and then it drove away. She came through the door looking flushed.

"Hello, hello." Ruth threw her purse into a chair and gave Sam a smile. "What are you doing up so late?"

He tried a smile back. "I was out of beer...."

"That's what bars are for." Ruth shook her hair back in that way he had always liked. She looked at him again, her eyes clear and pleasant.

"The company isn't as nice."

"Ah, a question of nice." She nodded. "We can do that. Would you like another?"

"Why not?"

"Susan?"

Sue shook her head, watching the television.

Ruth went into the kitchen and then came back and handed a beer to him. He looked at the can, and then her.

"You're not having any?"

She sat down on the other end of the couch and pulled her shoes off, and then pressed her hands against flushed cheeks. "Oh, no! I think I'm just fine."

"Been out on the town."

"Yeah. Just decided to get out a bit."

He snapped open the can. "It's necessary now and again, I suppose."

She yawned.

Sue suddenly stood up. "See you guys," she said and went off to her room.

"So," Ruth said after a long silence. "What have you been up to?"

Sam stared at his beer can. "You know."

"I guess you're still harvesting."

"You could say that."

"Yeah, work, work, work," she said. "I can't believe you guys. Going like that all the time. I don't see how you can do it."

"You're welcome to find out."

"You mean, come out there to watch?"

"Why not? There's a jump seat in the combine. Or you could ride in a truck."

"Sounds really interesting, riding around in rigs all day."

"It's the company."

"Ah, the company again."

The flatness in her voice told him all he needed to know. All he had to do was say he had to work in the morning and that would be it. Maybe a kiss at the door. Or not. And a wave goodbye. Or not. And no mess for anyone to clean up.

But as he contemplated that, it began to grow in him and then, suddenly, he wanted the mess. A big mess. Or at least as big as they could make it. Because, regardless of what she was thinking of him he wanted her to know there was more to it. Certainly more to it than just not coming around or not caring or just being thoughtless.

Sue had been right, though, it would not be Ruth's fault not knowing or having any real feel for what he was doing or thinking. He had simply been hoping, he realized, that she might have guessed.

Or, maybe she had. And if that was the case, it was time to stop pretending otherwise. But where to start?

"Anytime you want to come out, just let me know."

"I don't know," she said. "I'm so busy these days."

"It's no big deal."

She nodded. "Who knows? I just might."

He raised the beer and drank down the half of it, feeling his heart beginning to pound. And then he just let himself go. "I can see I'd better not hold my breath."

And there it was.

Her face went hard. "That's an interesting thing for you to say."

"So it's all going to be my fault."

168

"Why fight about that? Isn't this what you want? Now what's the matter?"

He finished off his beer. "Nothing. Everything is just fine. Like you say, it's just the way I like it, and just the way it is. And that's...," he had started off trying to be cynical and hard back at her, but then suddenly couldn't keep going in that way, "...and that's what's the matter."

Her look changed. "What?"

"I don't know. Maybe that's not how things are anymore."

She frowned. "I don't know what you're talking about. But more... I don't know what to believe about you."

"That's what's nice about friends. They do you the favor of getting around things like that."

"Is that your idea of what a friend is? Because, me, I don't think so." She looked at him for a long moment and he thought she wasn't going to say anything else. But then she shook her head. "I don't think so," she said again, even flatter than before. "And I really think that's all there is to this."

"I should have called, I know. Even Sue said..."

"I don't care what Sue said. I don't care what anyone said, or is saying. I'm telling you right now, it doesn't matter. Not at all. You did not even have to come over here in the first place. OK?"

Everything drained out of him. The fact was, he had not been sure of what he was really doing there, much less what he thought he might have said, and he regretted having gone over there, as she put it, in the first place. In truth, he had come back because he said he would. He had told Sue he would. But beyond that, there was no longer any reason for him to be there. It was a failed effort to go there earlier on, and it was now another failure that would only get worse the longer he stayed.

He set the empty beer can onto the side table and got to his feet.

"Thanks for the beer. I'd better be going. I'm really sorry for keeping you up. I really am."

She looked up at him.

"You really are going to be an asshole, aren't you?"

169

All he could do was stand there.

"What were you expecting?" she went on. "It's been weeks. Or nearly weeks. Hard to say. And one goddamn afternoon and all that went with it doesn't count."

"I know, but..."

She waited, but when Sam didn't go on she threw her hands at him. "It's hopeless, Sam. We sort of gave it a shot. And that's enough, don't you think?"

"I've been trying to explain."

"Oh, fuck the job, the job, the job. I'm so sick of that."

"It's true though."

"Oh, right. And you're... what? Trying to protect me? Afraid you might hurt me?"

"It's crossed my mind."

"I'm old enough to take care of myself. And, anyway... bullshit. Who is really protecting who?"

"You think I'm that selfish?"

"What do I know? But, regardless, you have the easier way out. All you have to do is leave."

"You think that protects me?"

"Who the hell knows what protects you, Sam? I sure as hell don't. But I do know that in spite of all your efforts, this has now gotten way more complicated than it should have."

"You mean, right now? Here? That's not all my fault. Just look at the way you came in. It was as if you were saying to me, oh, what are you doing in my house?"

"It's not a bad question. But I was talking about everything else."

"I wanted to see you."

"And I have wanted to see you, too. But evidently it's all just too complicated for you. And... I can now see, even if that wasn't a thing, you don't let anything happen to you anyway."

That one went straight to the heart. He had thought those very words lately, and often enough.

"I didn't want you to think that."

"But I ended up doing it. So, there we are."

He looked at her face, into her eyes, and then finally found what it was that would explain it. He swallowed. "You never called me, either, Ruth. I'm not the only one who held back. So, yeah, maybe it's been a lot of me," he said. "But..."

He was going to start, tell her about how it was, had always been. Being outside mostly, and never really being anywhere near something that made him feel anything other than that. But then, when he looked up at her he saw her eyes had no welcome in them.

He could see he had started wrong and, for whatever reason he probably would never had said the right thing anyway. And the brief moment of thinking he might finally just talk about all that, drained out of him. He saw how the anger had risen back into her eyes and could see that whatever was said from that point forward would just risk getting harsh, and then harsher. And he did not want that in any form.

He felt himself giving up.

"OK," she said. "That's enough." She evidently not only saw him doing that but felt the same way herself.

"It is," he agreed. He wanted to leave it there, but then could not help himself. "I could have hoped it wasn't."

A small thing, a sudden glimmer... it seemed that something flashed in her eyes. He could not tell what and, looking at her, could not see it again.

He began backing towards the door.

"Sorry," he said. He now could not look at her. He did not want her to see. Anything. But knew she would, and could.

"Sam." Ruth's voice changed a bit.

He glanced up at her, half hoping, but instead of seeing... something... maybe an invitation to continue... in her eyes, he saw something even worse than the anger. And suddenly he felt it come up in him, and now couldn't trust his eyes, and knew that could also be seen. He could be seen. And it was now too much. He got the door open.

"Don't," he said, trying not to look at her. "It's OK."

"You don't know..."

"It's OK. Really. I'm sorry. I'm so sorry."

He got out the door as fast as he could and down the steps. He did not know what was happening behind him but went down the street with the trees and houses rushing by him as though in a blur.

Anything... to get away from that look of pity.

There was that time before they had made love for the first time, when she and he, with Dan and Sue, had gone out waterskiing.

At lunchtime, they had eaten at a wooden raft at the far end of Edward's Lake. The raft had been small but there had been plenty of room for the four of them, and as they talked their voices had gone out across the smooth water, coming back echoed and muffled from the high cliffs around them.

After lunch Dan and Sue had gotten into the boat to fix something in the steering and ended up sitting in there talking with murmured voices.

Sam and Ruth found themselves left alone at the other end of the raft. Sam had sat with his right side away from her, there still being some bruising on his face. They sat with their legs dangling in the water and after a while Ruth laid backwards onto the dock, Sam continuing to stare out across the water.

"What are you thinking about?" she asked him then.

"Nothing," he said. "Except how nice it is here."

He turned around and looked at her for a moment and she looked back, her eyes deep, welcoming him in.

She smiled suddenly. "How did you end up in Gainesville?"

"My dogs got tired."

"I mean, really."

"I'm not kidding." He had not thought much about the circumstances for his being in Gainesville, but he suddenly saw it as being a little strange. Really, he had only stopped to get a hamburger.

He looked down into the water. It had almost been like fate, he thought. Then he looked at her legs, there in the water next to his. They were smooth and getting a bit red from the sun, and she was gently stirring the lake, her thighs alternating tightening and slackening as she moved the water around. His glance traveled up her body, taking in everything along the way. Her long slim legs, her

172

smooth hips, her wide shoulders and long arms. Her fine, strong hands. She was so beautiful, he thought.

"Do you think it's all that strange?" he said.

"Don't you? Even about us?"

"Well, if it comes to us, that is strange."

"Do you really think so?" her voice went serious. "I mean, how we met?"

He shook his head. "No. How in the world could anyone plan something like this?"

"I know it," she said. "But it just seems like there should be more to the way it happens."

He laughed. "How it happens is the last thing that bothers me."

"Oh, I see," she smiled. "You're only into the big questions."

His gaze faltered. "Does it really bother you?"

She looked at him for a long moment and then closed her eyes. "Not usually."

He had not said anything and she opened her eyes again and smiled. "I'm sorry. I didn't mean to get carried away like that." She reached out and touched his arm. "Don't worry, I'll get over it."

He looked at her face, by then picking up some sun onto her fair skin, and then at her hair, the soft waves tangled from skiing. He looked down at her throat, and then to where it went into the depression between her collarbones. He reached his hand out and ran his fingers along her shoulder to that place, and then up her throat towards her chin. Then his hand had dropped away. He had not known if he wanted her to get over anything or not.

"You think this could get serious?" he asked.

"I don't know." Her eyes were still closed. "Why?"

"I don't want to screw things up, is all."

"It won't be you that does it."

"Don't be so sure."

"I'm not. That's why I said that."

There had been nothing he could say. Any honest thing would only serve to tell her she was right. But he did not want to be honest. He wanted things to continue. The trouble had been that the way those things usually went did not seem right anymore, and suddenly he felt like he was at a place where any step he might make would be the wrong one.

For a moment all he had been able to do was to just stare at her face, and her eyes, and her golden brown hair, and her skin shining with perspiration beneath the sun. So easy, he had thought. It was all so easy. All he had to do was jump.

And then came all of those thoughts he had not wanted to think.

Spoiling it all.

At one moment he had been looking at Ruth and thinking how nice that seemed and in the next he had gone and seen the whole thing go past as it had to. They were going to get closer and closer and then one day it would start going the other way, until it fell as far apart as it could ever be possible to imagine.

Except that this time could be the worst. He could feel how this could be the worst ever.

Because there were a lot of ways things had been bad but none had something that seemed like love mixed in.

He had felt her right hand suddenly on his back. Only one hand, warm and soft, resting there as though just a place to put a hand. But he had felt himself, all of himself, going into it as if he was being held there.

She had begun moving her hand across the muscles in the small of his back and the sickness he had felt before came back again, and he had come close to groaning, but had not, and he had leaned forward and had caught some water in his hands and had pressed his face into it.

Well, he had thought as he had rubbed the water out of his eyes, it might have been the start of a mess, but it was better than nothing. He had been so tired of nothing.

He had turned around to look at her. Her hand had still been on his back. Her eyes were closed. He had looked at them, and then at her temples where the fine hair curled wetly there, looking at her in the way a wide landscape could be looked across from a high vantage point, seeing so much more than just the details of its features, seeing it as a place in the world in which one could belong.

He could tell her he loved her, he had reasoned. Sure he could. And at that moment she opened her eyes and saw him looking at her, and she sat up.

For a moment, she lowered her eyes, and then she raised them again, those flashing green eyes, and he was lost.

He just went into her, his whole universe. He knew he loved her, and it just took him straight into her, leaning to kiss her, and she lifted her face to him.

He didn't know how long they kissed but while it lasted nothing else existed but her soft, sweet mouth, kissing him back. And when they finally stopped, to take a breath, they could only stare at each other. Either amazed, or frightened, or overwhelmed by the great unknown. For himself, he had never known anything like it.

And then Ruth took in a deep breath, and exhaled fast, like she was out of breath. And, still looking into his eyes, said: "Do that again."

Even at four in the morning everything was still shit and he was still awake. If he had had any whisky he would have been drunk but he had nothing and that was part of the shit.

It was not that he was feeling bad, it was just that he could not find any way to feel good. So not being either one or the other, or drunk or asleep, and almost too tired to be so awake, he could have sworn he was dead.

He was thinking how if things were that way because they had somehow been planned, with few choices to make, then it all was a terrible crime. But worse was if things were that way with no choices at all. Then it all was a terrible joke. Whichever it was though, he could not be convinced right then that the deep mysteries of the universe mattered much. Because he really did feel dead, and the dead do not give a damn about anything more complicated than death, if that. He looked at the dark ceiling and blew out his millionth cold breath—lonely sighs in an empty room, filling the captive air. Then he heard the knock.

His breath stopped.

He listened to a wild silence and then rolled off the bed and crossed the room, his body still dead, his mind nakedly racing beyond thoughts.

He opened the door. For a moment he stared. Then his mind came back to him again, then warmth to his body.

It was cold there at the door. The balcony doors were open, and a small breeze was able to now make its way past him out into the hallway.

He shivered.

"You're right. We should talk."

"Yeah," Ruth nodded. "Right now though, what I'd really like is to get some sleep."

Chapter 19

HE arrived out at Harley's just as everyone was coming out from breakfast to load themselves into the back of Tyler's pickup.

"Problem?" Harley asked from inside the cab, looking towards Sam's old car.

"No," he said. He climbed over the tailgate, taking a seat on the spare tire.

"Hard getting up in the morning?" Carl said as the pickup began moving out of the yard and down to the highway. Dan opened his mouth and laughed silently at Sam. The rest of the crew grinned.

Sam looked at all of them and then looked away at the countryside going past. Everyone seemed to know everything. But regardless, if they wanted to joke around he was never going to join in.

Even early morning they could all tell it was going to be hotter than usual. The sun, two hours off the horizon, already penetrated uncomfortably into the air. For the combine drivers, it was with a sense of anticipation that they greased the running parts of their machines, looking forward to when they could shut themselves in with their air-conditioners. For the truck drivers, all they had to look forward to was a long day of sweating inside cabs, the heat coming off the hard packed ground worse than the heat of the air as they crept around the fields, their engines oven hot, with a chance that something, a radiator hose, the batteries, a hydraulic line, might fail. Walking around his combine, Sam could smell the heat in the dust. The stubble, drier than ever, crackled and shattered as he strode across it. They were into awfully good wheat there. So thick and tall-growing the combines were able to cut with their headers much higher. It was nice not to have to think about skimming dirt, and it was nice because the combines thrashed better in the good stuff. But there were drawbacks. Combines did not start fires. There was nothing hot on them at ground level. Trucks, though, could. Low muffler systems, hot transmissions, straw getting up into engine spaces. Good as a match.

He had seen stubble fires and knew how they could get going so fast that it was barely believable, eating up hundreds of acres before anyone could do anything.

Of course, a stubble fire was just that and only burned up the straw. But in mid-harvest stubble fields sat next to wheat fields, neighboring fields, and things could get very bad.

Next to his combine, Pete was filling the tank from the fuel truck. Pete put his hand against the side of the combine. "Fry an egg already."

Sam glanced at the truck drivers. "Those guys are going to be sweating."

"What they're going to be sweating, is not starting fires. The younger fellows need to be warned."

Sam looked out across the fields, the heat already shimmering like a mirage above the feathery heads of wheat.

"You'll be happy to have your AC today," said a voice behind Sam and he turned to see Harley.

"Pete says we should remind the younger guys to keep an eye on their trucks."

Dan, working on the next combine over, heard the comment and walked over. "You know? We need to let everyone know to watch out for fires today. I'll go do that."

Harley lifted his hand. "Carl's already done that. And he's gone to get the disk, like he said he'd do this morning."

"Right, right," Dan said. "Just saying." He gave Sam's shoulder a light slap. "Right lover boy?" He and Harley walked off towards the trucks.

"Field boss, my ass," Pete said in a low voice to Sam.

"What's that?"

"It was Carl started talking about taking precautions this morning. Said we needed to bring up a disk. Dan laughed but Harley said that was the way to do it."

"It's always the way to do it."

"I know. And I don't care who calls it as long as it gets done. I don't want to end up roasted out there."

It was the first really hot day. But the morning went well, the combines often filling with grain before trucks, burdened with the long run to Cresswall, could get back to them. Sometimes, the combines actually had to stop and wait, their bulk tanks almost spilling over with the wheat.

All that morning he had been cutting around a big hilltop by himself, working higher and higher on its golden sides until he came up on top, finding there a large and almost flat plateau and after a while all he was doing was cutting on the level.

Taking advantage of the ease of cutting, he would occasionally glance around at everyone else. The other combines were all together across on another huge hill. He could see where, up the draws on the near side, trucks crept up the transverse roads the combines had cut through the wheat, sometimes making switchbacks in a few of the steeper sections. The trucks would station themselves in line with the cutting combines in those places that were more or less level, and after filling would jockey themselves around and make their ways back down. For him there in the cool, pressurized cab, it was a pleasant thing to work that morning. The drivers remembered to swing over to him once in a while and he rarely had to stop long to unload. But by lunchtime, when everybody met in the big draw between the two hills, it had been different. To be out in the heat in the middle of all that massed equipment and the shimmering wheat field was suffocating.

Sally and her helper found them all sitting in the shade of their circled machines, hiding from the sun. She put the tailgate down and began to set out the food.

"You all look like you're expecting an attack."

Nobody answered. The combine drivers were almost stunned by how hot it really was. The truck drivers were just doing what they had done all morning and were moving as little as possible.

"Come and get it," she said, setting out the last plates.

No one moved.

"It ain't going to eat itself," she looked at Harley and shrugged.

At that Harley got up off the ground and the rest of them began to get up and go over to the pickup.

"What's the matter with all of you?" she said. "It's only a hundred and thirteen out here."

"Is that all?" Harley reached for the iced tea.

"The weatherman said it'll be over ninety the next few days."

"He's playing it safe." Sam dished himself some fruit salad.

"You know," Dan said. "This'd be a great day to go to the lake."

A few of the truck drivers groaned.

"See you later," Carl said.

"I wouldn't mind," said Tyler. "Do some water skiing."

"We did that," Dan said. "Right Sam?"

Sam did not answer, taking his plate over and taking a seat by his combine, his back against the big tire.

"I heard Sam was a pretty good skier," Carl said, loading up his plate.

"He's a champ," Sam said, taking a bite of coleslaw.

"When the boy keeps on his feet," Dan said.

Sam nodded. "Saw you on your ear a few times."

"Yeah, but I think you did it better. Falling down, that is."

"What were you doing," Harley grinned. "Skiing or doing a ...," he hesitated for a second and then said: "ménage-a-twa?"

Sam looked over at Harley.

"Dad was a paratrooper in Normandy," Carl said to Sam. "He picked up some lingo, here and there. But I think he meant to say menagerie, or something like that."

"That's what they called it," Harley said. "If you ever go to Paris, go to Pig Alley."

"I'll keep it in mind," Sam smiled. "But anyway, it was maybe one or the other."

180

"Or both," Dan said. "We had the girls with us there. So maybe more like a clown show. What did they call that, Dad?"

Harley's teeth flashed white. "Anything that was a mess was a ... merd total."

"That's what it was, then."

Carl pursed his mouth. "That's what you call going on a date?"

"Generally is." Dan looked around at the rest of the crew. "It is, ain't it?"

"I don't know about you sometimes."

"Yeah?" Dan said. "Well, we don't know about you all the time."

"That so?" Carl, having started back towards his shade, stopped at Dan's boots.

Dan raised his hands. "It's too hot."

After the initial roar of engines being started the big circle broke up and the harvest crew headed back onto the hills. Eager as they were all to finish it, they were also being prudent. It really was hot, and it could not have been drier. Everyone was aware of the dangers.

For the combine drivers, there was less worry about setting anything off. But they also knew their machines produced the main danger as they cut. All the chaff and straw waste, once separated from the wheat grains, got flung out the back of the combines, and even with the spreaders fanning it around clumping still occurred on the high stubble where the chaff could get picked up into the hot areas of trucks. Often enough Sam saw truck drivers stopping somewhere to dig straw out from around transmissions and muffler pipes. It was a bother for them, but it was obviously better than the alternative.

At about three, when the pale yellow dust was simply hovering fine and hot in the still air, he suddenly noticed something different about one of the trucks rolling towards him from ahead.

The truck was making to go past him, then swing around out in the stubble and come up from behind so they could run together side by side, letting Sam unload on the go.

Sam stared hard.

181

From a distance, he had only thought he had seen it, but as the truck went by he could definitely see the flashes from the darkness beneath it. When it came alongside he called over and they both stopped. While the combine was auguring out its wheat he climbed down and went around to where the driver, Tyler, was pulling straw from under his cab. Some of the straw was cooked brown.

"Just can't keep this shit out of here," Tyler's voice cracked in frustration. "Every time I leave the field it's there, and I know it's there within minutes after I come back."

Sam nodded and looked at the boy who was, according to Fred, his rival for Fred's job. He did not want to think of Tyler that way, because he liked him. But there was no getting around the fact that he, in many ways, had a strong claim to things. Tyler was practically a farm boy himself even though his family lived in Gainesville. Sam had come to know that all the boy wanted to do was work for some farmer, work around the machinery and in the fields, and maybe if he was lucky buy a few acres for himself someday. What he knew about farming already came close to whatever Sam himself had picked up from an itinerant lifestyle. And there was also how Tyler had a continuous life there with friends and neighbors who went all the way back to childhood.

From what Sam had heard, the boy was supposed to be smart in school although he mainly seemed interested in the sports.

He looked under Tyler's truck.

"I thought I saw some burning stuff falling off as you went by."

"Oh, no."

"I can't be sure."

Tyler frowned for a second, and then motioned for Sam to follow him around to the cab. Sam looked in at the base of the shifting levers where Tyler was pointing. Tyler had loosened the metal cover plate over the transmission. "That's so I can use the extinguisher," he said.

"You think that's necessary?" Sam could see it was a real worry.

"It wasn't my idea. Gordon started it. But we're all doing it."

Gordon was the most inexperienced driver out there and

worried the most about anything and everything. Yet he had everybody doing it.

"It's not a bad idea, I guess."

"Yeah. You can't imagine how nice it feels to get the hell out onto the highway again."

"You'd be surprised how often I've thought that."

Tyler did not exactly frown at what had been meant to be some sort of joke but Sam still felt a little stupid. "Anyway," he said, "it's sort of like you have an insurance policy there."

Tyler's face changed back to its usual friendliness. "I hope so," he said with honest emotion. "I've had a couple of real clumps get up there and start smoking and it really scares the shit out of you. Especially when you're in some place you can't stop, like when you're coming down the hillside."

Sam nodded and would have said something but his combine suddenly emptied itself and went into a high whine.

It stayed hot like that for the rest of the week but on Friday, only two or three days away from the impending finish of harvest, things just went worse. Not even the combines' air-conditioners could keep up with it.

Chapter 20

THEY were all cutting the last section, a big, deep valley up at Cammas-Dian that bellied five hundred acres for almost a mile between two long, soaring hillsides. In the morning they got most of the valley cut and by noon Sam and Carl had moved up onto the farthest hillside, running alongside a neighboring field.

The hillside was huge; it was like being on the side of a mountain. Sam had never seen so much wheat all on one smooth slope. As he cut he could see far ahead to where Carl's combine looked like a tiny green insect in the golden immensity. Far below, he could see the other combines working up the other side of the valley. It seemed a wonder they were in the same field.

At the very top of that hillside ran a fence line, little more than a fine line in proportion to the field, and he could see, on the other side, in a similar-looking field of a long valley that seemed almost as large, distant combines working as well, moving their way slowly up onto that mountain of wheat from their side. Everything seemed outsized.

But as big as the land was and the endless-seeming job it presented, and as hot as it was, he felt no fatigue. The knowledge they would be finished by the weekend made everything seem that much easier no matter how little progress they seemed to make each time they cut a swath.

There was a lightness to things and everybody felt it. Where before the days had dragged on from one to another in an endless repetition, with always another field to go to after the last, there was suddenly no other field except a small one back towards Harley's.

Like no other thing, that gave them energy for a last burst in the same way a marathon runner gains strength at the sight of the finish line.

For Sam, cutting along with ease through that high, thick wheat, he felt for the first time part of everything around him. The land, the machinery, the crew, the days and the nights of it, and for that matter the town and the life of it. He felt he was at last an element that fit as neatly as all the other elements fit.

Fred's conversation came back to him continually, and where before it was just a thing to think about, it became something he could imagine. He could imagine himself working on into the fall, then the winter, then the next spring, then the year beyond and beyond that, with the years then stretching out into a comfortable, easy landscape of his life. Would he always work just for the Petersens, or would things evolve? Where before he never had any ambitions for anything more than what he had been doing, could that change? Could there now be something else that drove him onward more than just what he rose to do in the morning? Could it be that Ruth could, had...

...and it was just upon the beginning of the thought of her that the day was swept away.

It had been a combination of everything. The blistering, fatal heat, the hip high stubble, the scorching dryness of the air and how the crew was rushing the work along in anticipation of ending it, all of that had finally come together to cause what they had all been trying to avoid.

He had been rounding the far side of the hill at the end of one of his long sweeps, lost in his thoughts and barely concentrating, when suddenly his radio burst into a cacophony of voices. Everybody seemed to be trying to talk at once.

He looked far down into the long valley to where the other machines were.

Sam could see one combine stopped and a truck rapidly moving away from it down the valley. Dan's voice was high-pitched, telling someone to keep going, keep going, keep going. All the other trucks were also turning and heading back down the valley, following the first one. He looked closer at the first truck, and caught his breath.

Directly behind it, as it ran down the valley, was a line of smudged patches in the stubble. On the ones directly behind the truck he saw no smoke or flames, but those farther back grew in size with flickers of bright red and yellow now shooting up along the smoky edges, rapidly joining together and increasing their strength. Sam could see even from that distance that the patches were growing too fast for anyone to do anything to stop the fire right there.

Carl's voice came over the radio. "Drivers, go unload. Gordon, you stay at Cresswall near a telephone in case things get out of hand."

"OK," came Gordon's voice. "OK. Cresswall. Telephone."

Sam saw Harley's combine, far up ahead, run down and swing directly over the burning patches in a rush, lowering his header in an attempt to bulldoze dirt. But the fires had now spread beyond his reach.

Harley obviously had the same thought and Sam saw him quit that effort and head up the hill to get himself between the stubble fire and the standing wheat and his neighbors, up on top.

"Let's try to get the stubble down flat," came Harley's voice over the radio.

Sam saw Carl pull out of where he had been cutting and start to shave back through the thick stubble in another line lower on the hillside. Sam, at his end, began doing the same, lining himself up with Carl's new mark. Harley was way below them, doing as they were, having somehow avoided getting his header plugged up with dirt from his plowing effort.

The fire, having consumed the thin strip of standing wheat at the very bottom, gathered itself rapidly and was now spreading widely towards both sides of the valley. Despite how the fire was spreading in every direction, everyone was now over on Sam's side of the valley. In the other direction, back across the valley towards Harley's other big fields, there was only stubble, and the fire could go for miles without jumping a fence.

Sam did not know if cutting the stubble was going to do any good but he set his header practically on the ground and began to mow it as flat as he could. What he would have liked to have done was just start bulldozing the dirt. But while that gave only a slightly better possibility of stopping the fire, it guaranteed ruining his header. Probably, though, he thought as he skimmed the cutting teeth as low as he could, they would all have to do that in the end anyway.

There was no wind to push the flames but the foot-high stubble was nevertheless going up quick and the smoke was getting thick. The long lines of flames now creeping up the hillsides were strong enough to be shimmering visibly above the stalks by then and were creating their own air flow, pushing them higher and faster.

Below, the black, burnt-out area grew steadily larger and uglier, as though a malignant growth, and the fire line became a wall of flame and smoke that was soon no longer just a material problem but now an actual threat to be feared.

Sam, Carl, Harley, and the other driver, a guy named Wally, were all cutting along a single line by then, creating an eighty-foot swath of shaved stubble along the entire length of the hill. Sam reasoned Dan had driven his combine out to the road to get the hose truck, or something. Or maybe it wasn't that, because normally that was something he could have left to the truck drivers.

At one end of the field's valley and hillsides was a highway; at the other were naked, dirt fields of summer fallow. If their line on the hillsides could contain the fire from spreading to the neighbors, they could get up to the head of the valley and keep the flames from jumping the road.

Unfortunately, back across their shaved swaths they could see tendrils of flaming chaff creeping across towards the unshaved stubble, and with a sickening feeling of desperation they turned to set up another run.

Carl's voice crackled over the radio. "Sam, you moved the disc up here, right?"

Sam punched his mike button. "It's down by the shed by the house. Want me to go get it?"

Carl was right, Sam thought, a little ashamed at having forgotten. But it was also a long way back to the barn and a combine did not go all that fast. It had to be tried though, the fire had to be stopped whether it was there, or a mile away.

"Dan?" Harley's voice rang out. "Dan?"

Silence.

Sam watched Harley's machine turn, its header lifting high, and go tearing down the valley.

"Everything hooked up down there Sam?" Harley's voice said.

"Yeah," Sam said. "Yes. Tractor's fueled up and the disk is hooked up."

"All right, Sam," Carl said. "We'll just try to keep shaving."

"Roger that."

Harley's combine disappeared into the smoke now rising thickly into the sky from the blackened valley. Sam, back to cutting behind Carl, after a few minutes noticed movement at the top of the hill, and saw a pickup appear along the fence line.

Although he had to concentrate, with his header so close to the dirt, he glanced constantly up at the fence line, hoping to see a tractor suddenly discing along it, cutting and churning the wheat down into a clean dirt sweep thirty feet across. If he saw that he would abandon what he was doing and go up to open up a section of fence so the tractor could get through to their side. Instead, he only saw the appearance of three combines at the top of the hill, cutting slowly as they tried to eat their way through the wheat there, taking into their slowly turning maws the whole plant in one big bite.

With more and more smoke in the air it was becoming hard for Sam to see behind him and at one point he stopped his machine so he could step out onto the catwalk to look. What he saw made his heart sink. Far behind, where the tendrils had spread, some of the flames had finally got up into the uncut wheat, and were building here and there into the truly massive swirls of fire which would create, finally, a large disaster of completely unpredictable proportions.

He got back in the cab.

He thumbed his mike.

"Carl, I've got to go back. It's into the wheat." Before he could lift his header he saw Carl's machine shoot up and turn back in his direction. Sam turned his machine around and headed straight at the flames.

There was a thing about car wrecks, Sam had once thought after having survived a particularly violent one, that if you came through them intact they were sort of exciting. The flash of danger. But while the memory of that thought flickered past him, he also knew this wasn't at all the same thing. The danger was definitely here, but because it was unfolding minute after minute it was possible to imagine fully and exactly what could happen. The biggest worry was that if the fire took over the hills it would become so massive that it would create its own wind and form towering walls of flame and, worse, a blinding blanket of asphyxiating smoke.

Sam could feel a real, growing worry in this and the tension was stifling within the muffled glass confines of his cab. More and more, as he was shaving along through the stubble, he was also trying to peer ahead and see if there would be any way to get out of that field.

He would have liked to have talked back and forth with Carl but he knew what Carl was thinking and concentrating on, and it would just be the same things. And it was with that thought, that he suddenly realized what it was that made him glad to be out there with Carl. Carl, like his father, had just blandly taken charge of things, getting things in order with a steady sort of efficiency. Taking care of what could be taken care of.

He did not know if many people knew this side of Carl. Quiet efficiency was a thing people did not often get credit for. And, for that matter, as it was with people who were like that, he probably did not even credit himself with it.

Sam was only about a hundred yards from the first of the big flames eating into the standing wheat when Harley came back into view, cutting up in front of him with the big wheel tractor and, just before diving into the flaming wheat, setting the disc hard down into the dirt.

Sam stopped and got out of the cab to watch. As he did Carl

189

came up alongside and stopped and got out onto his catwalk to watch as well.

Pulling the big disc, Harley went straight through the flaming line of wheat and where before there had been flames and smoke there was suddenly a strangely clean looking swipe of dirt, the rich, reddish-brown contrasting with blacks and yellows.

Harley could not maintain his tractor in the midst of the flames and now just set himself to go along in front of where the fire was burning. When he got to one end of the hill he turned and ran back in the other direction.

From where he was, Sam could not tell if Harley was enlarging his swipe there or going over the same ground. Sam looked up at the fence line and saw that the other crew had stopped to watch as well, making Harley the only moving thing out there.

Where Harley had disced the flames had stopped but here and there smoke shot up again as the fire found clumps of straw. Going as fast as he had, Harley had gone fairly shallow and there were some places where the ground had not been completely turned. But as Harley came back he ran slower, running the discs deep, and Sam could see nothing behind him but dark earth.

Sam, Carl and Wally got their combines going again and cut their way up to the top of the hill where they stopped to watch, waiting to see what to do next. Up there, watching Harley running up and down the field, Sam stepped out of the cab to stand on the catwalk, and looked over at Carl, who had done the same thing. Carl looked over, his face impassive but his eyes keen, and he nodded at Sam.

An efficient man who lived as a full element within his world, Sam thought as he nodded back. Did he get credit just for that? In Carl's case, Sam believed there were perhaps a few around that town that did. Hopefully Marilyn, no doubt Harley, and Sam could include himself. Even Daryl, over at the burger shack, seemed to appreciate the guy. The only one that did not seem to, was his brother.

Or maybe Dan could not—whether willfully or otherwise.

Truth was, though, that Carl was a bit like Harley, and it was only out in the fields, a place few people saw those men, that you could really begin to understand them. If, Sam thought again, you wanted to.

They watched Harley go back and forth and back and forth, and after a while it was obvious the fire was no longer a danger. Sam saw Carl get back in his cab, and listened to him tell the truck drivers to head back out into the field again. Sam looked into the half-filled hopper. He could still cut for a half mile or more. He got back into his cab and looked down the hill to find the edge of the standing wheat, ran up his engine, and pushed the transmission lever forward to begin gliding along the hillside, feeling the combine smoothly leveling itself as the slope increased. Maybe it was because of the previous two hours, but a sudden feeling of peaceful contentment came over him, an odd feeling of—how to put it?—of being exactly where he wanted to be.

Chapter 21

HARLEY came back to the field in his combine with Fred standing on the catwalk. Harley ran alongside Sam and waved for him to hold up. Fred climbed down from Harley's machine and came up Sam's ladder and stuck his head in the door.

"You have to go back to the shop. I'll keep going with your rig."

"What's up?"

"They need your help back there. Just go on out in the next truck."

Sam looked at Fred for more of an explanation but none came. He got out and walked down the hill to the truck road at the bottom and waited.

Back at the shop, he found Dan sitting on an upturned bucket, a dejected look on his face. Dan's combine was parked alongside the shop and as Sam walked by he saw the heavy header beam was nearly bent back into the tire on the left end and the reel was destroyed, splintered slats and twisted metal smashed back into the workings.

"Lovely, isn't it?"

He could only nod.

"Shit." Dan got to his feet. "So let's get it off."

Sam looked at the header again. It was definitely a two-man job but he could not see why he had gotten dragged out of his combine for something anyone else could have done. Like Fred, or even Tyler.

"You got me down here for this?"

Dan began undoing a hydraulic hose, something he could have done before Sam got there. Sam squinted at him for a second but then just grabbed a wrench. After a few minutes of sullen silence he said, "Where're you getting another header?"

"Pete went over to St. Pierre."

"They've got one?"

"Seems to be the case."

Bolts, and more bolts. And silence seemed to be the way Dan wanted to do it so Sam just did it that way.

When all was loose, Dan climbed up into the cab and backed the pivot out of the header and then ran the machine over to an open area where the new header could be installed. Sam, now undoing bolts on the ruined header's feed ramp, straightened up as Dan came back, and set his hands on the header.

"OK," he said. "What happened?"

Dan came to a stop in front of him, looking at the way Sam was looking at him, and then looked off towards the hills.

Sam wasn't feeling much patience about anything right then, and certainly not dramatics.

"Seriously."

Dan looked back at him. "Just a big fuckup all the way around."

Sam waited.

Dan finally sighed.

"Me and Tyler locked horns."

It happened. And often enough. Once in a while a truck, loading on the go, would move in too fast, creep too close, get jogged to the side, and that was all there was to it. It did not take much to damage a header.

Dan got himself a wrench and began applying himself to the other side of the feed ramp.

"I see," Sam said. "I imagine it didn't do much good to Tyler's truck either." There was not much else to say. Accidents happened.

They had been very lucky up until then. As far as harvests went theirs had been practically accident free, which was a rare thing. But he did not say it because, no matter what, accidents were always tough on those having them. The good thing was that nobody forgot about the first thing, and so practically nobody ever got too deep into recriminations.

"Tyler," Dan's voice went heavy with sarcasm, "has other things to worry about."

Sam, surprised, glanced over but Dan kept his head down. Sam remembered the truck racing out of the field, dropping fire as it went, and now knew it had been Tyler.

Oh hell, he thought, it could have been anybody. In fact, it was amazing that it had not happened before. It wasn't fair for Dan to crucify Tyler for that. Dan knew Tyler was a careful driver.

"Tyler had some problems?" Sam felt stupid with the question.

"He burned up his truck."

"Bad fire?"

"I don't see how he was still running. I'm surprised his fucking hoses or wiring did not melt. I don't know how the little fucker got out of the field."

Sam had seen Dan in many lights before, but he had never seen him work out his frustrations so directly on other people. Sam would have liked to tell him what he thought, but decided to just change the subject, not wanting to spend the rest of the afternoon on that line.

"Tyler's all right?"

Dan nodded but nothing came out of him. And there was more silence and Sam began to wonder if Dan was resenting the equanimity. But then Dan gave a shake of his head. "Fuck. I thought for sure he was going to just keep on."

"Keep on?" Sam frowned.

Dan's voice flattened out. "Tyler caught fire while we were unloading. Really caught fire. And he took right off, and, I don't know, then he just ended up in front of me like that." He made a curving motion in front of himself with one hand.

"Into the wheat."

"Yeah. And I ran right smack into the back of him."

"Oh, shit."

"I might have missed him, I guess." The weariness in Dan's voice deepened. "But God damn it, the kid was too erratic."

"It's hard to make fast adjustments when it goes suddenly like that."

"What a fuckup."

"So now what?"

"We wait around for Pete to bring the new header back."

"Where's Tyler?"

"He's driving Fred's truck."

"I see, and Fred's in my combine."

Dan nodded and after a second Sam nodded back in parody. "Really?"

Dan raised his eyebrows. "What?"

"Don't give me what. All this," Sam waved his hand around him, "is because you're so pissed off at Tyler that you couldn't even have him around to help you."

"Whatever." Dan set his wrench down and turned and walked over to the shed and found a couple of bales of hay to sit on.

Sam watched him go, and then looked back at the header. They were finished undoing the ramp and he set his own wrench down and then looked around at the farmyard. The heat seemed to have doubled in just the last ten minutes and he would have gone over to the shed, too, but he suddenly needed to get some air elsewhere.

Tyler's truck had been left over on the other side of the barn and he walked over, pulled the door open and climbed up to look inside.

Everything looked normal except down around the base of the shifting levers where Tyler had discharged his fire extinguisher.

He leaned over the seat and lifted the cover. There below the floor was the white mess of the chemical everywhere over burnt-looking surfaces. It was obvious a lot of straw had got up under there and become a serious fire.

Although Sam had not seen the actual accident he could remember how fast Tyler had taken off. He probably had a lot of smoke coming up into the cab and would have had no idea he was both picking up chaff and continually dropping burning straw as he fled out of the field.

Sam guessed Tyler must have panicked a little from the smoke and had gone in front of Dan. Maybe he had not been able to see at all.

Sam could understand how it could have been frightening with flames and smoke coming up around the cover plate, and the thought of all the diesel fuel in his tanks and of all the plastic and rubber surrounding him there in the cab. He took one more look and had to agree that Dan had a point. It was indeed surprising Tyler had gotten out of the field.

He went back to the shed and sat down on the ground, his back against a hay bale, across from Dan. And they sat there in the relative cool of the shade—which was not cool at all but not as bad as being in the direct sun—watching the wheat trucks rumbling by.

In the silence of their waiting, he found himself wondering what it would be like to have Dan as a full-time paymaster. Evidently, there would be moments of little mercy and, rival or not, he could feel a certain sympathy for Tyler.

They said little and after a while they both dozed off with the occasional moan and rattle of a wheat truck going by and the occasional buzzing of a fly. It was about an hour later when Pete showed up with a new header in tow.

By the time they got it onto the combine and all hooked up Dan had recovered his good mood. Sam and Pete had barely been able to go over the nuts and connections a last time before he revved up and rolled out to join the others.

Sam and Pete stood watching the combine disappear up into the field and then walked over to look at the truck.

Pete took one look and whistled. "This is going to take me two days."

Sam looked out towards the fields. "Need help?"

Pete laughed.

"Help a mechanic?"

Sam, still looking at the fields, nodded.

"No, anyway," Pete went on, "I'm just going to be doing a lot of disconnecting and driving all over hell and gone to find parts."

Sam would not at all have minded doing a lot of disconnecting and driving all over hell and gone but, nodding again, he walked over to stand by Pete's truck to listen to the radio chatter between combines and trucks. Harvest was back in full gear.

After a while he walked across the yard to the edge of the field and stood in the shade of a small wood building. The shade seemed a good place to be, and he watched the trucks going in and out, and after some more time went by it was as though he was in an entirely different day.

Chapter 22

THE trucks came out and the trucks went in and they all went in the same way up that wide draw, disappearing there around a far bend or came back out to the highway with their loads, with Sam watching from the shadows.

When the trucks came in empty they banged and rattled on their stiff springs. Coming out, loaded and ponderous, all there was to hear was the engine, pulling along deep and melodic.

As time went by and the day wore along in the heat, minute after broiling minute, and then an hour, and then another half hour, and there wasn't the slightest sign that anything would change from what had become of the day or how things were organized, Sam finally realized that as far as he was concerned, that was—as they used to say—all she wrote.

Tyler's truck had caught fire so he was driving Fred's. Dan had run his combine into Tyler but that had not been much of a problem with three competent mechanics to repair it. And Sam had done what he was told was needed and helped where he could and not where he could not and had not either burned up or crashed into something...

...and it was cooler to stand by the field in the shade of that little wood building where it was maybe only a little over a hundred degrees...

...and Pete, who was friendly enough but was also of that way mechanics tended to be when they were working, did not think the other truck would be ready until the next day, at best.

At first he figured there were a lot of ways he could feel about it but then changed his mind. There were only two. He could either be angry or not give a damn. He did not like either.

That he was forgotten about, there was no doubt. With work back to nearly normal nobody was going to be wondering about whatever had fallen through the cracks.

Under normal circumstances he might not have cared. But the way it fed into previous things put a cloud over what, after all, he had only recently come to feel. And all because of what? A goddamn unforgiving fit of temper.

Sam's face went grim, feeling things wash through him and he decided he was finished. It was just too hot, and too stupid, to be standing around like that. Far up the valley he spotted the black dot of a truck coming around the hillside and he walked out of the shadow of the building towards the dusty truck road in the field. Out of the shade the sun was staggering and he reached towards his pocket for his green bandana, but remembering he had lost it. When he got to the truck road he waved it down and it slowed to a stop. Tyler was driving it.

"Mind if I ride with you for a while?"

"Hell, no," Tyler said. "I can use the company."

Seated in the cab, Sam watched as Tyler went through his shifts in the first range. When they got to the highway, Tyler stopped for a second, leaning over to lift the cover plate around the shifting levers to peer below. Glancing over at Sam with a small smile, he dropped the plate and then clutched up into the gear ranges and rolled out onto the highway and soon enough the big truck, heavy with its thirty tons, was up to speed. Just before Cresswall there were some big curves in the highway and Sam watched how Tyler took them smooth and fast.

Really, the boy was pretty good.

"You know," Sam said. "I think I'd like to drive truck once in a while. Just to be able to go like this."

"I like it." Tyler grinned. "And except for the straw, I especially like it on days like today."

Sam felt the warm wind blowing past. It certainly was more comfortable to be moving through it and maybe even more comfortable than the flat air-conditioning in the combines.

"You feel like you're breathing."

"Yeah. Of course, today, I'm happy to be breathing at all."

Sam had not been inclined to talk about it but since Tyler had brought the subject up, he asked, "What happened out there?"

"Shit if I'll ever know. I was checking all the time. I think it was right when I came up alongside Dan."

"You must have got a clump right off Dan's spreaders."

"The size of it caught me by surprise. The whole cab went full of smoke and got so hot ... I mean," he shook his head. "I thought I was going to have to jump out."

"That fast?"

"Yeah. Like you said, it must have been a big clump of straw and it just lit up. But I did not know how much was going. Even if it had not gotten up through into the cab there must have been clumps everywhere up in the engine space, all of them suddenly dropping embers everywhere. But Dan kept saying on the radio, go, go, go, so I just went. If I had known I was a fire starter I think I would have just parked it there and tried to contain it."

"Dan was surprised your hoses didn't melt on your way out."

"They did afterwards," Tyler nodded. Suddenly, a small frown went over his eyes.

"I don't know what happened with Dan. He saw I was on fire. Christ, there was smoke everywhere. I couldn't see anything out of the cab. Next thing, bam, he's right into my ass end. I'm almost thinking he was still cutting behind me."

"He was."

Tyler glanced over. "Really?"

"What he said."

Tyler looked back at the road. "Man, oh man. If there's one thing about Dan, it's always that you have to be perfect when you're around him."

"I don't know."

"It's true. You have to go right down the line with him. Because if you don't, you'll either get blamed ... or make him fuck up, too. No margin for error."

Sam had nothing to say to that and he even thought about maybe changing the subject. But after a moment Tyler grinned stiffly and went on.

"Of course, when he's the one that fucks up..."

"You sound like you know him pretty well."

"Don't get me wrong. Dan's OK, I guess. But he's always been just the way he is. You know, he was my hero when he was in high school. He was the big athlete and everything and all of us little kids wanted to hang around him. But even then I remember how he was like that. During games, you'd see it. He'd just come unglued when someone else, or something, screwed up on him. One little thing and he'd be busting everyone's chops, kicking shit around. We all thought it was funny at the time, watching him. But like I say, he's an OK guy in his own way."

Sam could never forget that Tyler was his main rival for any possible job that might come along at the Petersens. But that did not affect how Sam liked him. He liked how Tyler made an effort to carry good impressions about people. He even found Tyler's sense of humor to feel like something familiar. The only difference he could see was that Tyler knew a hell of a lot more about what he wanted to do at his age than Sam had known. On top of that, Tyler had never had to be, or wanted to be, anywhere but in Gainesville.

"I hope," Tyler went on, "it's not going to be too expensive to fix the truck."

Sam could hear the real worry in the boy's voice. For whatever it was worth, Tyler wasn't about to offload his private little hells onto other people.

"It won't be that much," Sam said. He jerked his thumb back over his shoulder at the truck's bin. "Probably about half of what this load's worth."

"And the combine?"

"Two loads."

Cresswall had a couple of big elevators. There was no waiting in line and they went right in onto one of the scales. Three girls worked the scales and while Tyler was unloading, one of the girls climbed up and hung there at his window to talk with them. She wore a faded orange top and shorts revealing long legs. Sam was still a young enough man by anyone's account, but he could suddenly see one of the ways a guy could know he was getting on.

Rolling unburdened back to the field Tyler suddenly broke in on Sam's thoughts.

"Next Friday night I'm taking that one out."

"Well done."

"What do you think?"

Sam smiled. He could not say anything beyond: "I think she's pretty smart to snag an elevator job."

"I know, right? I didn't really feel like it was the big new idea when I asked her out." He suddenly laughed. "In fact, I almost felt like I was obliged."

"Obliged?" It took a second and then Sam laughed like Tyler had. "You know something," he said finally, "I think you're going to be ahead of your time."

Tyler looked far ahead down the road, his eyes seeming to see more than what was just out there, and then finally said: "I hope not."

Sam had only meant it lightly, but he could see Tyler did not take these sorts of conversations as meaningless, but before he could say anything Tyler glanced over at him in all seriousness.

"You mean her?"

"Oh... no," Sam lifted his hands. "But then again, who knows?"

Tyler nodded. "Yeah. I mean, how is it possible to get ahead of your time?" He shook his head. "Cause if you think about it, I think the only way you can be anything, is to get behind."

Tyler was now going fast and clean down the country highway, steering through the corners with both hands as lightly and easily as if it was only a car and not a fifteen-ton tandem-axle truck. But if he was driving easily along it was obvious he was now thinking of things.

And Sam, now staring at the road, found himself doing the same.

The truck banged across the bumpy ground as they went up through the draws and around the hills and finally, going over a big saddle, they saw the combines off in the distance on far hilltops. Tyler drove the truck into the opening towards the last big hills. The burnt area was now far behind them, far from where the combines were cutting, and it now seemed all forgotten.

"I'm pretty full," came Harley's voice.

They drove up to where Harley was cutting on top of a hill. Tyler maneuvered in beneath Harley's auger as he was moving along but Harley called over and said they could just stop and do it. Harley sounded happy over the radio and Sam glanced out his window at him. Harley grinned and opened his cab door to yell something. Sam could not hear it but thought Harley wanted some water. He grabbed Tyler's jug and pushed out of the truck, climbing down and then going over to the combine. Harley climbed down and, thanking Sam for the extended jug, took a long, full drink.

"Well," he finally said, wiping his mouth with his sleeve. "What do you think?" He had to raise his voice against the high-pitched whine of the unloading combine.

"Getting close now."

"Oh, yeah. We ought to have all this knocked off by tomorrow night."

"Be done Sunday?"

Harley nodded. "Just the stuff back by the house. By Saturday. Noon on Sunday latest, I figure, if we don't stop. Yeah."

Sam wanted badly to ask a few things. But if it had never seemed the right time before it certainly was not right then.

"The crew won't want to stop, this close in."

"How's Tyler's truck?"

"Pete's fixing all the wiring and hoses."

"Get her running this afternoon?"

"Doubt it."

"Tomorrow?"

"I'd say so. He seemed pretty confident."

Harley was pleased. "So all we ended up losing was Dan's header."

"Yeah."

"That makes it one hell of a harvest."

It was true. Only one accident the whole time. "It does."

"So what are you doing?"

"Not much. I can't do anything to help Pete. I asked, but ...," Sam's voice trailed off.

Harley glanced at him and then looked far off across to the other hillside to where Fred was cutting with Sam's combine.

"I suppose we could stop Fred."

"He's going fine."

Harley nodded, with a quick glance at Sam.

"Yeah, and we'd end up with the same thing."

"Odd man out."

"I guess you're the one on the outs until we get that truck back. At least for today."

Sam did not want Harley thinking he did not care but there was nothing he could say. "That's how it goes."

Above their heads, the auger suddenly began to whirl empty and Harley flashed a smile.

"I'll see if there's anything I can do down there," Sam said.

"You want to wait on the other truck tomorrow? You'll keep your combine rate."

"OK."

"Pete'll call you."

"All right."

Sam jumped back into the truck and Tyler was in gear and they were rolling even as he pulled his door shut. They followed Carl and Wally for a few more loads and then went down to the truck road to head out to the highway.

"Let's just stop by the barn on our way out," Sam said. "If Pete doesn't need my help I'm just going to head home. Since we all came up from Harley's in your pickup, I'll take that and get back to my car at Harley's. You, or someone, can take the crew back to Harley's tonight with a field truck, where you'll find your pickup. If that's all right with you."

"Sounds good," Tyler said. "The keys are in it."

Before long Tyler was pulling to a stop by the barn.

"Thanks for the rides," Sam said, climbing out. For half a second, looking back at Tyler, he felt he might say something else but in the end just nodded.

As Tyler drove off Sam walked over to the burnt-out truck.

Pete and his pickup were gone.

He stood there for a moment, and then looked up at the sky. It was still hot, the sun still well up. It would be many hours before the natural light was gone and they could even cut into the early evening.

He stared towards the hills.

What it came down to, he thought, the reason he was standing there alone and out of the action, was simply because Dan had felt more comfortable being in a completely rotten mood with him—throwing his anger all over to hell and gone—than he would have with either Tyler or Fred. Just flat-out bad manners. For one thing. And for another, because in the face of Tyler's clear conscience or Fred's experience, that sort of anger would have put Dan in the wrong.

The irony was not lost on him.

On the outs, indeed.

The big engine of Tyler's pickup roared to life and he drove away down the road to the highway, and then fast down the highway, the big field tires humming as they put Cammas-Dian behind him. It was a nice pickup, he thought, feeling gears slide smoothly into position beneath his hand. Just the type he would have liked to have had. As he drove along he looked at the hills going past and breathed the air.

And while it was a slim possibility he could now even hope, as he went along, he would not see Pete coming the other way.

Chapter 23

THE next morning, even before Sam had his boots on, Pete called from the farmhouse at Cammas-Dian.

"Nah," he said to Sam's question, "the truck's going to be out of it for the rest of the day. But maybe I'll have it ready for Saturday. Sunday at the latest." The mechanic did not sound optimistic.

Sam took a stab at it. "You'll need help getting it back down."

"I suppose so, I don't know. But in any case, I don't want to be around up here alone."

"What?" Sam half laughed.

"Seriously. It's strange up here."

"Strange?"

"Yeah. I think the people in this house are renting or something from Harley. The first time I asked at the house if I could use the phone, there was just the lady. She was nice. Gave me a cup of coffee. But next time I came back her husband was at the door."

Sam laughed outright. "You think that's strange?"

"Bit paranoid."

Sam stared at his feet for a second. "So, when did they finish up?"

"Must've been around ten. Running under the lights. The trucks went back to Harley's full because the elevators were closed by that time."

"So, they did get the field finished."

"Far as I know. I haven't seen anyone up here."

"They wouldn't have taken the combines down the roads at night?"

"I have zero idea. All I know is nobody's been up here, so I'm assuming they didn't leave anything up in the field."

Sam could not make it work.

"In any case," Pete went on, "everybody at dinner last night ... almost midnight ... was talking about getting things over fast. I know some wanted to get up real early. I wouldn't be surprised some were up by four."

"It gets that way."

"I suppose. Jesus Christ, though, you should have been there. You'd have thought it was a party. Harley broke out the beer to celebrate the end of Cammas-Dian... or something."

"More likely something."

"Yeah. But look who's still here."

Sam tried again. "I can come up."

"No, I've got just a lot of hook ups to do, and one big trip over to Harrington."

Sam looked down at his stockinged feet again. "Right."

"Well. I'd better be getting at it."

"Yeah."

"I'll give you a call if I need help."

"Thanks."

There was a pause, and then Pete sighed. "Later on, buddy."

Sam hung up.

He looked out the balcony door. It was a beautiful morning, cooler by far than the day before.

He went out on the balcony and looked across the quiet town. Gainesville was basking beneath a light blue sky. There were some clouds, the first he had noticed for days. The weather had finally changed and the heat would not be as bad. In fact, it was going to be pleasant. He went back in the room and picked up the phone and dialed.

"Hello?"

"Good morning."

"Sam? All's OK? She's not here you know."

"Right, right. Spokane. Her aunt."

"And some things she can only do on a weekday."

"I just wanted to check."

"Aren't you working?"

"Yeah. I just wanted to check."

"I'll leave a note in case, but I don't think she's getting back until Saturday evening. I have to go to work, right?"

The rest of the day he wandered around. Bought some food. Bought a burger and ate it in the park. Got his oil changed. That afternoon, on a whim, he drove down to St. Pierre, the town Ruth was from. He had never seen it and it was way smaller than Gainesville with only a few big brick buildings on Main Street. It was hard to tell if those had been the only big buildings ever built or if others had burned or fallen down. One of the buildings was a former hotel which now had a bar where the lobby had been, the upstairs rooms all seemed either vacant or unused. He went in and found a few old men, and got a beer and said hello. One of the men had known Harley's father, but that was as far as Sam got with talking to anyone. Despite the lack of conversation, he ended up staying later and drinking a few more beers than he would have wanted but nevertheless managed to get back up the road to Gainesville that night.

He could not imagine Ruth being from that town.

Saturday, he sat in his room for most of the morning, then he gathered all his clothes and took them over to the laundromat. While sitting there waiting for his clothes to cycle through, he found someone had left, alongside some hunting and fishing magazines, some old, dime-store-style westerns. He took a couple of them with him when he left and spent most of the rest of the day lying on his bed reading about evil ranchers, damsels in distress, and solitary heroes.

Sunday morning was spent much like the day before, except for now he could fill the hours by continuing to read about windswept mesas and dusty cattle towns—he found he liked the way the stories were written—and then he went and had lunch.

Same as Friday, he decided to go for a drive, but this time it was completely aimless and what might have just been an hour's loop turned into a couple of hundred miles of back roads all the way down to Walla Walla and back, before he finally made it back in the early evening. He was barely up to the room before the phone rang and a bit later Ruth arrived, carrying a bunch of packages.

"I thought you'd still be out harvesting. Then I saw your car."

"It's finished."

"Oh, boy." She took a seat on the arm of his chair, leaning on his shoulder. "Must feel good. But isn't there always a big... a last dinner or something?"

"Usually, I guess."

"You look gassed."

"I am that."

"God, what a weekend," she sighed. She went over to the bed and began opening packages she had brought up. "But you're finished now so there won't be any more like it, right?"

"Hopefully not."

She sighed again. "Come here," she said. "Try this on."

"You bought me a shirt?"

He pulled off his shirt and slipped into the new one, a white shirt with button down collars. The sort they wore in offices or with jackets. Or in any case, it wasn't a work shirt. She buttoned it up and looked at him. "Like it?"

He wiggled his shoulders. It fit perfectly. Neck... arms.

She stood there, watching his face, and she took a deep breath. "Oh, thank God, you like it. I was a little worried."

"You don't know your own strength."

She looked into his eyes and then stepped towards him, putting her hands on his waist. "You really have had a long day."

"Sort of."

"I'm sorry I wasn't here."

"You can't be here all the time."

She gave him the long sort of look that he had seen Sally give him on occasion as well, as though they either did not understand what he meant, or understood way more than he thought he meant.

"I hope not."

Sam looked down at the shirt. "I really do like this."

"I figured you were going to be needing it."

"You did?"

"Yeah," she nodded. "Out of curiosity, is it possible Sam Lawrence owns a suit?"

It slowly dawned on him what she was talking about. He freed himself from her hands and went to the closet, pulling out a dark gray suit. "Even have some black oxfords."

"I'll be damned," she laughed. "When did you ever need that?"

"You don't want to know."

"Anything to worry about?"

"Not at all," he said, putting the suit back. "But I did need a shirt."

When he turned, she had come back to him and put her arms around his waist. He was just about to kiss her when something he had long wanted to ask her came to his mind. Something he felt comfortable enough to now ask.

"Can you tell me something," he said, looking into those eyes, always those eyes, that whenever they were around he could look nowhere else.

"Remember when you asked me out on a date to go fishing?"

She laughed. "You mean, saved you from yourself."

He smiled. "What made you do it? I mean, you didn't do it just because Dan was being a smart-aleck...."

"Not at all. It was completely honest, directed at you."

"That's what I'm wondering. You barely knew me."

"Yes, Sam. And that's why I asked. Because I wanted to know."

"Know what?"

"If you were who I was seeing."

She had a playful look in her eyes that Sam couldn't help surrendering to. "Alright, fine. You're either going to tell me, or not, what it was that attracted you, or whatever it was."

She laughed. "You really don't know, do you...?"

Somewhere in the back of his mind, a strange feeling of déjà vu came over him. "Know what?"

"What a woman might find attractive in you."

"That's why I'm asking."

She laughed again, but this time her body shook. "I'm not so sure I want to tell you."

He slid his hands up her arms nearly to the shoulders. He didn't care anymore. He could just feel how she was his, and he was hers.

"Ok," she went on. "I'm not going to go down the list, but for starters, I just wanted to find out if all those soft-spoken good manners were genuine."

Sam stared at her for a moment. "That's all?"

Ruth's eyes were still playful, but now something earnest came through them. "You'd be surprised how important that is."

He looked into her eyes and saw the sincerity there, and could easily have asked any number of questions. But instead, he just let himself go and kissed her, in the only way he knew how to kiss her.

Although it was quite late, they were still up talking, and then a knock hit the door. Sam opened it and Dan walked in, his face bright red. "So here you are." He spotted Ruth and smiled. "Hiya."

"Hi yourself."

They all looked at each other for a moment, and then Dan raised his eyebrows.

"Not going to offer me a beer?"

"Would you like a beer?" Sam said.

"Yessir."

Ruth went into the kitchen while Sam led Dan out to the chairs and small table on the balcony. Streetlights from below cast a faint yellow light up through the trees, and from far off they could hear the sound of a band playing over at the Fireside.

Dan took a seat, stretching his legs towards the balustrade, looking out across town.

"I can see why you like it here," he said.

Ruth came out with three beers and took a seat, handing one to Dan.

He took it, and took a long drink. "God. I just realized how wiped I am."

Sam nodded. "When did you finish?"

"Today."

"I figured that."

"Yeah. Well, it's finished now, thank Christ."

Sam looked away.

"But you know," Dan went on, "I don't want to ever have to finish like that again."

"That so?" Sam's voice went flat and he saw Ruth glance over at him.

"Well, nothing really. Going sixteen hours straight two days in a row just sort of gets to you."

Sam counted back the hours and could not make it work. Even without counting the several hours Dan had been drinking they would have had to start an hour earlier than usual.

"What time did you start?"

"Same time as always. I mean, it was pretty much the same by the time we got down from Cammas-Dian."

Confusion swirled around Sam. "You worked last night."

"And the one before. We had dinner both times at three in the morning."

"You didn't work today at all."

"You kidding? I sort of woke up some time after lunch."

"Pete told me you'd be working."

"What would he know? He's been up at Cammas-Dian with that goddamn truck. We finally had to send Tyler to help him. Hey, anyway, where the hell have you been? I tried to find you all afternoon."

"I found him home," Ruth said.

"Been around mostly ..."

"Well, fuck that. I couldn't look all day. You don't want anyone to find you, that's your business." Dan finished off his beer with a long pull and then jumped up to get another from the kitchen.

Ruth eyed Sam. "So that's what the long face was all about. You didn't work at all this weekend."

"I was told to wait. So..."

"Whoop-de-doo," Dan sat down again. "Harvest is ohhhh-ver," he drawing out the last word like the howl of a coyote.

Sam saw Ruth was amused. Well, why not? Good old Dan was,

in fact, pretty amusing when he was drunk. Or he could be. And it was certainly preferable when he was that rather than the other thing.

"What are you doing?" Sam patted a pack of cigarettes in Dan's shirt pocket. "Taking up smoking?"

Dan glanced down at his shirt. "Oh, yeah." He smiled. "I mean, no. I lost Fred somewhere."

He pulled Fred's cigarettes out. There were some matches stuck inside the cellophane.

"Want one, Baby Ruth?" he asked her.

She smiled at him.

"Oh, yeah. You quit."

He shook up a cigarette and looked at it, pulled it out and stuck it in his mouth and took a match and lit it. He took a serious drag and blew the smoke out like a pro.

"Didn't know you were a smoker," Sam said.

"Ain't anymore, neither."

Sam looked at the pack. "So how is Fred?"

"How do you think he is?" Dan's gaze wavered from Sam to Ruth. "Oh, who knows. Who the hell knows. He lost his cigs and I lost him. Old bastard..."

"You were with him earlier?"

"Yeah. Haven't seen him for most of the afternoon, though. But that doesn't matter. Fucker's in such a grouchy mood." Dan gave a big yawn.

"Why's that?"

"Well, he was giving me this whole raft of shit for a while. Tyler and all that bullshit. But I know it wasn't that. Just his back, you know. What else? I got tired of it. Another few months, if he keeps on going, he won't be able to do fuck all." Dan waved his hand in frustration. "But do you think anyone can tell him anything?"

Dan was talking as though Sam knew all about whatever it was.

"It can't be easy for him."

Dan shrugged. "How much more time does he need? Don't you think a year's been enough?"

"Enough?"

"Nobody's pushing him. He knows exactly what the situation is. All I'm doing, all it is I'm doing, is reminding, is all. That's all. He won't do it by himself. And that old bastard is just making things all that much worse. He can really be a stubborn old asshole when he feels like it."

"You know I like Fred, right?" Sam said. He felt Ruth's hand on his arm.

"Nobody's pushing him. He knows exactly what the situation is. All I'm doing... I'm not fucking pushing. Everyone tells me I am. But, I mean, everyone can see he won't do it by himself. And Dad refuses to see what needs to be done."

"What are you talking about?"

Ruth leaned toward him. "Sam ...," she said quietly.

"You seeing this?" He said just as quietly back to her. "This is... all the time."

"Hey, you know what?" Dan yawned again. "We've got a few days to play here in front of us. I'm thinking let's have a barbecue tomorrow."

"Uh... Monday?" Ruth said.

"Can you get off?"

"Only way is to call in sick. And I had a day off Friday already."

"And Sue?"

Ruth looked at Sam with an ironic smile and answered Dan without looking at him. "I can ask."

"OK. OK. I can get all the barbecue, and all the meat and stuff. Don't worry about that."

"We won't."

Sam smiled at her.

Dan leaned back, collapsing his chin towards his chest. Then he suddenly sat up again, looking at Ruth.

"Hey, is Sue home?"

"Where else would she be?"

Dan began to get to his feet, but Ruth pushed him back. "Daniel Petersen, you will not go bother her at this time of night. You're drunk and a mess and she needs to see you like she needs a sixth finger."

Dan grinned.

Ruth gave Sam a beseeching look. "I'm going to go crash. I've had enough stimulating conversation."

"Sure."

Ruth went, closing the French doors behind her.

"You know," Dan said, looking down the balcony. "This isn't all that bad. I can see why you stayed here."

"You said that."

"You know, she's a pretty good girl."

"You're talking about Sue, I hope."

"No... I'm talking about Ruth."

"Don't."

Dan gave Sam a wink, thinking he was joking. "Yeah, right?" He looked off across town. "Ah, yes. I wonder what the poor folk are doing."

Sam took a breath. "Why do you make it sound like Fred's being odd or something?"

Dan looked at him. "You really don't know? If you kept your ears open, you would know a hell of a lot more."

"Of what? Stuff that isn't my fucking business?"

The anger in Sam's voice caught Dan off guard. "Things get around."

"They seem to. I wonder what else I'm going to know that I don't want to?" Sam's face was now hard, as angry as his voice.

A look crossed Dan's face and he got to his feet, suddenly and much more quickly and smoothly than Sam might have expected. "Hey," he said. "I've got to go. Don't be a stranger."

"What?"

Dan hesitated at the door. "That's not what I meant. Never mind. I'll be giving you a call." He went through the door, crossing the room and saying goodnight to Ruth.

When he left, Ruth got up and went into the bathroom. After a while Sam heard the shower. He went in and sat on the edge of the bed. The room was now dark, but a dim light came through the diaphanous curtains of the French doors, the heavy drapes tied back. The light was partially from the streetlamps through the trees

215

on the street below but mostly it was from the full moon sailing high over Gainesville.

Just over a month, he thought. Just like Harley predicted.

Chapter 24

IN the dim, pink light of dawn, Sam stood beside Sue and Ruth's house trying to peek into what he knew to be Sue's bedroom window. He was barefoot in the cold, dewy grass, far back in the side yard between that house and the neighbor's and the air was silent. Not a car, not a dog, not a bird was to be heard. He looked towards the street and then back at the window. Nothing could seem more dead, he was thinking, than the way a house was at that hour in the morning.

He stared at the window. If Dan had only been up when Sam had knocked at the front door, this would not be necessary, waking everyone up. But there was no choice. He moved closer to the sill. The window drapes were closed and he could see nothing.

He rapped the tip of his finger against the window pane.

Nothing stirred.

He tried again for longer. Nothing.

He did not want to start off the morning going back to beat on the front door, waking up everyone including the neighbors, but just as he was about to do that a hand appeared, brushing the drapes to one side.

It was a man's hand and it was attached to an arm that came off from one side in the darkness.

The angle for Dan to see him was wrong so Sam moved. Dan, though, at that moment rolled over on the bed and pushed the drapes wide open, filling the room with a diffuse, morning light just as Sam got to where they could see each other. There, he also found himself looking at everything else.

In deep sleep, with one arm curled back behind golden hair, Sue lay arched into the rose light, her bedsheets all but slipped away.

Sam took a step back and, seeing Dan's eyes come into focus, jerked his thumb towards his car. And with that Dan's hand let the curtain fall.

There had never been a barbecue but through some odd process Sam found himself going fishing with Dan. Leaving Sue and Ruth's they spent some time getting over towards Idaho to where they were going to fish. It was farther than Sam would have gone, having long before found good places much closer to Gainesville. Once they got there Sam set out fast, roaming upon that nearly treeless stretch of river, trying to see what he could do with what morning hours were left. He had no luck at all and when he finally made it back to where he had started he found Dan sitting on a huge rock, his shirt off in the hot sun. Although he had a line in the channel that swept by below him, what he really was doing was drinking beer and getting sunburned. Sam had learned that Dan did not like to fish any more than Sue did.

Sam had gone by the car as he was coming back, and carried our lunch along with his fishing gear. When he got to the bank he stopped to look at Dan's choice of a fishing spot. It was terrible for that but it was a fine place for lunch. He stepped off the bank, going across round stones out to the big rock.

"How're you doing?" he asked as he clambered up.

"Nothing so far."

"You been here all morning?"

Dan pointed down at the channel running next to the rock. "All I have to do is sit here and say hello."

Sam looked at how the stream was going past the big rock. Better fishing would be just about anywhere else, if there was such a thing as fishing on that sun blasted river. But Dan had wanted to come to this specific place although Sam could not see why except that maybe he had come here at some point with others. A memory, or something.

Sam sat down. "I don't think there's anything in here."

218

"Sure there is."

"How would you know?"

"I think I know my country better than you."

"Hmmm," Sam let out, and with a dumb show of enthusiasm flicked a wet fly out into the current and let it drift down around a rock to where he knew he could ignore it. He looked back at Dan. "You should put a shirt on."

Dan poked a finger to his chest and then put his shirt back on. "You'd think, all the time we work outdoors," he said, "we'd be more browned up."

Sam opened his pack and took out some sandwiches wrapped in wax paper, and from his creel he pulled out a couple of the beers that had been soaking in the river.

"Hope meatloaf's all right?" Sam said.

Dan took a bite and after a moment said, "Ruth's a good cook."

"You're assuming." Sam unwrapped his own.

"Not at all."

"Well, you're right."

After lunch Dan returned to his nap. Sam watched the dark water of the river going past the big stones. Wide and shallow there, except for the channel next to the huge rock, the river in that place made its way across a flat plain. Fields came right to the straight-sided banks of the river, ten to fifteen feet in height and lightly grown over with stiff scrub brush. There were very few trees and none at the place where they were sitting. From the top of that huge rock he could look out across the countryside where everything was bright and hot beneath the vast expanse of sun bleached sky. He did not think of much although at one point, remembering how the day had begun, he thought about Dan and Sue and how they were so different in so many ways. And yet there they were, drawn together by something they saw in each other. Or did not. Especially where it came to Dan. Although Sam could admit that it was very possible Sue was a better judge of what there was to see in Dan or not. To be fair.

He smiled. When it came to that, he thought, if he was going to be fair all around, there could be plenty of people who might think the same sort of thing when it came to himself and Ruth.

He looked down the river and gave his line a twitch, seeing the wet fly surface for a second before getting pulled back down into the swirl behind the rock, and then went back to looking out across the fields and off towards Idaho where the purple foothills of the Rockies made a hazy band along the horizon.

After nearly an hour Dan sat up and looked around. "This isn't all that bad," he said.

"Getting to appreciate fishing, eh?"

"Ah, yes..." Dan stretched. "Wonder what the poor folk are doing."

Sam drew his breath in but held back the sigh. "Not farming wheat."

"We can't all be sharecroppers."

"Wasn't saying anything more than you were." Sam picked up his pole and reeled the line in. "What's everyone else doing? I mean, nobody's really working, right?"

"Even farmers take a few days off."

"I know."

"Well, plans are going along for Carl. We were thinking of going through all the combines and equipment, get them dusted out and put away, but even Fred said that could wait."

"What's he doing?"

"I don't know," Dan yawned. "Same as usual."

"He's sort of an old work horse, isn't he?"

"He's an old nutball, is what he is. Stupid motherfucker wouldn't know what to do with a vacation even if he took one."

Dan picked up a round stone sitting in a depression on that big rock and chucked it across the river at a clump of bunchgrass. A chirp-trill rang out from the clump and a red-winged blackbird flew up out of the rushes. Sam watched it going away, flashing black against the shimmering yellow of the stubble fields. He took a breath.

It was like being a cripple, he thought, to have to sneer at almost everything. "Why are you always going off on Fred? Like he's odd or something."

"He is."

"Compared to... you?"

It took a moment. "No. Compared to himself."

Sam frowned.

Dan picked up another stone and threw it across the river. "You don't see it because you haven't been here long enough."

"That again."

"You wouldn't notice."

"You know ... he was the one who brought me out to the farm in the first place. And I worked with him damn near every day right up to farming. I've got to know him pretty well."

"Doesn't matter. You wouldn't see it because he wouldn't show it. But we've seen it."

"Seen what?"

"Difficult. Stubborn. And he's getting impulsive."

Except for the story of Fred's brief marriage Sam could think of nothing Fred had ever done that could be considered impulsive. "I don't see that."

"Whatever."

"You make him sound like he's sick or something."

Dan took a pull from his beer. "If I make it sound that way it's because it's true."

"A bad back ain't sick."

"That's how you think?"

"I don't think anything."

Dan looked away off across the river.

"You've got no idea."

An ominous feeling came over Sam but he did not want to ask outright about Fred. But he could ask about something else.

"You know? I've had a conversation or two."

"We know."

"So, if you don't mind, does any of what you're talking about have anything to do with things I should be thinking about?"

Dan's eyes squinted and for a second he looked like he was about to say something serious. But then a different look—one Sam knew well—replaced it.

"You know," Dan gave Sam a big grin. "It isn't always about you."

Sam frowned. "Is everything a joke?"

Dan started to laugh, but about halfway through wheezed to a stop. Sam's face told him that maybe there were better things to talk about.

Chapter 25

THEY were staring at the ceiling with Ruth snuggled against him.

"So what is it?" she sighed. He realized she had been awake as well although maybe not as long as him.

"Good morning."

"Good morning, nothing. You're pondering."

"No, no."

Her hand fell on his chest with a thud. "Oh, no you don't. Out with it."

He might have thought that putting things in words he had been thinking about for nearly an hour would have been easy. But it was not. "Do you know Fred Rosenbauer?"

"Just what you've related about your days."

"But... before?"

"It might be that Dan mentioned his name, but I don't remember. Nothing to remember. Why?"

"Dan said he was sick."

"Is he?"

"I don't know. Dan said he wasn't himself. And that's what I've been cogitating..."

"Pondering."

"... pondering about. How that explains a few things. Like how things went when I first started out there, and then things after that didn't make sense. But also about how things are suddenly going in a different way."

"Different?"

"Fred's retirement... I didn't know anything. But it's clear that it's been a thing out there. And I seem to be in it. He talked about it, right open with me, the other day. And then Dan did yesterday, but in another way. And Dan wouldn't say but I can tell my name's come up."

"What was it that didn't make sense?"

"Things before. Things that sort of clouded my thinking about the Petersens."

"Which were?"

"Doesn't matter. Just a few things this summer and a few other things in the spring in other ways. I've been thinking this morning that I dropped into something, without knowing it, family things even. And now, although it hasn't been said right out by anyone, it could be that the Petersens are thinking of offering me a full-time job."

"I thought you were full-time already."

"I mean permanent. Fred's job."

"Would you accept?"

"Sure."

"Fucking hell, Sam," Ruth said at long last.

"What?"

She let out a breath. "Never mind."

He turned his head to look at her. "And you talk about me..."

"It doesn't matter. But... and I'm just saying... I don't think you ought to listen to Dan so much."

He smiled. "I don't think I do. But even so, why not?"

"Because I don't know what he talks about."

Now he laughed.

"No, really," she went on. "What I meant was, I don't know exactly how he puts things and I think you believe him a lot."

"He says things often enough that don't pan out the way he thinks, or plans for, but I've never heard him tell any outright lies."

She shifted her legs beneath the covers. "Not a liar, exactly. He just puts things certain ways that leave you feeling, I don't know... skeptical."

"I didn't realize you distrusted him this much."

"Haven't you noticed how everyone takes Dan with a grain of salt?"

"He's a regular enough guy."

"Oh, please. You guys. That's all you need? You don't bother wondering about what he thinks, and why?"

"I'm his friend, not his psychiatrist."

"You don't think about why he says what he says?"

"Yes, I've tried that," he admitted. "But mainly I just try to deal with what he does."

"Fair enough. I just get the feeling you sometimes don't want to understand things about people."

"That's quite a thing to say."

"Yes," she nodded. "It is."

He nodded back. "Well, I don't know what to say to that. It might be true, but what difference would it make?" he smiled.

"I'm not joking."

"Ok, then, are there things I need to understand about you?"

He smiled again but she did not smile back.

"Is that all this is to you?"

"Honestly, I don't know. It's a little early for me to be examining Dan Petersen, let alone myself."

"OK. But I'm saying it's important, or it's going to be important, to understand him better."

"What's there not to know? He's sort of a friend and sort of an employer. What else matters?"

"Well, if that's all it is to you, I guess you'll be just fine working for Mr. Perfect."

"Mr. Perfect?"

"That's Sue's name for him on some days."

"He must be more talented than I thought."

"That's what he'd like people to think."

"Plenty of people do that. It's not so terrible."

"It is with him. And it is for Sue. She really likes to be with him and can handle pretty well the way he can get sometimes. She's beginning to think they might have a chance."

"You don't sound convinced."

"Not my business. But she's always wanted to feel secure. You have no idea. And the awful thing is that they've known each other all their lives. And now look what he's doing."

"What's he doing?"

"He's starting this damn pedestal thing."

"Oh..."

"Yeah, oh. And she worries."

"To the point she's talked about it."

"That's not a hopeless thing, Sam. It helps her keep things in perspective. I don't have anything to say, you know. Dan is just Dan and you either take him or leave him. I think you know that."

"Sure. But Sue likes him."

"A lot. And he's got good qualities."

"Yes, he does. And he can sometimes get himself settled down enough to be like a friend."

"How nice. All I wish, is that you could tell your friend to get his act together."

"What's the chance of that?" Sam smiled, but once again she was not amused. "OK. Anyway, if it means anything, he told me he loved her."

"He said that. Exactly that."

"No, not exactly that. But close enough that I believe his words."

"You put a lot of stock in that."

"He told her. I'm sure."

"He told her that back in high school. And then...," Ruth laughed but not with humor.

"Oh, Christ." Sam looked up at the ceiling. "So if Sue knows so much about Dan, then she's aware of what she's getting into. It must be what she wants."

"She does. But she's holding back a bit, watching to see if he starts going sideways. And I don't mean about his talk. He's always talking, talking, talking. I mean starts thinking about her in some way and then do the same thing to her that he did to others. To Marilyn and to... and like what he did to Marilyn."

It had only been a short pause, short enough that he could let himself pretend he had not heard it but that the only thing he heard was Marilyn. Marilyn.

He thought about Marilyn.

And as for Marilyn, he was not surprised. All the signs had been there all along and it all fit. All of it. Thinking of Carl. Things said. Things seen. And that would have been enough, but suddenly he knew he could not push it all away. She wanted him to talk... talk it would be. So he threw something out, something she could deal with if she wanted. He could live with it, either way.

"Why are you telling me all this?"

"Because, if you're going to work out there..."

"All right," he smiled. "Don't worry. I won't let Dan corrupt me."

"I didn't say he would."

"You said not to listen to him."

"Yeah, I did, didn't I..."

He did not mind. He had let himself turn it over, let it go this way and that, and in the end knew he not only did not mind but did not care as long as he could be sure that she did not care in any way. And that seemed to be the case, but he also wondered if they, and not just she, would have to deal with it. It was not something he would have cared about, but Ruth was right. He would have to be dealing with Dan, and for a long time, and he had to keep that in mind.

Ruth was dressed and making coffee. He sat at the table, cleaning his work boots, the leather laces oiled and stretched out on the windowsill. "So," he rubbed a spot of wax into a boot. "I guess you and Sue aren't planning to go to the wedding?"

"Uh, no. You think Sue wants to watch the first big love of her boyfriend's life getting married to his brother?"

"And you?"

"Solidarity."

He picked up the can of wax, wiping the rag into it, and said lightly. "For Sue? Or Marilyn?"

He just could not help it.

Ruth went to set the pot onto the stove, her shoulders giving him what she wanted to answer. And it was enough. The way she stood at the stove told him she was quietly crying. Not a bad sort of crying, but the sort that comes from having had to finally deal with the thing that he had been wrestling with since before dawn—a thing she had to then also wrestle with.

And as far as he was concerned, it was all now dealt with for good. Although he knew two things. That some day they'd talk about it, and that he knew he had nothing to worry about.

Chapter 26

SAM opened the shades to a brilliant blast of daylight. The old, four-story hotel, the Upton, had a corner restaurant and when he went down he had lunch but mostly drank coffee, and he was still drinking coffee when Dan showed up. To the waitress Dan pointed at Sam's cup and said "please." Somehow, that made Sam feel better for the first time that morning. Or afternoon. Or whatever it was.

Dan gazed out the window at 1st Avenue. "Nice day."

Sam looked out the window at the bright sunshine, cars and people going past. It was a nice September day out there. A warm and sunny Saturday and people were walking around in Spokane just like that was all there was to it. He looked back at Dan.

"Did you just get up?"

"Been up and around for a couple hours."

"You're kidding."

"I've even been for a walk."

"Good for you."

"Over to the park. You'll never guess who I saw."

"Jesus?"

"Lonni and that girl from St. Pierre."

Sam groaned inwardly.

Dan shrugged. "Now that I think about it, you look more like Jesus this morning... I mean, the day after."

"OK."

"They were over there feeding the ducks. Or Lonni was. Like a zookeeper."

"She has the training."

"She likes to look after things."

Sam felt whatever there was of the day go flat. "This where you want to go?"

"Oh, c'mon."

"What the hell did I get into?"

"If you asked Lonni, not enough."

Not even Dan could have guessed how close it had been. A big tavern, dark, with deep places people went into like hiding. The main thing had been the music, so loud nobody talked about anything but just did whatever it was they were going to do.

For a while there had been a lot of people Sam and Dan knew who were going to the wedding. Later though all Sam could remember was himself, off in some small place, drowned in whiskey and beer, deaf from the music, blind to all the other people in that smoky darkness, and nearly smothered by Lonni.

Even there the next day, Sam couldn't remember what had stopped the mindless rush. What had stopped it? And that was a problem. He couldn't remember. He hoped it had been him, but he just couldn't remember.

Dan smiled. "Why'd you leave?"

"Yeah, right?"

"What is this? To fuck or not to fuck?"

"More like to fuck things up or not fuck things up, is the question."

"Wow." Dan pursed his lips. "Ethics."

"Can't go that way?"

"Sure. Or else you're just worried it might get back?"

"Well, ethics can work that way, too. Whatever works."

"Shit." Dan looked out the window. "Have your cake and eat it. You think everything gets around? You'd be surprised at the things that don't." He shrugged. "I mean, I get what you mean, your attitude. Clear as day. But I'm telling you, maybe things aren't like what you think. Ever think of that?"

"My attitude?"

"Your way of looking at things."

"That would be interesting. But whatever. Just do me a favor.

Don't tell me any of the things everybody knows that haven't gotten around."

"I've got to tell you something," Dan leaned into the table. "With attitudes like that you can end up in some pretty big crashes."

"That right?" Sam looked back at Dan for so long Dan got uncomfortable.

"Just saying."

"You might be right. But if that's the truth, then it would probably just be good sense for anyone who knew it, to steer clear." He smiled. "Don't you think?"

If Dan had anything to say he dropped it and grabbed for the menu. "Maybe better get something," he said. "It's going to be a long day ahead."

"You can say that again."

Dan ran his finger down the sandwich list. "It's going to be a fucking long day ahead."

The wedding was in the late afternoon at Coeur d'Alene. Sam and Dan drove over to Idaho and found Harley and Sally's motel and stayed there for a while, playing some cards with Harley.

"So Marilyn's from Coeur d'Alene. That's why she wanted to get married here?"

"It's for luck," Harley grinned.

Dan grunted. "She's come so close so many times, I think she'd believe in anything."

"Dan," Sally said. "You promised."

"Oh, Jesus," Dan held his hands up. "Nobody's going to be able to say anything from here on out."

"All depends, Daniel," Harley dealt out the cards slowly. He wore an impressively well-fitting dark blue suit with richly-tooled black cowboy boots, buffed to shining perfection. Sam looked at the farmer's face and could see he was thinking about more than just Dan's way of saying anything that came into his mind. Sam could see that Harley was mulling over a large range of things, and he could not help wondering how deep things had gone from the time before when—as far as Sam could figure out—it had also involved

Marilyn. Harley set the last card down and picked up his hand.

"Did you get the bathroom hooked up?"

He was talking about an old farmhouse Carl and Marilyn were going to move into.

Dan eyed his cards and pursed his lips. "It's all set except for wiring the hot water."

"When're you going to do that?"

"Before they get back," Dan shrugged. "I'm going to do it tomorrow, or Monday." He glanced over at Sam and gave him a look. He had told Sam he planned staying the entire weekend in Spokane.

"All right," Harley said. "We don't want them to be without hot water."

"No."

"And while you're at it, get the area down below the house mowed down to look more like a lawn. So the place doesn't look abandoned."

"What do you call an old farmhouse that hasn't been lived in for thirty years?" Dan looked at Sam. "Even when we bought that land, nobody had been living in it for twenty years. We just used the barn for hay."

Sam remembered it from haying, and had actually stepped inside just to take a look. "Seems a good, solid old house."

"You checked the roof?" Harley went on. "And the electricity works everywhere? The new fridge, and the oven? Got the furnace cleaned out and running?"

"I said I was taking care of things."

Harley grinned and looked at Sam. "I know it, Daniel. You're the big boss."

It was a joke. Of course.

Everybody knew how Dan liked to take over. Actually, in a lot of important ways, Dan was in fact the boss. He did a lot of the calculations. He decided what the price of things were. Trouble was, Sam suddenly reflected, Dan could sometimes seem to put as much of a price on things he did not own as on those he did. Dan was very thorough when it came to what belonged to whom. But Sam personally knew, as well, how Dan honored his promises about getting things done.

"Just because I want to make sure things are right." Dan shrugged. "Just because I make a few suggestions."

Harley laughed and Sam smiled. He would not have smiled before but found it now seemed the natural thing to do.

"A few suggestions. Hell, I wouldn't be surprised if you'd chosen the color of dress Marilyn was wearing today."

"Go ahead and joke. But have I been wrong?"

"No. You're doing just fine."

"That's right, old man." Dan punched Harley on the shoulder.

"Watch out now," his father said.

Then everybody grinned. Even Sally, who had been watching television through it all. Sally nodded at Sam. "So, what do you think of these two?"

"I don't try."

"What do you mean?" Dan punched him. "Huh, boy?"

"Who are you calling boy?"

"You, boy." Dan punched him harder.

"I'll boy you, buddy. Anytime." Sam punched him back.

"Yeah?"

Dan's eyes suddenly had a gleam and he reached down and grabbed the leg of the stool Sam was sitting on and pulled up hard, tipping Sam over onto the floor.

Sam's first reaction was to retaliate but then he had a strange moment, as though something had just focused. He looked up at Dan.

Dan laughed down at him.

"Say what, boy?"

Sam got to his feet and for just a second had the urge to tackle Dan. But he also knew he could not do anything, at least not without sending all the cards and chips between them flying.

"You just wait."

"What's the matter?" Dan grinned. "Haven't you learned how to sit yet?"

Sam picked up his stool and set it straight, but before he could sit down, Dan upended it. Dan laughed as Sam picked it up again. But Dan was too fast, and had it over again.

"What's the matter, boy?"

"Oh, man." Sam picked the stool up again and that time sat down quick and hard upon it. Dan reached out, but Sam put his full weight on it, making it so that if Dan really wanted it upended he would have to stand up.

"You two are going to wreck the motel," Sally said.

Dan nodded. "Well, if the boy ever learns how to sit down, we'll be all right."

Sam picked up his cards. "Whose turn is it?"

"Dan's," Harley said.

"Course it is," Sam said.

Dan took a look at his cards and tossed down a red chip. "Get used to it, boy."

Sam glanced at his hand. He saw he had a full and he stared at it for a second and then folded it and set it next to the pot. "Right." He stood up. "I need just one more cup of coffee somewhere."

Dan grinned, showed his pair of tens, and patted the pile of chips. "Just can't stop winning. That's twenty bucks there, right?"

Sam dropped a twenty on the table. "I'm going to stretch my legs."

Dan stood up, too. "Not a bad idea."

"You boys don't get lost," Sally said.

"It's Coeur d'Alene, Ma. Nobody can get lost." Dan went out the open door.

"Meet you at the church," Sam said to Harley and Sally, and followed Dan.

Harley began gathering the chips and cards together. As he was putting Sam's hand into the deck he saw what it was. He only looked at it a second and then looked out the door at Sam and Dan heading towards the parking lot.

"Almost ready, Ma?" he said without looking at her.

Sally laughed. "I've been ready for years. Are you?"

"If I ain't now, I never will be," he looked over at her and grinned.

"Going to be an interesting day."

Harley gave his wife an affectionate smile, and then looked back out to where Sam and Dan were getting into Sam's car.

"It will be that," he said.

With Dan inside helping Carl get ready, Sam and Harley talked out on the church steps. Harley nodded at people going past, shaking a lot of hands and saying a few words. It was not going to be much of a ceremony but the number of people showing up kept growing by the minute and after a while it became obvious many people were going to have to stand. Sam glanced inside at one point and saw men shifting from the pews to let the women and children sit. He was surprised by the number.

"Marilyn's got quite a few family and friends over here," Sam said.

"Heya Pat. Heya Billy." Harley turned to Sam. "You have no idea. If I told you about all of them you'd get the impression Carl's marrying into half the state. Hi there, Judy, where's Phil? Oh, there he is. Heya Phil."

"And this must be Danny?" someone said.

"No, no," Harley said. "This is Sam. Friend of the family."

A half hour later the stream had trickled to the last few stragglers. Sam was looking into the church wondering how anybody else could possibly get in when he suddenly felt Harley's hand on his shoulder.

"I've been forgetting to give this to you all day." Harley pulled out an envelope. "Here you go. No, don't just put it away. Look to see it's all there. It also goes back to when you were farming with Fred."

Sam opened the envelope. Harley said it was not only a harvest check but for some previous wages. He looked. And then he looked again.

"That's generous."

"No. It isn't."

Sam was stunned. No other outfit he knew paid wages like that. He suddenly had to deal with an entirely different appreciation of the Petersens, or at least Harley Petersen.

"You sure this is right?"

"Yep. I was going through the accounts and saw what you'd been getting. Did you think you'd been paid in full?"

"I didn't work all the time."

"We pay monthly wages."

Sam let that sink in. "I didn't know I was hired on that basis."

"That's the only basis we work on. Farming's full time, whether it is or isn't."

"Just seemed generous."

"I told you it wasn't."

Sam stuffed the envelope in his pocket and nodded. Damn, though, he thought. It was a hell of a check. A down payment sort of check.

"Thanks."

Harley nodded. "And that reminds me of another thing. When are you going to tell us?"

"Tell?"

"For what Dan asked before harvest."

Sam frowned. "What did Dan ask?"

"You know, Tyler's been hound-dogging me about it, in one way or the other, for weeks now."

"Tyler?"

"But it's up to you."

Dan, Sam thought. Once again, here he was, hearing things coming at him sideways and—once again—it involved Dan. Under other circumstances he would have said something but given the circumstances just decided to pretend he was aware.

"Well, sure, it's true that I'd been wondering if there was more work for me."

"Why were you wondering that?"

Harley had turned to shake a few more hands and as he did so a frustrated look came over Sam's face. But he cleared it before Harley turned back to him. "Fred's done and we have to replace him starting next month. Dan said he wasn't going to ask you again, and I have to agree. We don't have the time."

Despite himself Sam could not help his voice rising a bit. "Yeah? Yeah, I can understand."

Harley raised his eyebrows.

"So?"

Sam stared at the farmer for a moment and then threw away every particular thing he was thinking.

"Yeah, I want it."

"Good. I'll tell Dan to tell Tyler."

"He's a good worker."

"Oh, Christ, yes. And maybe if what we're looking at this winter comes through there'll be a lot more work. But he'll have to wait a spell."

They did not have anything more to say. It was that simple and he was hired on for good. He was no longer what he had been, anywhere, before. He could feel how really different that was with nothing more to worry about and very little more to get straightened out.

And with that, suddenly, they were alone on a porch again. Everyone else inside.

And once again they both just stood there, happy to have settled some business, some things understood, and now just standing there on that wide church porch looking out across a sunny back street in Coeur d'Alene. No harvest moon hanging above them there, Sam was thinking, and as well, no memories of other times in other places. Just standing there waiting for a wedding to begin. After a moment Sally came out of the church to grab Harley's arm.

Sam stood there a while longer and then Sally came back out.

"C'mon now, Sam. I've got all the other boys finally collected. You're keeping them waiting."

The pews and side alleys were so full Sam had to walk straight down the main aisle of the church to where he saw, tucked behind an arch, the side door where Dan was staring out across the crowd. Dan spotted Sam and made an impatient motion. Sam followed Dan down a hallway and then into a small storage room full of fold-up tables, choir gown racks, candle holders, folding chairs. A couple

dozen men were in there and on the other side of the room someone
had scrawled in chalk on a rolling blackboard:

RIP CARL PETERSEN, ESQ
CONGRAT$-$ULATION$
MR$. MARILYN PETER$EN

Carl was standing at one end of the room chatting with six or
seven men who were evidently his groomsmen. Sam had never met
any of them and it was obvious they were all close friends. He
looked at other groupings and saw Fred, who looked back and gave
him a wink. Before Sam could go over to talk to him Dan came up
and handed him a glass full of champagne.

"Here. You're celebrating, too."

"Sure." Sam held it up towards Carl, catching his eye. "Here's
to it, Carl."

Carl held up his own glass. "Thanks, Sam. And here's to yours."

"Mine?"

"Looks like we're going to be seeing a lot of you around now."

Sam looked at Dan. "I see."

Fred walked over. "Glad to see you here."

"Did not expect me?"

"I never expect anything, anymore."

"Fred figured Tyler would be getting his job."

Fred growled, "I never said that."

"Didn't have to."

"If there's one thing I'm not going to miss, you little shit, it's
your ass-umptions."

A few of the nearer men laughed.

Dan went over and filled Carl's glass.

"What the hell are you trying to do?" Carl said. "I'm going to
hardly be able to stand up in there."

"You can't go in there sober."

"Why not?"

"Because I'm not."

"You're not the one getting married."

238

"What do you mean?" Dan smiled around the room. "We're all getting married today."

"That may be. But I'm going to be wearing the ring."

"In your fucking nose."

"Very original."

Sam downed his champagne. "You're going to do all right. Marilyn's all right."

Carl took his eyes off his brother and looked at Sam.

Sam had come to know Carl a bit and had come to appreciate that slightly chivalric quality he had. But he now found himself looking into a steely pair of eyes that were both completely aware and dead serious. And something else that flickered for a second. Humor or anger, Sam was not sure. And Sam regretted having said anything at all.

Carl looked down at Sam's suit. It was a good suit, but Sam suddenly felt cheap in it. Carl looked back up at Sam's face. And where before his face had seemed hard, it now showed a sort of kindness, his eyes showing an easy humor.

"Look," he said. "I don't want to spend much time on this, but keep this in mind. My brother's always on the outside, has always been, judging and controlling, and trying forever to force himself into everything, anywhere. But he's always on the outs, with everyone. I've known that forever, and you'll see all that soon enough. Or maybe you already have. He'll always find a way to be jealous and be a jerk about things, but it won't matter." He nodded at Sam seriously. "It won't matter, you understand? You won't have to be defending yourself all the time. With any of us. Got it?"

Sam was already speechless, but then Carl leaned in closer and said in a low voice something that astonished him completely.

"And so, also, don't ever bother trying to compensate for what he says or does. Especially not with me. For one, I don't care. And secondly, it doesn't matter. I'm not like him. And it's obvious to everyone you aren't like him, either."

It was a strange feeling that came over Sam, as though he had just stepped through a doorway into another world, and although he felt relief to find Carl showing he was aware of what might have been some of Sam's concerns, he just nodded carefully. Anyway.

Carl, still looking at Sam in that friendly but somewhat impenetrable fashion, now seemed to see something and he reached out and put his hand on Sam's shoulder.

"Just ignore him most of the time." He smiled. "I find that works the best. And you will, too."

Sam tried to make a smile of his own.

Dan, seeing them like that, came over and laid his hand on Sam's other shoulder. "Yeah," he said, raising his glass to everyone else in the room. "Here's to Marilyn. Fine, finer, finest."

Dan poured more champagne into Carl's glass and then raised the bottle and drank off what was left.

Carl looked at his glass, then at his brother, drank it off and—faster than anyone could have expected—hurled the glass across the room, smashing it to pieces against a steel coat rack.

The effect was perfect, total silence.

"Oh, shit," Carl's face went red. But Sam could see he wasn't embarrassed.

Dan looked at his brother. "Wow, man. Just... wow."

Someone working for the church stuck his head in the door. He saw the broken glass on the floor and the empty champagne bottles and the full one in Dan's hand.

"A little accident," Carl said tightly.

A thin whine came out of Dan's nose.

Someone else coughed.

The churchman looked at them for a moment longer and then withdrew, closing the door with a careful click.

Carl looked straight up at the ceiling. "Oh, fuck me." He looked at his brother. "Satisfied?"

"That was pretty good."

"OK," Carl said. "Enough of this. Let's get this on the road. Ben?"

One of the men went out the door and soon enough another man, a young minister, came in to get Carl and his men.

Dan walked off towards the back of the church and Sam looked for where he could stand somewhere along the wall under the columned and arched side aisles. He had barely found a spot when he was surprised to find Carl, out of nowhere, suddenly coming back to him.

"Hey," he said. "Could you do me a favor?"

"Sure."

"Soon as you can, at the reception, see if you can take Danny off somewhere." He leaned slightly in and raised his eyebrows. "OK?"

Sam looked straight at Carl. It was a clear request and the message behind it needed no elaboration. "I will."

"Thanks." Carl just nodded and walked back to the front of the church and in a little while the organ roared to life with the wedding march.

It went pretty fast from there on out with the minister speaking and then Carl and Marilyn saying the things, and then they were married, and Marilyn was a legal part of the Petersen clan and everyone emptied out of the church almost as fast as they had got in and they all went off to the reception to celebrate.

Chapter 27

HE stood with his back against the bar listening as people talked around him. Around and around. He said nothing because all of what they were talking about was about him.

"Lots of unused old houses are on the older homesteads," Sally was saying. "Like the one Carl and Marilyn will use. How about the old Jorgerson place? Such a beautiful old house. Three stories with that big porch going nearly all the way around, and that turret with those round rooms. You even rented it one time, I remember. Just needs to be swept out..."

"Oh, Ma," Dan said. "That old place is so dried up. And, anymore, the road up would need grading to be usable. Pre-fabs are easier to set up."

"All the pumps on those places work fine, Dan," Harley said. "Just need to get the electricity sorted out."

"In any case," Dan went on, "he needs to get out of that money sucking hotel. What a waste..."

"I like it," Sam said.

"Why don't you just sell him the Jorgerson house?" Sally was going on. "We never use that farmstead, and you yourself said we can't claim the old houses as farm buildings."

"We use the hay barn," Dan said.

"And he'll let us do that," Sally turned to Sam. "You'd let us do that, wouldn't you?"

"If I what?" Sam said.

"If you owned it."

Harley waved his hand. "Do you know how hard it was for Dad

to take in the Jorgerson farm?" Harley gave Sam a look. "People think we just snatch up old farms like this and that when they become available. But some of these places end up being a necessity. That place has one of the few wet coulees around here."

"You'd still have the land," Sally said. "I was talking about just the house and a few acres around it. Just like when you sold the old Miller house to Fred."

"Well, whatever. But even if he just lived there we'd have to take a look and see how the roof and floors are doing. And that old knob and post wiring..."

"It's just fine," Fred said. "If you don't touch it."

"But can it carry a load?"

"It can just fine. It's not like he's going to be running a welder in the kitchen."

"Always need a few more outlets."

"Knob and tube is fine," Fred insisted. "Unless you want to insulate, and if that's the case you might as well take the walls back to the studs and change everything."

"You do that," Dan said. "You might as well knock it down and put in a pre-fab. Or maybe just a double wide. Pour a slab and be done with it."

Even Carl, coming over with a few of his friends to get drinks and hearing the conversation, pitched in.

"I know where you can get a pretty good used pickup." He gave Sam a big, friendly pat on the shoulder. The second that day.

Sam looked at him.

Carl pursed his lips, but as he did so a glimmer of amusement came into his eyes as he realized he was now stepping into something the same way Sam had done with him before. "Just something to think about," he said, and moved away.

Sam listened to them talk about it until they were no longer talking about it and then, one by one, they had all drifted off elsewhere. He was only alone for a minute though before he saw Lonni walking towards him.

He took a breath.

"You been avoiding me?" she said.

"Yes."

"Why's that?"

"You look good in that. What is it? Your going-to-weddings dress?"

"I wear it to funerals, too, honey."

"Practical."

"Keeps me neutral. And actually," she looked around, "sometimes you can't tell one from the other."

"Now, now..."

"I ain't saying."

"Nobody has."

"But they make it seem they have."

Sam shook his head. "If anyone has, it's only from Gainesville. These people from over here don't seem to have what you're talking about."

"The anyone... you mean the Petersens."

"Some of them."

"Meaning Dan."

"Yes," Sam breathed out.

Lonni looked off at the crowd. She was drinking something green with ice cubes through a straw. Without looking at him she said, "Why'd you run out on me last night?"

"Run out? Last thing I remember you dragged Dan out to dance."

"Did you think I was going to take advantage of you and get you knocked up or something?"

"Getting that fixed up isn't cheap."

She laughed. "In my book, the father pays."

"So you say."

"I don't play that way."

"That's what I'm thinking. Anyway... it was drunk."

Lonni opened her mouth but before she could respond a couple of women came to the bar. One of them looked Sam up and down and gave Lonni a wink.

Lonni took his arm and pulled him. "For a guy who was too drunk, you were doing OK."

"Drunk is drunk."

She squeezed his arm and leaned towards him. "Well, if that's how you are drunk..."

Sam could not help himself from glancing off across the room.

"Oh, I see." She took her hand from his arm.

He frowned. "No," he said. "C'mon Lonni, don't do that to me."

The words were a complaint, but it came out more like an apology, which in a way it was, and Lonni's smile came back. She was simply irrepressible and Sam could not help but smile, himself.

"Oh?" She said. "So what are you doing after..."

"Hey!" Dan came out of nowhere. "What're you still doing, standing over here? Still haven't learned how to sit down?"

As usual, Dan's timing was awkward and for the second time that weekend Sam was fine with it. "Hey."

Dan grabbed a bottle of whiskey from behind the bar, the hired barman just watching. Dan was not yet staggering, but he was definitely flushed and well on his purposeful way. He gave Sam and Lonni another smile, and then winked at Sam.

"Or is it you've got yourself a date?"

Lonni squinted her eyes. "You're doing OK, it seems."

"Well, I wasn't the best man..." he grinned at her. "But then, that must make me the best brother." He put his arm around her waist. "So that entitles me to a kiss from all the pretty ladies."

She smiled, but when she opened her mouth to reply Dan covered it with his own, bending her back under his weight. When he finally let her up she gasped. "Oh God, Danny! You taste like every fucking whiskey barrel between here and Kentucky."

"Smooth as silk. And even smoother going down."

"So goes the rumor."

"I don't spread rumors."

"No. You start them."

Dan shrugged.

"Can't hurt to advertise."

"I'm guessing more bait and switch," Lonni said.

"Any time you'd like a proper demonstration, sweetheart..."

"I'll take your word for it."

"Never take a man's word. You women should know that by heart."

"What should we take?"

Dan laughed. "Start with the money. As always."

Lonni gave Sam a look. "There are things besides money."

Dan was far enough along in his whiskey to be focused more on his own sense of humor than anything else, but not so far as to miss the look Lonni gave Sam. He leaned towards Sam, whispering nearly as loud as his regular voice. "Like I told you, boy, you got no reason to play Mr. Perfect."

"Mr. Perfect?"

"Yeah, right?" Dan grinned. "That's what I told both of them. I told them you were far, far from that."

Sam's smile flattened out.

Dan took a drink and put his arm around Sam's shoulder. "As for money," he glanced at Lonni, giving her a sly grin, "it's a good thing you're not worried about that. And as for you," Dan gave Sam a pat on his shoulder, "you just need to... go... with... the... flow."

"I'll try to keep that in mind."

Dan was looking across the room with a small frown and his arm dropped from Sam's shoulder. "I'll be right back," he said. And he was gone.

Lonni watched him leave, biting her lower lip. "If he's still walking by midnight, I'll be surprised."

"He's pumped up."

"Why not? But I'd never have guessed he'd be so happy about it."

"That Carl and Marilyn got married?"

She let out a short laugh, as though he had just said something ironic. "Yeah," she said. "Nothing like payday, eh? I don't think even Danny planned how well this works out for him."

"Planned?"

"No, you're right. Planned isn't the right word. I don't think he's that smart. Expected or hoped, maybe. But I never guessed he was this mean."

"Dan's not mean."

Lonni's eyes rolled. "Yeah, whatever. I'm just saying I don't think he saw it. But he's making it all seem to go that way now."

"Making what?"

"Just what you think," Lonni's mouth twisted into a smile again. "Carl gets the door-prize and Danny gets the... something. And all just by not going around calling Marilyn the Whore from Coeur d'Alene."

Sam looked at Lonni with dismay. "I... aren't you her friend?"

"The problem for Danny was how to get away from what an ass he'd made of himself. Making his family—making the whole town for that matter—think he and Marilyn were a number, when in fact she never wanted anything to do with him. And good old Carl just comes along and picks up the pieces. And now Dan's just trying to figure out what to do with it. I'm guessing he doesn't know yet. But he'll figure something out sooner or later, or be trying something. Just you wait and see."

Sam felt glum. "The door prize." He was not quite sure what he was hearing being talked about, but remembering Ruth's conversation, and even things like a look on Sally's face, or Harley's, or even something in what Fred had said, he knew Lonni was right somehow. Dan would be figuring things.

Lonni nodded. "There's a lot of that going around. But it has...," a bubbly laugh began to shake her words, "...it has a bright side, you know."

Sam felt himself want to laugh as well. "I'm afraid to ask."

Her voice was nearly lost in a giggle. "The bright side is the... what do you call it?... moral superiority!" The last words came out in a near shriek causing a few people nearby to look over and grin at her.

Sam sort of laughed and looked around the reception. Near to them were a lot of Coeur d'Alene folks who all seemed to know each other but, as before, he saw Harley and Sally circulating among them—especially the older ones—as though he knew them all well. At the far end of the room Carl and Marilyn were surrounded by the men Sam had seen earlier, joined by a number of women.

"Those are all Marilyn's friends?"

"Oh no, some. Mostly the women."

"Carl's that well connected over here?"

"No, those are his college friends."

"College."

"When he was down in Pullman."

Sam could not think anyone had mentioned that. Or maybe they had. "At the university? What was he studying down there?"

"Baseball."

"I see," Sam smiled, but he was nevertheless impressed. "He played in that program..."

"Then... something, something. Marilyn told me he got drafted really early and then something happened and it ended. And he never went back."

"He got hurt."

"I don't know."

But Sam knew. He looked at Carl's friends and then realized what it was that made them all seem similar. Tall and broad-shouldered, all were fifteen years beyond university but also built in that strong, easy-flowing way baseball players carried most of their lives. And he noticed how those young men would also greet and talk to the older guests. Well-mannered and polite. And Sam, in one way surprised to see Carl had so many friends like that, in another way was not surprised at all.

Down at the far end of the hall, on a raised stage, Dan suddenly appeared carrying a drum and a cymbal. Behind him were a couple of other men, carrying other musical instruments. Evidently, Dan was in charge of setting up the band. He almost said something but Lonni broke into his thoughts.

"They do look happy, though."

He looked at her and saw that she had been looking at Carl and Marilyn as well.

He looked down at his empty glass. "You want another one?"

"A double."

"A double what?"

"A double whatever."

Sam went down the bar to talk to the bartender, trying to explain what he thought Lonni had been drinking, and when he returned he found Lonni talking politely to some women. He nodded at them, handing Lonni her drink and backing away, avoiding her eyes.

He wandered through the crowd, going past people without looking at them, and then suddenly spotted a couple of people coming in through a side door. The smoker's door. He went over to it and went out.

Outside, it was dark and quiet and the air was cool on his face. He breathed it in deeply.

Alongside the lodge building was a small park and he could see through the big trees Lake Coeur d'Alene, smooth and even darker than the night, house lights glimmering like stars fallen to earth along the far shoreline. He stared at the lake, almost succeeding in not thinking, when someone came out of the lodge behind him. He did not turn around although he knew if it was anyone it was going to be Lonni. And then the door-prize, or some damn thing, was suddenly standing next to him.

"What are you doing out here?" Marilyn asked.

"Giving the dogs some air."

"The way I saw you go out, I thought you were leaving."

"I must have an interesting way of going out doors. What did I look like? An escapee?"

"That. Or maybe a thief. Or maybe both."

He pulled his jacket open. "Check my pockets?"

"Don't have to." She shook her head. "There's no loot in there. I already looked."

Sam let his jacket fall closed.

"You see? How could I be a thief when there's nothing to steal?"

She nodded. "Maybe for you the loot's somewhere else." There was something in her eyes that told him it was no innocent remark, but when she saw she was not going to get a rise out of him she went on, "In any case, not much of a detective, am I? Or a thief, either."

"No, you're not. But I'll tell you what you are."

A hint of a smile. "What?"

"You're the Gem of Coeur d'Alene."

She continued to smile but then turned and looked out at the lake, her face calm, and she lifted her chin a little.

He looked at her and thought how beautiful she really was. She had always been that, of course, but now there was also something else, something that was different about her which made her seem more assured. As though she had nothing to prove. It wasn't an obvious thing, but just some form of tranquility in her eyes which made her, if anything, even more beautiful. But there was something sad, or if not sad, wistful.

"You know," her voice rose softly into the evening air, "I really felt like that once, Sam."

"I'm not joking."

"I know you aren't." She glanced at him. "You never do. That's one thing I know about you. That's one way you and Carl are alike."

"And one thing I know about you is that you're again a gem, regardless of how you've maybe felt."

"I could hope."

"You'll see."

"I like your optimism. I guess, then, that makes me the thing worth stealing."

"And Carl did."

"That's a nice thing to say, Sam."

"My wedding contribution. It's not much but you don't have to exchange it, either."

She looked at him and then stretched up to give him a kiss on the cheek. "You know something?"

"What?"

"You really are like Carl."

"I wouldn't say that. And even less after tonight."

"You don't get what I'm talking about."

Sam smiled. "You know something? All day today people have been telling me things about me. Don't you start."

"I'm not telling you anything. I was just saying you have the same thing Carl has, that's different from a lot of people. I was just going to say you're one of the few who are just who they are."

"That's not much of a feat."

"See? You wouldn't know." Marilyn smiled back. "And anyway, I've heard some of the talk. Don't be worried about being a topic of conversation. You'll get used to it. We all had to at one time or the other. Until you get figured out. And they mean well. They really do. Regardless of what it sounds like."

"They haven't figured me out?"

Marilyn laughed. "People who are who they are, are always the ones people have the hardest time with."

"I don't know if I'll get used to it."

"It'll go away. Time will take care of that."

"I'm not sure."

Marilyn leaned her head back. "I know what you're talking about. You think it just goes on forever. But it doesn't. It goes along, gets shaken up, then goes on along again. That's not what I was talking about. I was talking about... well... myself."

"I didn't mean that..."

Marilyn smiled. "Look. There are two different things here. I saw you talking with my best friend there, not too long ago. You imagine we don't talk?"

Sam shook his head.

She leaned towards him. "Just remember this. No matter what you might hear, this is all about Carl and me. Best friends, not so best friends, doesn't matter who... me and Carl are going to make sure what we have always stays that way."

"Good to hear."

"Believe it."

"I do."

Marilyn laughed. "Dangerous words."

"What?... Oh."

Marilyn gave him a thoughtful look suddenly. "You know, I remember when you first came to town, and I can even remember thinking how you were so easy-going. Soft spoken. And Lonnie said she'd rarely met anyone so easy to get along with right from the start.

251

How she trusted talking to you, and how easily people became your friend."

"She said that?"

"Everyone says that. Sally said nearly the same thing. You haven't noticed how everyone treats you like they've known you forever?"

"No."

"You're more in with people in this town than some people who've been here all their lives." She smiled. "You seem to have a knack. No wonder Dan's jealous."

Sam's mouth fell open, but before he could say anything Marilyn sighed. "Why is it I always get into these sorts of conversations with people at weddings. And this time my own."

Sam laughed, but then thought of something. "Speaking of your best friend, your other best friend, could I ask you something?"

"About Lonni?"

"Yeah."

Marilyn looked at him for a moment. "Sam, you've got nothing to worry about. She knows all about Ruth."

"Then... why?"

She looked out at the lake for a moment. "I don't know. I guess she figures that until there's a ring on it, she's got a chance."

Sam nodded. "You might mention it to her, that she should start to figure that. I mean, the first thing."

Marilyn grinned in surprise. "Already?"

Sam held up his hands, laughing. "No! No. Just... there isn't an atom of hope. Regardless. OK? So if there's any way to get that understood, without me losing her as a friend, too, I'd want that."

"As for that, I can't say."

"Then that'll be how it goes."

She nodded. "Right. OK, I've got to get back in before they've decided I've run away. And that reminds me of why I came chasing out here after you in the first place. I think Carl asked you something earlier?"

He had forgotten. "Yes, he did."

"Make it happen, please."

"I promised."

"Good. It starts tonight. We're going to start getting some air into things."

"Air?"

"Distance." She nodded. "Barriers." She turned to go but then stopped for a second and looked back at him.

"And maybe you should start, too."

"Me?"

But Marilyn had already turned to go back inside the lodge. Leaving him there in the dark.

He looked back out across the surface of the lake reflecting steadily those small house lights from the far, dark shore covered with heavy forest. From somewhere off down the lake he thought he could hear a small outboard motor, some late fisherman coming back from an evening's trolling, maybe, but other than that the air was still and the water was black and smooth, undisturbed by any movement except an occasional slow heaving as though the entire lake were taking a deep, sad breath. After a moment he was surprised to find himself blushing.

Maybe it had just been all the alcohol, him and Marilyn talking like that. Maybe just sodden sentimentalism. A ring on it, indeed.

He frowned hard and then looked down at his glass. A last drop. But as he was bringing it up to finish it off the movement extended out suddenly as though making a silent toast out to the lake. To Marilyn and Carl. Maybe. Or maybe to something else. And then he drank it off.

He did not want to go in, but he had promised. And he realized he was going to now have to go get Dan out of there.

And he was wondering about that when for the second time that night someone was suddenly there, a dark figure coming around the far corner of the building.

"Oh, hell," Dan said, seeing the door. "Not really good here, either." He walked over to a tree and straddled the grass in front of it. "Fuck it. Just like every other dog in town."

"Let's get out of here," Sam said.

"Yeah?" Dan said over his shoulder.

"Yeah."

Dan shrugged. "Roger that. Let's get out of this place and go somewhere better."

Sam smiled. "Good idea."

Dan began to walk towards the door to the lodge but Sam did not move. Dan looked at him.

"What?"

"I'm gone already."

"OK. I won't be long."

"You've got five minutes or you're finding another way."

Dan went inside and Sam went around the lodge to the lot and found his car. He stood by it in the dark until Dan finally came out. Dan was swinging a bottle by its neck. When he came closer he tossed it to Sam. A sealed bottle of whiskey.

Behind the wheel Sam started his car. "Where to?"

"Drive. I know just the place. A great place."

Chapter 28

THE great place was west of Coeur d'Alene, only a mile or so from the state line. Sam had come over to these state line bars a few times and did not like them but Dan said this place was as good as any they were going to find.

A big bar, built to handle all the nineteen- and twenty-year-olds coming over from Washington where the drinking age was twenty-one, its crowd nevertheless looked more like cowboys and cowgirls than what would have been seen at the other bars spread along the highway. Even the music was different. The college bars blasted away with various forms of rock-and-roll, where this one had a country-western band thumping away over a sea of bobbing hats on the dance floor.

A multitude of tables filled the space between the dance floor at one end and the neon lit bar at the other, but even after their eyes adjusted to the gloom it was impossible to see much in that mass of customers. Sam and Dan stood there for a moment, and then made their way through an aisle in the tables towards the back of the room where beneath the green glow of hanging lamps a line of eight or nine pool tables, separated from the rest of the bar by a series of wooden railings, were served by another long bar flowing along that wall. It was evidently a chosen destination for unattached men, although here and there a few women stood at the bar or played pool.

They went along the bar and found an open spot. Dan leaned his head over the bar and caught a barman's eye. Sam leaned against the bar and gazed back at the crowd.

"So, here we are."

Dan nodded. "Home sweet home."

"It'll do."

"It will. And best of all we won't be finding anyone from the wedding over here."

"Would it matter?"

Dan laughed. "You'd want to run into someone?"

"Don't start."

"About what?"

"Don't."

"Two shots of Canadian and two schooners," Dan told the bartender and then looked back. "You know something? Just sort of realized it." He squinted up his face. "But it's going to be fun watching how all this navigates from here on out."

"All what?"

"The whole shooting match. Carl and Marilyn, a few other people. And I think especially you."

"What do you mean, navigates out?"

"Get along. Get installed. Make a life out of things."

"How's that going to be all that interesting?"

"Transitions, man."

"I didn't know you were a student of human nature."

"It's what we do, isn't it? People? Watch each other all the time?"

"Actually, no. We don't. Or not all of us."

Dan made his mouth round. "Oh, I see. We're not into poking around, sticking our noses into other people's lives, are we?"

"I didn't say anything about you."

"Near enough."

Sam shoved a couple of bills across at the bartender, and picked up his shot glass. "Near enough, maybe." He held up the glass towards Dan. "Here's to your future amusement with all of us. Or to whatever the next chapter of the story turns out to be."

Dan picked up his glass. "To the next chapter."

"You do know you're as much a part of it as everyone else."

"You're schooling... me?"

"Not like you're thinking. You talk about observing and having thoughts. I'm just saying you can do that all you want, but remember the same thing can apply to you."

Dan made a slight nod. "I'm aware."

Sam inwardly shrugged, thinking, no, Dan, you are not. "Never mind. Let's just let go for a while. I've had enough of it, pretty much all day."

"So that's what's been bugging you."

"Nothing's bugging me."

"Yeah, right."

Sam frowned.

Dan raised his eyebrows. "Really? All day long you've been staring off into space, looking like... I don't know... someone's stolen your fucking car."

"Stuff happens. Like you say. Changes."

"Nothing that big."

"No? Seems like some things are changing or coming to a close. Even for you, if you don't mind me saying it."

"Nah. Not for me."

"See? That's what I mean."

"What?"

Sam had half a mind to go right into it. Say straight out how tired he was with, first, how Dan had to always have an opinion about everything. And second, the dishonesty he used to avoid seeming responsible. But what he had told Dan was the exact way he felt. He had had enough for one day.

"I thought we could get away from the talk."

"Drunk talk."

Whatever, Sam thought. "So ...?"

Dan looked at the tables. "Want to see if anyone wants to play some cutthroat?"

"I've been watching."

"Haven't seen any... guys?"

"You mean sharks? Not this time of night, I would think."

"With all these drunk hats? Easy pickings."

"I don't have that much on me anyway."

"I just don't like them."

"Me neither. And anyway, no, I haven't seen anything like that."

Sam watched in one direction and Dan the other and then Dan nudged Sam with his elbow and walked over to a table where he stuck a twenty-dollar bill under a cushion. He looked at the closest men. "Four man spots and stripes?"

Two men stepped forward, and after introductions, one of the men started racking the balls.

Sam found some chalk and started dressing the tip of a cue. "I can't afford to lose more than three games in a row," he said to Dan. "But if we win three in a row, we're leaving."

"For sure." Dan pulled out a quarter, got the nods, and flipped it up and down onto the green baize.

Sam and Dan played, and won and lost just enough to keep going, and because it was a social activity and they were still wearing their suits from the wedding, they found themselves the object of some teasing and it was mostly good natured and the drinking went along steadily for them and everyone around them, and once in a while someone brought out a bottle of something they had snuck into the bar. Here, a pint of whiskey, there gin, and once even some schnapps, which tasted terrible after the whiskey and beer, and it all became louder and more friendly there around the pool tables and there were even some women who had wandered over from the dance-band side, attracted by all the good-natured activity.

Gradually the pool tables became the loudest part of the bar, louder almost than the band sometimes. But still friendly and nobody could complain. There was nothing the band or the managers or the bouncers could do about the rowdy loudness since it was friendly. Everybody was just having a good time and if they got a little loud it was no sin. They could not kick anyone out for being loud and friendly on a Saturday night.

So on it went and it got louder and louder and as time went on some of the women began drifting out of there because of how loud and friendly everything was getting. That maybe it was getting a little too loud and friendly. But nobody who stayed seemed to mind... and then someone threw a punch.

If there had been fewer people or less noise or if everyone had known each other it might have been over quickly. But it was a big, loud crowd of random men in a bar where there wasn't much holding them together except noise and liquor and within the space of seconds the whole world fell apart.

The punch was thrown a couple of tables down from Sam and Dan, and the flailing that followed caused a sudden swirl, as though by gravity, bodies seeming to get pulled in that direction. Maybe some of the men thought they were trying to stop things, or break things up, or were just wanting to watch, but however it went it was too fast, too much like an attack, and other punches got thrown and soon enough it went bad because there were just too many men back there who felt there was only one way to deal with trying to either stay in one piece, or let others know how they felt.

Sam, trying to get around the corner of a table to where he thought he could get free, got pushed back by two pool players who were wrestling each other, trying to throw each other down or keep from being hit.

He ended up backing into another group with someone in the middle throwing his arm around in big, sloppy hooks, and the whole lot of them, Sam included, went tumbling.

Sam managed to crouch sideways and tried to squeeze his way out from under the weight but got pushed backwards. He tried throwing his other leg farther back to keep his balance but something blocked it and then something else caught him just behind both knees and he went down to the floor in a tangle of bodies and legs.

From where he landed, nearly under one of the pool tables, Sam could see if he did not move he was sure to get kicked in the head.

He made a violent effort to get out from under and he almost did but he came up into something else and an elbow just missed his face. Then another that he was able to block, pushing it to create some space so he could at least get to a wall and get something behind him. Then he got suckered.

Right behind the ear, it felt like he had been hit with a brick, and more than anything the idea that he had maybe been hit with something other than a hand made him lose his temper and he swung his right arm, putting all his weight and anger behind it, not caring where it landed.

He connected just below a cheekbone and a little on the mouth. A nasty place. Sam got immediately shoved into someone else, propelling him into others and then tripping and going down onto the floor again.

In that second, his anger cleared, and he found himself thinking how there seemed more than just a bar fight going on. Something more deliberate and hateful.

He moved forward, found a clearing and stood up, and taking a few steps, it seemed to him as though things to the right and left of him were suddenly slowing down, maybe the fight itself having run itself out. There seemed, at least, less fast movement. Some breathing room. Sam tried to spot Dan. And that was when the bouncers swarmed into it. Beefy ex-jocks, weightlifters or bikers, they came in from the dance bar side in a hard, offensive line, a dozen or more of them, and next thing Sam knew everything went from being a little better to much worse.

The bouncers grabbed anybody, throwing them as hard as they could against walls and across pool tables. They were obviously loving it way too much and Sam tried to get out of it but one of the players, swung around in a half circle, kicking his feet around frantically, threw around his fist and caught Sam on the head right behind his ear in the same place as he had been hit before. Sam did not even feel himself collapse before he blacked out.

He came to as whoever was holding him ran him fast out the door and threw him onto the gravel of the parking lot.

Sam wasn't the only one out there and someone next to him put a hand on his shoulder for support. Sam knocked the hand away and got to his feet.

It was black out there in the night, and beyond the big parking lot lights cars on the highway were streaking by bright and glaring. Sam walked into the cars, going across the lot like it was a heaving ocean. He finally got all the way through them and found, beyond the last line of cars, an expanse of dry, wild grass, and he went down onto the grass on his hands and knees, breathing slowly.

For a time it seemed like that grass was the whole world there below his face and beneath his knees. He saw his hands in it, and then his mouth began to salivate and his stomach went sick, and then he was sick and sick, and each time feeling like death's hell.

After a while his head began to go bad with pounding. Sometimes even a sharp pain that he did not like at all. Testing and wary, he stood up and leaned against a car, paying attention to the pain. For a few moments it went even worse but then, in holding himself stiff and upright, he felt the pain lessen. Relieved, he moved off carefully to find his car.

As he walked he was surprised to discover how much steadier he felt and, step by step, even more surprised by how easily he found his car.

He pulled open the driver's side door and sat down, his legs out the door. It was only after a full minute that he realized Dan was over on the passenger side, his door open as well.

"Shit."

Dan nodded. "Some days are bad. Others are worse."

Sam rested his elbows on his knees and stared at the ground. It looked far away but also very clear, as though he could see right through it. See right through all of it.

It was not good to have vision like that, he thought. So crystalline and perhaps even worse than the vision the swather accident had brought on. But if the clarity was awful it at least had the virtue of not lasting long. He straightened himself up and twisted around into the seat.

"Didn't I tell you it was a great place?" Dan said.

Sam took slow breaths.

"You all right?"

"Give me a minute." Sam listened to how his voice seemed like it was coming from somewhere else.

"You sound like you got hit."

"Good guess."

"Why'd you let that happen?"

Sam marveled at how many ways he could hate Dan's sense of humor.

Dan rocked his head, stretching his neck. "I'm getting tired. You coming out of it?"

"I'm just out of it, period."

"What do you want to do?"

"For starters, get the fuck away from this hellhole."

"I didn't mean that. Do you need someone to look at you or something?"

"No. I'm just a little out of it."

"Well, I'm a little drunk."

"What a surprise."

"OK, all right. I'll drive."

They switched sides and Dan got the car headed towards Spokane. Just over the state line they saw a dozen or more motorists stopped, the lightbars of state troopers spinning behind them.

"DUI city," Dan said. "All your lights work?"

"Just watch the speedometer."

They drove along in silence for a few miles and they only relaxed when Dan took the Dishman exit to drive into Spokane on the old highway. "How did you get it?" Dan asked once they were off the highway. His tone of voice was measured. Sam found himself liking that.

"I got it a couple of times out of nowhere."

"You're lucky you're not out cold."

"Maybe." Sam felt better to have some humor coming back.

"What a crazy place."

"I didn't see where it started."

"Some guy punched a guy in the face. I didn't see what led up to it. After that, you know, buddies..."

"How did you get out?"

"I backed to the other side of the railings. When the bouncers showed up I cleared out." Dan hesitated. "I didn't see you."

"I might've been on the floor. And then I got helped out."

Sam looked at how his hands were torn from the gravel. Dan glanced over.

"Where do they get those guys?" Dan said.

"Animals."

"Yeah. But I suppose it's one way to stop things fast."

"To hell with that," Sam spat out. "To hell with them. I mean... fuck... them."

Another mile went by and then Dan let out a laugh. "And so ends the marriage celebrations for Carl and Marilyn Petersen. Happy ever after."

Sam looked over. "Mind telling me something?" His voice was flat, but calm.

"Sure."

"Were you going to ask me if I wanted a full job out working for your family?"

Dan stared at the old highway.

Sam did not wait for him. "I was just wondering."

"Why?" Dan finally said. "Problem?"

Sam nodded. He could be easy too. "No. Just a question."

Another half mile or so passed. "Sort of sounds important."

Sam could see no matter what was said Dan was going to turn the question sideways. It was masterful gaslighting and Sam knew that only an outright quarrel would get a straight answer. He was too beat up for quarreling. "It could sound that way."

"Not if it isn't."

"It isn't."

It was only about a mile further when he heard it. Dan, talking under his breath, saying "I suppose I'll now have both you and Carl ganging up on me from here on out."

It was barely audible, but Sam was sure it was meant to be heard. And for once he wasn't going to let it pass. He did not know how far Dan would go with these sorts of things, but as Marilyn had said, there needed to be some lines drawn. "Is that what it's all been about for you, all this time?"

It was a direct question, but there was no response, and from there on into town, nothing was said.

In Spokane, Dan found an all-night place and Sam bought some aspirin, the cashier giving him a good look over. As Sam turned to go he saw his reflection in the glass door. His hair was all over the place, his suit dusty, and his tie askew. He frowned, pushed past the door and walked back to the car, patting the suit as he went.

"It's just got dust on it," Dan said. "Nothing's torn."

Back at the hotel they got their keys, the clerk handing Sam a note as well. He looked at it and only wondered how she knew he was staying there. He stuck it in his pocket.

Dan thumbed towards the cocktail lounge. "Last call's in an hour."

"I'm going to call it right now."

"See you in the morning." Dan walked towards the lounge.

Sam went over to the reception, and made an arrangement for Sunday, and then went towards the stairs.

Up in his room Sam stripped off his clothes and stepped into the shower, standing under the warm water until the day was gone out of him. Drying off, he worked the towel carefully around his head. There was a good-sized swelling behind his ear, sore, but the skin was not broken. He took four aspirins, pulled the heavy drapes shut, got into bed, and flicked off the light.

"Fucking hell," he said. Holding himself very still, he could almost say he was comfortable.

He knew he would have no problem sleeping once the pain went away. It only took three quarters of an hour for the aspirin to take hold.

Chapter 29

DAN'S car was long gone by the time he checked out of the hotel on Monday morning. His car was parked on the street right next to the hotel and he found another note, stuck under a windshield wiper. It was a follow-up to the one from Saturday night.

"Your buddy's helping me get my car back. Hope you're feeling better. Maybe I'll bring you some chicken soup!"

He looked around and then went and stuck it and the other note under the windshield wiper of a car parked behind his. A morning mystery for someone.

He had taken more aspirin on Sunday, sleeping the rest of the time, and his head was no longer hurting much, the swollen lump not as tender. Leaving Spokane there was almost no traffic except the occasional long-haul eighteen-wheeler and pickups.

With his window down the cool morning air blew in and for a long way he just let it go like that. But as time went by and the miles gathered under his tires he gradually became less numb and there was no doubt. At first he tried to tell himself he was just feeling sorry for himself. Making little things big. Or else it was just fatigue. Fatigue would be the best because all it would take was a good night's sleep. But as the highway wore on it all went away, leaving him feeling flattened with nothing but the unpromising panorama of the Palouse hills rolling past beneath a cloudless, breathless sky. The tire-scarred and stubbled flanks of the hills were blurred a dull yellow, or graying brown where harvest fields had been turned under. In the deeper draws, trees were still full-leafed but with a heavy, tired green, and the weeds beneath the trees had gone to seed and were burned to light browns and yellows by the sun. It was about noon, having felt hungry for almost an hour, when he saw the road sign for a town ahead. He did not know the place and could not see it from the highway, it being hidden somewhere up within the endlessly shifting hills. He took the town's off-ramp when it came along.

He followed the secondary road north for a ways and finally saw the town appear with its massing of trees and the inevitable grain elevators. He drove in, going past the sign that said Welcome to Carlington.

The town consisted of one main street with some side streets where the houses hid beneath the trees. Carlington looked little different from any other farming town—humorless and static, with solidly built frame houses, a few of the nicer old ones with gables and wide porches, beneath old, overgrown chestnuts. Two big grain elevators towered at one end of town and at the other the white steeple of a church punctured the sky. He drove along the main street, found the restaurant and angled his car up in front of it.

A small café, it advertised its specialty, homemade pies, on its window. As he walked in he saw a couple of employment notices, one for farm labor, the other for a mechanic, taped in the window. Inside was a long counter with round, swiveling seats, and along the wall were small booths. A few men were drinking coffee at the counter and he took a seat a few seats down from them. The waitress came down, youngish, small and trim, and gave him a cheerful smile.

"Could I get a club sandwich?"

"Sure," she said. "And coffee?"

"Yep."

The café was fairly quiet and pleasant and as he drank his coffee and waited for his order he found he was back on the road again, spending all his time trying to figure out what he was heading for.

The problem was, if it all seemed so much like the eleventh hour of something and he was neither ready for it nor even sure he really wanted what was happening, he knew it was no one's fault but his own. Whatever his hopes or plans might have consisted of, he realized none of those people in Gainesville could be blamed for not knowing any of that, and for two simple reasons. He had barely known himself.

Had he ever had plans?

Maybe something vague, but in any case, even if there had been hopes or plans now it was too late. He had let it all go too long, only focusing on his discontents, without thinking about what could actually happen if he was treated differently. In a way, he thought, he had been acting just as petulant as Dan. Except with one variation. Dan was exactly where he felt he should be.

But if Sam could admit he had never really thought about what he wanted, he suddenly knew with certainty what he did not want.

And it was not about whether Gainesville was a good or bad place. He had been worse places. The problem was that the more he had let himself drift into the way things were, with no effort to establish a feeling of being his own judge of what he should do, the less he felt he existed. As though he had thrown whatever it was he was, completely away.

The whole week and the whole weekend he had practiced being nothing. It had been like letting go and letting someone else drive. And it was not a good feeling.

He was staring at his coffee cup when the waitress appeared with his lunch.

"Get you anything else?"

"Just keep the coffee coming."

"You're easy to please."

"Some days. I guess."

The waitress gave him a smile. "You don't sound like you believe it."

Sam saw one of the older men down the counter look over at him and wink.

"It isn't that sort of day," he said to her.

The smile slightly drifted from the waitress's face. "Oh, do I ever know what you mean."

Sam nodded.

She pursed her lips, and then something came across her eyes.

"Want the newspaper?" A sly sort of smile crossed her face. "The want ads?"

Seeing the look on his face, she laughed out loud. "Boy," she said, "did I get that wrong...!"

Sam smiled. "Actually, you're not far off."

She went down the counter and reached for a newspaper stuck next to the coffee machine. As she did so, she glanced at the two old men.

"What're you looking at?" They both grinned and she shrugged at them. She brought the paper back to Sam.

Sam unfolded it on the counter. The paper covered the doings in half a dozen towns very nearly over to where Gainesville sat on the other side of the county line. School news, town councils, utilities, merchants' associations, and some countywide stories. There were also miscellaneous news items and a feature story the editor had worked up about a farmer starting up his own bank. There were a lot of stories that looked like they had been written by agencies, the fish and game department, the forestry department, and things being done by the agriculture department down at WSU. Sam guessed that was how this little weekly paper managed to fill its pages from one week to the next. He knew Gainesville was included in a paper like this one, printed in Harrington, but he had never actually read it.

Having flicked through the pages, he did take a look at the jobs page. There were office and housekeeping jobs, journeyman carpenter or plumbing positions, something at the hardware store, and a half a dozen notices for farm or ranch work.

"Since when do farmers advertise?" he said to himself. It wasn't meant for anyone to hear but the closest man to him, heavyset and with thick white hair combed back in a style forty years gone, turned.

"We don't. If you're seeing something in there it means it's something you don't want. And, anyway, those are from way the hell over by the line."

"Towns that don't even have a restaurant," said the other, an equally heavy old man with thick glasses magnifying frank blue eyes. "Let alone a seed and feed store."

"I'd think it'd be all the same."

"Pretty much," said the first. "But they don't get people coming through over there. Not like us."

"Not like you." Sam nodded. "You don't advertise for help."

"Never had to. Just put up a card around town, and they find us. Even Judy has a board." He turned to look at the waitress and wheezed out a low, rumbling laugh. "You going to tell him about that, too?"

"I figured he'd find it," she said. "If he wanted to."

Sam saw her give him a sideways glance and it was just long enough to cause him to reflect on how she was a good-looking woman. And although she had a clever eye, he could also see a well of genuine likeability. And she seemed to be looking back at him with something that looked like the same sort of thoughts. But whatever they were, he didn't want to know. He just didn't want to know anything, anymore. He looked back at the first man.

"I wouldn't have thought there was all that much work."

"There's always work and plenty of it, but depending on the time of year. Right now, we're all sewed up. No need for hands now that everything's in. Not until spring. My name's Bill, by the way. Don't like much talking to someone without knowing their name."

"I'm Sam."

"And he's Don, and that's Judy over there, giving us that look of hers."

"What look's that?" she said.

"Like you're about to give us what's for."

"And you would deserve it."

Bill looked back at Sam. "Anyway, we're all done here."

"Then why, over there towards the west, are they still looking to hire?"

"The usual turnover. Like Don said, the towns out there don't have much to offer. Not like here." He looked over at Judy and winked at her the same way, earlier, he had winked at Sam.

Judy rolled her eyes.

"Just putting in a word for you, hon," he grinned at her.

"I'll do that myself, thank you. If I feel like it."

Bill looked back at Sam. "It's that feisty temper she's got, does her in."

"As it does us all," Sam said. "But... I'm guessing those aren't permanent jobs."

"Nobody hires permanent anymore," Don said. "I haven't had to do that in ten years. Fifteen?"

"Fifteen," Bill said. "Hell, maybe twenty."

"Permanent hired hands," Sam said. "They exist."

"There's a few, but most of them are older than us even."

"Nobody needs to hire permanent hands anymore."

"Buyer's market. What with Mexicans coming north and the general flux, there are always fellas showing up."

"And anyone can learn to drive a tractor. Or even a harvester."

"But in the winter?"

"Everything's pretty much planted. Don't need to do much but just go over the equipment. And we don't do any ranching around here. Farther west, they have those scablands, so they can grow hay and run cattle."

"Sewed up."

"Like the man said," Don said. "Farms here go deep and everyone knows their business."

"How many generations?"

"Mine goes back to the 1870s."

"About that, too," Don said.

"Nothing much shifts around."

"You mean newcomers?" Bill shook his head. "There's none of that. Everything's been settled for a century." He looked at Don. "I can't even think of a place getting sold to a newcomer."

Don looked at Sam.

"Hope you're not a newcomer."

"Oh, no."

Bill laughed. "Could you imagine someone coming in now to buy up farmland and start farming? First of all you'd have to be as rich as all get out. And rich people, they ain't interested in work."

"You looking for work?" Don said.

Bill nudged him with his elbow. "Judy thinks so, I'm thinking."

Arranging plates and glasses, she turned to give him a warning look. "Bill..."

"He ain't no newcomer," said Don, who nodded at Sam. "You ain't no newcomer."

"Well, I'm not rich."

Bill let out a laugh. "Well, we are."

"On paper, we are," Don said. "But we're too dumb to know what to do with it so we just keep rolling it over." He looked at Bill. "So don't you go on bragging. I think Sam here, he doesn't have to be told."

"It's funny how everything's all sewed up, though," Sam said. "I never really thought about it much. But it's true."

"True enough. But, to be honest, pretty much all was taken up by the first people in. Got those big land grants and from there on out it was just family and on down. The only thing is that when it does run out, it doesn't get bought up separate, but gets folded into the neighbors, them buying up each other. Hasn't been a new outfit started up since..."

"Since after the war," nodded Don. "Not out here, anyways. But, want to hear something interesting? Like I was telling Bill earlier before you came in, my grandson, he was telling us about how he'd gone out fishing over on the other side, gone out there to the San Juans, at the resort out there, and he drove around the island just to see it. Said he had no idea there were farms out there. I wouldn't have thought so, myself."

"Islands?" Sam said. He did not know much about the state, west of the mountains.

The first old man nodded. "Never heard of them? San Juans? Big islands between us and Canada."

"Vancouver Island?"

"No, that's so big it's more like the mainland. These are filler islands, in between. And the thing about them, Johnny was telling us, is that they've got some sort of, what they call a, microclimate, and the thing is..."

"They can grow just about any damn thing," Bill said. "Seems they grow anything from oats and wheat... to strawberries."

271

"And the thing is," Don went on, frowning at Bill for interrupting him, "they're offering cheap land to anyone who wants to start up something. And Johnny, he was surprised, and even went around the town hall over there. The main island." He looked at Bill. "You know the one, with the resort John Wayne went to, to go fishing with all his pals."

"How the hell would I know about that?"

"Well, he did."

"Sounds like he was serious," Sam said. "Your grandson, I mean."

"No, no," said Don. "He was just curious. He's always interested in everything. Says you've always got to be aware of what's going on."

"And he's right," Bill nodded.

"Anyway," Don went on, "And that's all. But it was interesting. But, not for us, of course. We were just talking. Interesting, like Johnny said, to know there were still opportunities. We wouldn't. Fellas from this side of the mountains, you know... we don't...," he waved his hand, "that side... all those Seattle folk, and the Canadians... boats and stuff..." Don shook his head and made a face.

Sam grinned.

He had long since figured out there was more separating eastern Washington from the western side, than just the Cascade Mountains. "Yeah, but to have his own farm."

"He'll have his own farm, if he wants it."

"You were saying the land was going cheap over there?"

"You wouldn't believe it. He said as little as a couple, three thousand, could get a down payment."

"That's nothing."

"Nothing at all. But people don't think it's farming, an island and all. That's why it's what it is. I guess."

"Sure," Bill said, turning to Don. "But it's not just the farming, you know. But who you do it with..."

Bill looked over at Judy again, and then turned to give Sam a ragged grin.

Sam immediately looked down at the paper, turning the pages

over to the back, and when he looked up again Judy had gone back into the kitchen.

He nodded at Bill and Don, pulled out his wallet and covered the payment with a more than decent tip, and stood and walked out and then down the main street's sidewalk in the bright sunlight until he reached the main cross street. Standing there a moment, looking up and down Main, he tried to fall into the mood for getting back on the road again. But it was difficult. Carlington was quiet and peaceful and it was like being on another planet.

On the other side of the street was a small bar. He suddenly thought he could stand a drink. It was Sunday after all, he had nowhere he really had to be, and he found it appealing to waste a little time in a place he had never been in and would probably never see again. He walked across to it and went inside.

Sam drank his beer in the cool darkness, letting the day slip along, and felt how good it was to be somewhere where there was no one he had to talk to, no one to tell him anything, no one to tell him to sit or stand, or especially tell him of the things he could not know but would, eventually and inevitably.

He glanced out the window at Carlington's main street.

Just as easily there, he thought. It could just as easily have been there. If he had been an hour earlier out of Montana. Or his gas tank a bit lower. Any number of reasons. And maybe he would have ended up exactly the same, outside of how there might have been no one in Carlington who would tell him one damn thing beyond what he needed to know, or knew already.

All that time gone by, he was thinking. All that time running from place to place and it always turned out the same. In the same place.

Nowhere.

Except this time, he had really put his foot in it.

It was a lot easier to not think about the Petersens but he could not get around Ruth.

No matter how clearly he was beginning to see things, Ruth made it impossible to keep things separated. He knew that staying in Gainesville was going to change him, and not in any way he would ever have wanted, no matter what he had. He would change.

She had to know that, too. No matter all the things that had gone before, his coming and going, her doubts and frustrations, they had always been, when they had managed to be together, that thing they had been at the very start. With nothing else attached.

She had never really meant Gainesville to him before. But all weekend, all morning, that had been growing inside of him and it was as real and as unyielding as the Palouse Hills folding in around him like an infinite sheet, entangling and wrapping him as though a shroud, a clinging, suffocating tissue of time and place from which nothing, and certainly not a man who did not know much else of what he wanted, could escape.

Going back over it, and then going back even farther, he started unreeling the miles. First Gainesville went away, and then Bozeman before that, and then Montana, and before and before, Kansas and Missouri, out to California and back, and Colorado, but then so much farther south, and it seemed to him as though the whole country was just like that. All of it different and every bit of it exactly the same, with him unconnected, moving in it but never in it.

It was true he had never tried. Never thought about it. Thought about what it could be. But even if he had not done so, he had always thought he had the option. To make a choice and move into something so easily, so effortlessly, as in any old dream.

A warming morning, a blue sky, and high above white clouds would be tumbling in from the Pacific.

Out from the mainland, the ferry went smooth and fast over the dark water, the sluicing froth of its wake the only thing to disturb the flat surface of the strait.

Sailboats sat here and there and far away on the calm inland sea. With barely any wind at all, there was no ambition to be sailing, everyone just drifting on the tide with only an occasional flap from the sails to announce the presence of any breeze at all, any impetus, but never enough to think about, let alone to try to harness. Most of the sailboats would be small, but once in a while a very big one, with all that white sail hanging from its masts, looking like it could sail away forever if only it had just the smallest whisper of wind to provide an inclination.

Everywhere else, close to the north, farther away to the south, and directly ahead, would be the islands.

Some were small, just big enough for one house, or some not even that and just a place for seals to congregate. Some were larger with a few houses along the beaches or up on the hillsides hiding among the dark trees. As the ferry went among them, their steep sides black with forest, they moved past like a crowd jostling. Following the ferry as it rushed along, seagulls would spin in and away. Out on the calm water, groups of them would sometimes be floating together, forming islands of their own. White and squawking, busily doing nothing, they would ride along unconscious of the blackness below and unperturbed by the ferry.

For a while it would all be the same with the ferry gliding across the glassy surface, the water reflecting the clouded sky and the islands and the sailboats moving slowly. Then there would suddenly be more boats and the ferry went into the big channel winding between the larger islands until approaching the big one at the far western end of the archipelago. The big island's dark, hummocked hills became a forest of tall trees as the ferry edged closer, and there were steep banks and rock cliffs. Houses began to be seen and a few of them had stairs down to small docks on the water where boats and small sailboats were moored.

The ferry slowed and then allowed itself to nudge heavy up against the massed pilings of the dock, and the ramp went down and the air went suddenly hot as the breeze of the ferry's run was forgotten.

For a moment there would be the sound of cars starting up, and the smell of pent-up exhaust, and then would come the movement and escape out across the ramp and up into the town that clung there to the hillside above the harbor.

Up through the town then and then out into the interior, the island a series of hills and valleys broken with small farms and wooded hills.

The forests were mainly dark evergreens but, it being almost autumn, in that darkness of firs, spruce and hemlock was the occasional blaze of color as an isolated hardwood, a maple or oak turning red or gold, revealed itself. For a while it would be as though it were the mainland, going along that road out of sight of the water. But then the road would rise up onto the northern ridge where the sky fell down across the distant hills, and far away would be the other islands, dark in the sunshine like old whales sleeping.

The further south the road went, where the salt winds were strong and only grass could grow, a gravel road led down to the beach and then became nothing but a track bumping around hillocks and dunes until it went no farther.

At that place were big rocks where below was the roar of the surf, crashing and shimmering as the waves came in and then ran away.

Only some blankets and an old sleeping bag, but it would be warm and the ground would be smooth and somehow even soft. The breeze at the south end of the island was strong with the smell of the sea and, listening, after a while the sound of the water would go to a murmur in the blackness of the night and then it would go to nothing. And there they'd be.

But maybe not. It could go either way, or maybe completely some other way. In any case, there was no getting around the other thing.

It turned out he had been wrong, worrying about things that did not exist. But now he had something real he would have to be dealing with. And evidently forever. And even though everyone felt he would do just fine, there was just one problem.

He was the one who would have to live with it.

Chapter 30

WHEN he finished, she would not say anything for a long time. So long, in fact, he would begin to think she would never speak to him again. So long he began to almost hope she wouldn't. But then she would.

"So that's it?"

"Yeah."

"And your solution is to leave."

"I wouldn't call it a... solution."

"How do you know you can't stay?"

"I can't find a way to pretend anymore."

To his eyes it seemed she wanted to say several different things. Different emotions crossed her face, some questioning, some unsure, some angry.

"You don't look happy to me. I'd have thought it would have been a relief to have finally figured it out."

"How can I be?"

"This has been your problem all along."

People say it is always best to be prepared for the worst, he was thinking, but they never actually expect the worst. So when the worst happens, being prepared does not help at all.

"Which was...?"

"You've never let yourself be a part of it. And I'm pretty sure that isn't just the case for here."

It was true. Not nearly the truth or basically the truth, it was the full thing. But there had been a difference.

She saw his face and thought he was disagreeing. "It's true,

Sam. But the real problem is that you think that you're the only one who feels you're the odd man out."

Loaded down with a lot of things, he did not feel like adding other, more personal failures into the mix.

"Aren't I?"

"In a way. But you come at it thinking that everyone else automatically feels the opposite way."

"You feel differently than I do."

"You're right. And... think about what that means, Sam." She took a breath. "Think about it."

He did not understand her. He wanted to, but she seemed to be talking about something completely different.

"So, what do you think I should do?"

She did not even blink. "If you don't know yourself, there's nothing anyone can say that will mean anything."

"You don't care?"

"Didn't say that. I'm saying it was always up to you."

He did not have a response to that. There had been other times when he had also not known what to say, and he would find himself going silent not so much because he could not find something to say, but because he was hoping the silence would resolve everything.

Even though he knew it never did.

And he would see how she was looking at him, and how she was not saying anything now. She was letting him be the one to say something, if anything was to be said. But he could also see that she was no longer waiting.

Chapter 31

HE could not imagine it any other way, and just the thought of it made him frown with pain. But with that thought he also suddenly realized where he was, seeing the counter in front of him come into focus. He looked up and around at the bar, wondering how long he had been off in a fog like that.

His movement caught the attention of the barman but he shook his head and then checked his watch. It had not been as long as all that but it was enough.

He left the bar, retrieved his car, and drove out of Carlington to the freeway.

High up in the west clouds had come up. That suited him fine. He was tired of the heat and the dryness and the sameness of the sun every day. Maybe it would rain like hell for a week, he thought, and everything would go to mud and be completely impossible. That would be one solution to the immediate problem of going to work or not. He reached behind his ear, feeling the throbbing tenderness there. A lot could change in a week.

Something mindless began on the radio and he flicked it off. The miles swept beneath him, the fields going endlessly past on either side, and all the time the clouds built higher and higher into the sky with some darkness forming under the ones farthest off in the direction of the Cascades, and the day was very hot and the air coming through his window smelled of dust, dirt and straw.

It came at him continually. Scenes big or little and all of it was bad and in all of it she was there. Sometimes hurt, sometimes indifferent. But mostly just looking at him. It was those eyes. And it was like that for mile after mile and no matter which way it went there was only the one thing that never changed.

He almost missed the exit to Gainesville. When he got down to the main road into town, that stretch of the old highway, he drove slowly in, looking at the places. The burger shack, the gas station, the feed and seed store and implement store, then down Main Street past the restaurant and the bars, not many cars in front of Bob's, or The Hearth, and then all the way down towards the church and the grain elevators, where he turned the car around and came to a stop next to where the residential streets began at that end of town. He parked there under a heavy elm tree and shut off his motor.

As the motor ticked quietly he gazed back up Main Street, watching a few cars and pickups moving around up there but no one out walking on the sidewalks in that heat. And as he watched, fatigue came over him and he could feel that if he sat there much longer he would just fall asleep. Dead tired. Both physically and ...

He knew he was just one of the last of that movement of people, of that way things had once been—and not so long before as all that—where a man felt he could get things right just by going somewhere else. But there was no somewhere else anymore. That was the difference. The moving around, it was true, had made him feel alone and sometimes even lonely. But nothing made him feel more alone now than knowing there was no somewhere else.

Driving towards the center of town, and it looked completely different. Jarring colors. Busy and bustling.

It was like driving past shadows. An orange pickup went past the other way. There was a grin inside and Sam waved at it. Farther along at a corner there were a pair of overalls and he waved at them, too. Driving on, he suddenly saw the first recognizable thing. Dan's pickup, parked in front of Bob's. He looked at the other cars and trucks there and he knew almost to a man who was in the tavern. Pete. Carl. Which was strange, but he did not want to know about any of that. He drove to the hotel and parked his car in back.

He was going up the steps into the lobby, then up the stairs. Then down the hallway on the thick carpet that was not so thick anymore, in fact so threadbare that if someone were listening they might have heard footsteps on it.

Before he got to the door Ruth flung it open and stuck her head out.

Sam spread his arms. "Honey, I'm home."

She laughed and came flying out at him, jumping on him, and they both went falling down to the floor.

His head pounded and he could feel the heavy fatigue of the road in his limbs but neither of those could compete with how it felt to have contact with her again.

She had him pinned to the ground and she was laughing so hard at what she had accomplished that she could not speak. It got him laughing too, and they lay there, the laughter shaking their bodies uncontrollably, letting themselves go into it almost as though making love. Finally though, the wave passed, and they calmed to breathless resting, punctuated by an occasional weary laugh. It seemed strange, how hard they laughed. Almost as though it was not really laughter but more like the release of something almost fearful.

"Well," he said, "it's good to see you, too."

Her face, buried into his neck, rubbed against his throat.

"I've been going nuts around here this weekend."

"Hmm," his hands moved upon her back and shoulders in an absent-minded way. "What would that be like?"

She bounced on him.

"I've spent most of my weekend thinking of what was going on over there."

"Ouch," he said. "Me, too."

"What?"

He laughed.

"Don't do that," she said. "Go all cryptic on me right now."

"Cryptic?"

"Yeah, all mysterious."

"Me?"

She smiled. "The world champion." She bounced again and he wanted to laugh but in doing so he bumped his head on the sore place and he frowned.

She saw his face. "What's the matter?"

"Someone bumped my head."

"Oh, no! Not your head!"

"I've even got a lump."

She made a sympathetic giggle.

"Let me feel."

He turned his head. When she touched the swelling she laughed. "Now I know I should have been there."

"Not funny," he grimaced.

"I thought you'd be here earlier," she said. "Dan's been by already."

"I got hung up."

Her hand went down onto his shoulder and her other came up, and she held him. He did not move, letting himself be held like that, feeling her beneath him. But finally, he sighed, and got himself to his feet and pulled her up and with him into the room. It was when he closed the door that he felt the awkward thing finally come, beginning to happen.

"Ooh, boy," he sighed.

His voice sounded strange to him. She came up against him and slipped her arms around his waist, staring into his eyes. He picked her up and carried her to the bed, lowering her onto it. He lay down beside her, but neither spoke nor looked at her.

"What's this?" she asked after a while. "Was it all that bad?"

"You couldn't imagine."

"Don't bet on it," she laughed, but when he did not say anything she went quiet. She began to also see it, or something at least.

"What, Sam?" she finally said.

He could not imagine how to begin.

"What?" she said again. "Something that's going to be really as bad as all that?"

He knew of one thing that she might be thinking, and as though he might be answering that he said, flatly, "No."

He looked at how beautiful she was.

"But also yes. I mean, you know I'm in love with you."

"Yes." She smiled, but her voice was suddenly strained. "How terrible."

"It is for you."

"I suppose you're now going to try to tell me you love me too much."

"Worse."

He saw she was now just going to wait him out, so he went right to the end of it.

"What it is," he said, "is that if I lost you I think I'd die."

For a moment neither one of them spoke. She was looking directly at him now but there was nothing soft in her eyes anymore.

He had spent most of the morning imagining her look at him in any number of ways but none of them in the way she was looking at him right there, and he was filled with dread.

He closed his eyes for a moment, avoiding hers, as though to escape to somewhere he could be alone. But he knew that would be it, and it would be the final time he would ever be able to be alone inside himself like that, and outside of everything else. At last he opened his eyes and looked at her, thinking: why did she have to be the most beautiful thing he had ever seen.

Her voice came, a soft whisper.

"What are you trying to tell me, Sam?"

And there he felt it go, all the miles and miles of it, and the pain in his head came back, a soft rapping that got increasingly harder, and harder, until it began to pound insistently. Pounding and knocking.

"I'm trying to tell you I feel I'm dying right now."

Chapter 32

THE knuckles were rapping hard against his door and he opened his eyes and looked up at a burly middle-aged man carrying a grocery sack.

"If you're drunk you better get your ass out of here before Harry finds you."

Sam squinted. "Who?"

"Harry," the man said. "Harry Sloan."

Sam shook his head.

"The chief of police, who happens...," the man pointed his thumb down the street, "to live in that house over there."

Sam pulled himself upright. "I was just tired from driving."

"Maybe. But if you don't want to answer questions and take a breathalyzer you should find some other place."

It wasn't a threat, and Sam nodded at the man, started his car, and drove back down to the business district. He stopped for a few minutes to cash his check, putting the thick pads of large bills into his two front pockets. He then drove straight to the hotel.

He did not know how long he had been asleep but where everything had been sunny and hot, the light had changed. Overhead there were now dark, heavy clouds and a wind had sprung up bringing the iron smell of rain.

Stepping onto his floor's landing at the hotel he could see his door at the end of the hall was open and he could feel a slight breeze and knew she had the balcony door open as well to air things out. He had told her he would be back Sunday, but she had evidently decided to stay overnight until he finally came back. She already had a smile on her face as he came into view, but she did not get up because she was sewing something and had everything in her lap.

"Finally," she said. "Seems you're the last one back. Sue called yesterday and told me you and Dan had a rough night. Dan, like you, only got back this morning."

Sam could only stare for a moment but not because he was tired or did not want to talk about the weekend, but for what he was looking at.

Next to the bed stood two suitcases, one of which he had never seen. And next to them were his fishing poles, his boots and hats, and a full cardboard box.

She made a last stitch and stood up, holding up a pair of his jeans, and he saw she had sewed back in place a belt loop he had torn out during harvest.

She folded them and put them into the box.

"There," she said, and turned to him.

"What...," he opened his mouth.

"Don't." She stopped him. "The last three days I've thought about this in so many ways, but in the end just realized... it has to be now. This is the time."

"The time..."

She came up to him and put her arms around his waist. "My biggest worry was that you would just keep going and I would have had to chase you down."

"I wouldn't have done that."

"No, I don't suppose you would have left your boots behind."

Sam looked at Ruth as though he had never seen her before and she stood there, letting him do that. And then she walked up to him and gave him a kiss, and turned to grab her suitcase and his fishing poles.

"I don't want to stay around here one minute more than you do. But if we don't get moving..."

For maybe five seconds, ten, Sam could only look at her, look at the room, incomprehension slowly giving way to understanding in the same tingling way feelings returned to a numb limb. And then he picked up the box, and his boots and suitcase and they headed down, silently, neither of them able to speak to the other as turmoil and a growing sense of wonder at what they were doing washed over them.

But Sam also knew he had to say it, just to be sure. "They finally offered me a full-time job, you should know."

"And you accepted, of course."

"I did."

She looked at him. "And... was it for me, or for you?"

"Pretty sure it was both."

"And you feel good about it?"

"Felt."

She nodded, and he saw that it was enough.

Down at the car, he set the things down on the grass and went in to pay off his bill. When he came back out he saw she had everything in the car. He looked around.

"Where's your car?" Even to himself, his voice sounded thick.

"It's now Sue's. She dropped me off."

All he could think was how beautiful she was. And then he looked up at the hotel and the balcony on top where he could see the deskman setting the chairs back against the wall. The deskman turned to go in the door but then stopped for a second and looked down at Sam and gave him the only actual look of interest he had ever seen, and then something even more extraordinary. A smile and a wave.

"See you around, Sam," he said.

Sam smiled back and shrugged. "You never know, Merle."

He turned to look at Ruth. Then held out his keys to her. "Better that it's you."

When she had got settled behind the wheel she looked over at him.

"East? West?"

"Already been east."

Neither of them said anything as she drove them out of the downtown then past the farm and implement stores to the connecting road, drove through the underpass, and then swung onto the on-ramp up to the highway.

It was a few miles before she looked over at him and smiled.

He looked over at her appreciatively. "You were pretty sure of yourself..."

She looked back at the road. "I am now."

He nodded, and saw how her eyes sparkled in the last of the sun, her opal throwing turquoise and blue flashes.

"All the same," Ruth said after a moment. "Any ideas?"

"Maybe," Sam said. "But that's a whole other conversation."

"Oh boy!" She laughed. "A conversation!"

She glanced at him, and saw a large smile come over his face.

As the old, maroon-colored car disappeared far down the freeway towards the west, the big clouds continued to float in, thicker and darker across the endless succession of Palouse hills, their deep shadows interspersed with where the sun still burned down bright. And far and wide the shadows became thick and smirched as rainstorms gathered and fell across the parched, yellow hills. Summer had reached its end, and trees were heavy and dark in the unfarmed valleys and here and there could be seen a tractor, chopping and discing stubble back into the earth, the land having given up its bounty for the year, its surface now being tended to let rest. Every so often a hawk, a thick red-tail or a lanky Cooper's, could be seen wheeling above the tractors, or just watching with erect attention from a wooden post along the field, and pheasant and quail moved cautiously into the fields, gleaning whatever grain got left behind, with one eye for the ground and the other for the hawks or the tractor. And other than for those few obstinately industrious farmers tempting their fate with the weather, the land had become quiet, and Nature had returned to reclaim her leased domain.

Deep back in the hills, on a rock outcropping beside a long hay field, a mama coyote nuzzled along in search of mice beside a tired old barn, now empty and unused and half falling down. Behind her two pups followed, nosing and nudging each other. At one point she got interested in a hole and began digging at it, ignoring how her pups were now engaged in a tug of war with an old piece of faded, green cloth they had found, pulling and yanking each other around with growls and feigned indignation. But then a jagged streak of lightning rent the air, its thunder exploding upon them, and sent all three of them, thick tails flowing low behind them, back into the shrubs and trees of a rocky, scabland hillock where they, along with the other natural small residents of the Palouse, the marmots, rabbits and squirrels, the rattlesnakes, raccoons and skunks, made their homes. It was only by sheer luck they dove back into the opening of their den before a fury of thick rain came pelting and hammering down.

As the rain now fell outside in a sustained drumming, one of the cubs was paying no attention, chewing with concentration on the green cloth, her triumphant prize. Her sibling glanced over for a second but she glared back at him and, with a sniff, he went back to looking up at the opening to the den where the relentless waves of the downpour blew past. And with that she stretched out even further on her belly and returned to chewing in earnest, letting out the occasional happy grunt.

ABOUT THE AUTHOR

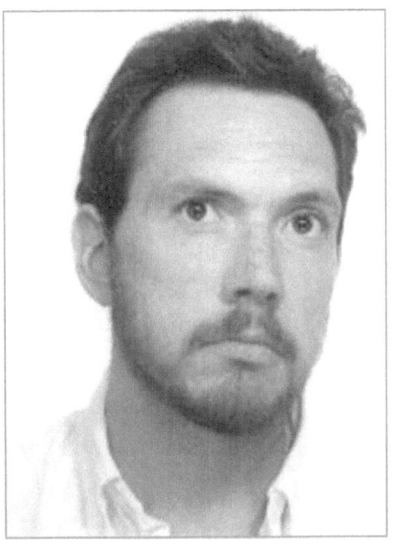

Marc Lloyd Heberden was born on 20 March 1956 in Spokane, Washington. His early years were spent in Pullman and later Tacoma. After his studies at Western Washington University in Bellingham and the University of Washington in Seattle, where he earned a degree in journalism, he worked as a newspaper editor and award-winning journalist. Moving to Europe in the early 1980s he wrote for newspapers and magazines and began writing short stories, novels and screenplays. Since 1999 he has lived with his wife Christine in a small town southwest of Paris where they raised their three children, Maurine, Joyce and Cliff. His novels include *Outside Man*, *The Big Tide*, *14 Days in July*, *Feeney's Part*, *The Norman*, and *Feeney's Last*.